Decisions of the Heart

Decisions of the Heart

Joan Virden

authorHOUSE®

AuthorHouse™
1663 Liberty Drive
Bloomington, IN 47403
www.authorhouse.com
Phone: 1-800-839-8640

Published by AuthorHouse: 9/10/2012

ISBN: 978-1-4772-6764-6 (sc)
ISBN: 978-1-4772-6763-9 (e)

Chapter One

Clear Water Cove
Lake Tahoe, Nevada

Threatening dark clouds hung over the lake and the wind whipped up roiling waves which lashed the pleasure boats anchored in the cove. As Carolyn Robertson watched from her bedroom, a flash of light lit the surface of the water, pulsing like a grounded aurora. Fascinated, she stepped closer to the window. The multicolored wash of brightness stretched across the deepest part of the cove, hovering a few feet off the surface to the left of the old railroad pilings that marched out into the bay like tired old soldiers. Then as suddenly as it had appeared the brightness vanished and the surface of the lake returned to its dark, storm tossed state.

Carolyn felt a shiver start at the base of her spine. It traveled up her back and raised the hairs on her neck. She trembled. Something had caused her to wake from a sound sleep and had drawn her to the window. It had

1

been years since Sirena's ghost had made an appearance in Clear Water Cove. Had she returned? What could she possibly want from them now? She forced a laugh. She was being foolish. It was probably just a searchlight from a boat lost in the gale, or a high-powered flashlight from one of the lakeside homes whose owners were watching the spectacle of the storm.

Pulling her nightgown tightly around herself, she walked back to bed where her husband, Tom, was sleeping soundly. She sat down carefully on the edge of the bed and eased herself under the covers, pulling them up to her chin. Tom grunted and his arm reached out for her. Gratefully, Carolyn nestled against his strong muscular back and tucked her legs behind his. She would mention the strange light to him in the morning. He knew all about the ghost that had haunted them twenty years ago. He would consider all the possibilities. Tragedy had followed the discovery of the blue diamond necklace belonging to the ghost, but now it was at the bottom of the deepest part of the cove where it belonged, surely *she* was content with its return.

Heavy rain lashed the house and the pine trees brushed against the roof making strange scraping sounds, but with the warmth of Tom's body and the protective feeling he gave her, she soon closed her eyes and slept.

Chapter Two

Clear Water Cove

Bright sunshine and blue sky followed the nighttime storm and the beach at Clear Water Cove filled with weekend visitors. Shrill laughter from a group of young children made Evan Burney look up from the book he was holding. The Saturday afternoon beach bunnies had settled into their usual sunning spaces close by. Pretending to read had only been a cover from where he could check out their sleek, young bodies. At twenty-seven, Evan had learned to look and appreciate, but not touch. There wasn't a female of legal age in the bunch. Still, he grinned, he could certainly appreciate the view.

As he watched the group of high-spirited children, he noticed they were gathered around an object lying on the beach. They jabbed at it with sticks, and one brave boy grabbed it and threw it up in the air while the others screamed with delight. Curious, Evan put down his book, untangled his lean, tanned body, and strolled over to where all the excitement was taking place. As he neared the scene he paused, it couldn't be, but it was! The children had found his old tattered, but still intact, swim trunks he had lost when he was seven.

Ignoring their protests, Evan reached in the circle and grabbed the faded, tattered garment.

"Hey, mister, give it back, we need it," called out a little girl with long, blonde curls. Evan patted her on the head and tucked the small suit under his arm. He walked back to his chair and sat down, disregarding the admiring glances of the teenyboppers clustered around his beach chair. The tall handsome man, with his dark brown eyes, black hair and incredibly long eyelashes, fascinated them. They had moved their beach towels closer, hoping to attract his attention.

He paid no mind to their stares and laid the small faded suit out at his feet. How well he remembered the day he had lost it. Now here it was, back on the beach-twenty years later! The storm last night must have torn it loose from wherever it had been. The trunks brought back old memories.

He had been young and stupid to try to steal the blue diamond necklace from Jenny's parents. Then, being the conceited little brat that he was, he had lost it, along with his trunks, while showing off his diving skills from the pilings.

His heart was pounding as he unzipped the deep pocket in the side of the trunks and reached in. His fingers found a hole where the stitching had rotted out. Empty of course, what did he expect? Did he think for a minute the necklace would still be there? He picked up his book again, but couldn't concentrate. The diamonds had been in that pocket when he dove in the lake. They still had to be out there, somewhere. He remembered lying in bed the night he lost the necklace, promising himself when he grew up, he would find them again. He flipped the suit over, and then handed it back into the hands of the little girl who had stubbornly followed him.

"There you go, it's all yours. Don't know what you see in a pair of old kids swim trunks, but there they are, have fun with your game." Giggling, the young child grabbed the small suit and ran back to her friends, who were waiting to see if she would be successful.

Evan watched her go, and then realized why they wanted the trunks. They were making a sand man and had managed to fit the trunks around him, making their sculpture more real in their childish eyes. He put down his book, and clasping his hands behind his head, he closed his eyes.

The years had gone by so fast. He had grown up here at Lake Tahoe, arguably the most beautiful lake in the world. Born with a silver spoon in his mouth, he had attended private schools and then went on to Harvard where he graduated with a law degree. Now he could only come back to this idyllic spot for a few weeks in the summer. The uncomplicated days of his youth were past. He sighed, wishing Jenny was here with him. Friends since they could toddle, he had always hoped they would have a future together. He had watched her grow from a charming, plump, curly headed child into a slender young teenager. Now at twenty-six she was a stunning red haired beauty. Their houses at Clear Water were close, as were their parents, but now Jenny was off in Europe somewhere, painting and doing whatever else you do in Europe when you are young, beautiful and as passionate about life as he knew she was.

"Excuse me, but would you help me with my suntan lotion?" The husky voice surprised him. Opening his eyes, he saw a tall blonde teenage bombshell standing over him, her tiny, red bikini barely covering her already tanned and flawless body.

"Look, sweetie, I would love to help you, but I'd probably get arrested." He heard laughter in the background and the girl's face reddened.

"Fine, I'll find someone who's not so old." She flounced off, trying not to show her disappointment.

Disturbed by the memories the appearance of the old trunks had invoked, Evan got up from his beach chair and picked up his book. Slipping on his flip-flops, he headed across the hot sand and climbed up the bank to where Jenny's house stood. He had parked his candy apple red, Corvette behind the Robertson's house. It was only a short walk from Jenny's to where his parents lived, but he preferred to drive. As he made his way up the steps he heard wolf whistles from the beach. With a grin, he turned and waved to his appreciative audience of teenager beauties.

Chapter Three

Las Vegas, Nevada

Streaming white cirrus clouds raced past Jenny's window as the big 747 settled into the landing pattern over Las Vegas. Beside her, Diego Rivera patted her hand and leaned over to kiss her cheek.

"You're almost home, baby. Just a few more days and everything will be taken care of."

Jenny turned toward the darkly handsome man sitting next to her. Her stomach churned. She would only be carrying his child for a little while longer. Did she really love this man who had talked her out of having his baby? He seemed so sure and confident that they were doing the right thing. But if he really loved her, wouldn't he want the baby? Her chin trembled and she tried hard not to think about what they were about to do.

"I guess you're right," she replied faintly. Then looking back out the window she asked, "Are you sure this is a good doctor?" The words came out shakily and Diego squeezed her fingers.

"Do you think I would have anyone but the best?" He saw her eyes begin to swim with tears. "Jenn, we're doing the right thing. Neither of us is ready to settle down and get married. I love you, but I know you want your art show in New York. You're finally getting the recognition you have been hoping for. A baby would only complicate our lives. You have worked so hard to get this opportunity to exhibit your paintings. Come on, cheer up. At six weeks this baby is only a glimmer in the ether."

"Maybe, but I've always wanted children. I don't want to do anything that might jeopardize that. And," she said, her voice quavering, "I already feel like its alive, growing inside me."

"I suppose that's normal, sweetie. You'll see. Dr. Blackwell is great. He'll make it easy for you."

Diego settled back in his seat. Why hadn't he been more careful the night they partied in Madrid? He had too much to drink that night and so did Jenny. The closeness of the beautiful girl had been so tempting he had been careless. Now he had to deal with ending the resulting pregnancy – and a nervous and emotional woman. Did he love Jenn? Maybe. He didn't really know what love was. He had played hard and fast all his life. He came from a noble Spanish family who were well titled, but no longer wealthy. Even so, he had never had to work a day in his life, always finding beautiful, rich women who could support his life style. With his good looks and charm, it wasn't difficult.

Six months ago he met Jenny at an art gallery in Paris and she had taken his breath away. Beautiful, talented and passionate, he had instantly become besotted with her. Now he was paying for his foolishness. The biggest mistake he had made was getting involved with a woman who wasn't going to support him. He couldn't bring himself to tell her she needed to. As soon as this was over, he would go home and get back on the fast track, but he was enough of a gentleman to see her through this first. He didn't know why she had insisted on coming back to the States, and of all places Las Vegas, to get the procedure done. European doctors were good at abortions, probably more used to doing them than Blackwell.

He met Dr. Blackwell one summer while he was living with a wealthy widow in the south of France. With his talent for attracting beautiful women, he had helped the vacationing young medical student have the time of his life. Now he would ask him to return the favor. It would take every cent he had to help Jenny, but he would never admit to her how little money he had. The plane tickets and the doctor's fees would empty his account, even though Blackwell had promised a break on the cost of the procedure. He needed to get back to his hunting grounds and find a lonely, rich woman – fast.

The warning light came on and the flight attendant walked past, checking on their seat belts, making sure their seats were fully upright and tray tables put away. The plane dropped suddenly and the wings dipped, the hot desert air causing it to buck and rock. In a few minutes the broad expanse of Lake Mead could be seen out of the right window with Hoover Dam rising white and majestic at its base.

"That's quite a sight!" Diego exclaimed. He leaned over Jenny's lap to look out her window. "Have you ever been to Lake Mead?"

"I've never even been to Las Vegas!" Jenny said her eyes serious. "Lake Tahoe has been my home all my life. I never wanted to live anywhere else. It's the most beautiful place in the world!" She squeezed his hand. "I can't wait for you to see it, Diego."

Diego took a deep breath. Jenny thought he was coming home with her, but his plans did not include Lake Tahoe, or Jenny. However, he would wait until this problem was taken care of before he told her.

"I would love to see your beautiful lake, Jenny. The sooner we get you to Dr. Blackwell, the sooner you'll be home."

Jenny looked at him curiously. That sounded odd, almost as if he didn't plan on coming with her. No, he wouldn't leave her now; especially after all she was going to go through to make him happy. She tightened her seat belt. This was going to be the most difficult thing she had ever done in her life, and the scariest!

The glitz and glitter of the Las Vegas Strip came into view, and in minutes the heavy aircraft had settled smoothly on the runway of McCarran International Airport. As the plane eased to a stop, Jenny released her seatbelt and stood up. She took a deep breath. For Diego's sake and hers, she hoped this would go well.

Chapter Four

Clear Water Cove,

As the smell of freshly brewed coffee wound its way up the stairs, Tom woke up. He groaned, rolled over and looked at the bedside clock. Seven! It was Sunday. Why was Carolyn up so early? All he had planned for today was a round of golf and lunch with Carolyn at the club. His tee time wasn't until ten! He lay back on the pillows and listened to the cheery sounds of breakfast being prepared by the woman he loved. "Oh, what the hell," he mumbled, and throwing the covers off, he stood up and stretched. Even after all these years, he didn't want to waste a minute he could be sharing with his wife.

Carolyn heard the shower running and smiled. She knew Tom couldn't resist the smell of breakfast cooking. She was still debating whether or not to tell him about the strange lights she had seen last night. She hated to bring up anything to remind them of the tragic events that had taken place twenty years ago.

She was setting his plate of bacon and eggs down beside a steaming cup of coffee when Tom came into the expansive, country kitchen. He grabbed her and kissed her on the mouth.

"Hum, breakfast smells wonderful, but not nearly as good as you!" He patted her firm behind and touched her breasts lightly. "I'm all showered. Can breakfast wait?" He couldn't quite figure out how this woman still awakened his passion the minute he touched her.

Carolyn laughed and pulled a lock of his wet, curly blonde hair. "Not this morning, my love. I have something to tell you. It's a little weird, but I think it's worth discussing."

Tom looked stricken, and then with a sigh he pulled out a chair and sat down. "Okay, you have my full attention. If something is more important than making love to your handsome husband, I guess I need to hear it."

"Seriously, Tom, the strangest thing happened last night. Something woke me up. It seemed to will me to go to the window and look at the place on the lake where Jim had his accident. When I looked out, a bright light appeared. It wavered and flowed just above the water. It was brighter than any light a flashlight could make. It was unlike anything I have ever seen. If you have seen the Aurora Borealis, well…that's what it looked like, only smaller, and it stayed just above the water. It was fascinating, but frightening. Then, just as suddenly as it began, it disappeared. Gone. Nada. There was only the darkness and the storm." Carolyn slid down on Tom's lap and put her arms around him. "You don't think it could be Sirena again, do you, honey?"

Tom hesitated. Anything was possible. Before he had actually had his experience with Sirena, he would have laughed at anyone suggesting a ghostly apparition, but he had seen her and heard her.

"I sure hope not. I can't imagine why she would be making an appearance again. She has her necklace back, and no one has bothered her for a very long time. She should be happy to leave us alone. I believe what you saw; I just don't have an answer as to what it was. If it was Sirena's ghost, I have no idea what we can do about it. Just wait and see if anything else happens, I guess."

Carolyn kissed his forehead and got up. "You're right. If she is back, and if she wants to be noticed, she did a good job. Hopefully, that's it. However, I have a feeling we haven't seen the last of her."

"Maybe we have, but maybe not." Tom said, between bites of egg. "Today, my love is Sunday. I don't have any real estate deals to worry about, and my golf buddies are waiting for my professional guidance. I'll try my best to remain calm and not worry about ghosts. I'll see you at lunch."

"You rat! You're making fun of me now." Carolyn smacked his arm and he yelped, pretending her light punch had hurt.

"No, I'm not," he said earnestly. "I know you're serious, but really, what can we do about it? If it happens again, maybe she will let us know what she wants. Until then we're pretty much at her mercy and I am not going to let it ruin my day. Now, let's eat your superb breakfast, and then go get beautiful so I can show you off to all my friends at the club, who by the way, are already so jealous of my lovely wife they can hardly stand it."

"You goof. I am over forty, and not exactly flush with youthful beauty. You're friends are full of it." Carolyn protested, but loved hearing Tom tell her, he still thought she was pretty. "Okay, I'll leave it alone for now. I think

I'll run over and see Sissy before I go to the club. I hear Evan is up for the weekend. It's been months since I've seen him. I should catch up on all the gossip."

"Yep, that's important," he teased. "I know you and Sissy. But, I might suggest you don't mention the ghost to her. Hearing about Sirena would probably remind her about Jim, and other things she would rather forget. Wonder if she has ever told Evan who his real father is?"

"I don't know, and it's certainly not for me to ask. But, if I ever find out, I'll let you know."

Carolyn left Tom to his breakfast and went upstairs to get dressed. She wondered if Evan still had any interest in Jenny. At one time, she had been sure they would get engaged. She was still hopeful. She wished Jenny would come home. This Diego fellow Jenny kept talking about when she called seemed so foreign, but of course he was! She had always wondered if it was Jenny's desire for adventure that had taken her so far away, or something else!

Chapter Five

Clear Water Cove

Carolyn knocked on the door of Sissy and Allen Burney's palatial mountain home. When there was no response, she opened the door and walked into the two-story high foyer, her footsteps echoing off the marble floor. Carolyn was never comfortable inside this modern structure of glass and metal. It seemed out of place in the forest setting, but it *was* magnificent.

"Anybody home?" she called up the winding staircase, and was immediately rewarded by an answering voice from far down the first floor hall.

"We're in the kitchen, Carolyn." Sissy's high voice came back faintly. "Come on back. Evan's here."

Carolyn entered the large chef's kitchen and was immediately caught up in a bear hug.

"Hey there, Carolyn, how've you been?" Evan said as he released her and stepped back to give her an appraising look. "You look beautiful, as always. Where's your lovely daughter? I was hoping she'd be home by now? Has she moved to Europe permanently?"

"Oh, my, I certainly hope not!" Carolyn laughed. She looked up at the young man she had watched grow from a beautiful baby into this strikingly handsome man. Her heart gave a little lurch as the deep brown eyes locked on hers. With his curly black hair and sweeping long eyelashes, he looked so much like Jim. He was wearing beige chinos, a black, cashmere sweater and tennis shoes. Carolyn thought he looked more handsome every time she saw him.

"Have you heard anything from Jenny lately?" Sissy asked. She was wearing a brightly colored Muu Muu, which covered her overweight figure. She smeared a large roll with jam, and took a seat at the long, granite topped, kitchen island. Sissy's face still held traces of her youthful beauty, but the years had put weight on her once slender figure, and her fair skin showed the affects of too much sun and too many medical procedures. She still acted spoiled and girlish, but their years of shared experiences made Carolyn overlook it.

"She called last week" Carolyn said with a smile. "She said she might be coming home for a visit, but would let me know. I haven't heard anything from her since. I really hope she decides to come home, I miss her so much." Carolyn looked at Evan, hoping she could tell if he was excited about the possibility that Jenny might be coming back, but his face was turned away from her and she couldn't see his expression. "She told me she would bring Diego, her new friend from Spain."

At the mention of Diego, Evan turned around. From the look on his face, Carolyn knew he hadn't entirely lost his feelings for Jen. "Diego, who's that?" His eyes darkened and his posture stiffened. "Some playboy she met in Spain?"

Carolyn suppressed a smile. "No, actually she said they met at an art gallery in Paris. I don't think it's anything serious, or at least she hasn't given *me* that impression."

Evan relaxed a bit, but his heart was racing. If a man was accompanying Jenny all the way home from Europe, it had to be a little serious. He knew he was probably making too much of it, but he couldn't help it. He hated the thought of Jenny being with another man. "Is she coming home to stay, or is this just a visit before she goes back to Europe?"

"I don't know, Evan dear." Carolyn said. "If I hear anymore from her, I'll let you know. I'm sure she'll want to see you. Are you going to be up here very often this summer?"

"Depends, I guess." Evan didn't want to say much. He had already let his feelings show more than he intended.

"Carolyn darling, do stay and have lunch with us. I'll tell cook to set another place." Sissy patted Carolyn on the shoulder and tossed her long, expensively frosted, blonde hair back behind her shoulders.

"Thanks, but I promised Tom I would have lunch with him at the club. Why don't you and Allen join us?"

Sissy's face darkened. "Allen's off somewhere playing tennis. Sometimes I think he loves that game more than his wife and child."

Carolyn could sense there was more to it than tennis. Allen had to know Evan wasn't his son. There was no way this tall, black haired, brown eyed man could have come from the genes of a blonde, blue eyed woman and a short, red haired, blue eyed man. Anyway, he looked exactly like Jim. She often wondered why Sissy and Allen hadn't had any children of their own. It must be hard for Allen, living with the knowledge that the heir to his fortune was another man's son. She hugged Sissy.

"I'm sure that's not the case, dear. Anyway, if he comes

back in time, come on over to the club. I have to run. I just wanted to stop by and say hello to Evan. But if you can't make lunch, come by the house around five. We'll have cocktails out on the bank. The evenings have been beautiful, and the sunsets spectacular.

"Allen should never have built this house way back in the woods. I am so jealous of you having beachfront property, Carolyn. You'd think with all our combined assets, he would have listened to me and bought property on the water." Pouting, Sissy followed Carolyn out to the door and saw her into her jeep. She looked at the old, battered vehicle, and made a face. "By the way, isn't Tom ever going to buy you a new car? Honestly, Carolyn, that jeep is at least twenty years old!"

Carolyn smiled at her unhappy friend. She loved her little jeep, and would keep it until the tires fell off. She had never felt the need for extravagant cars or clothes to make her happy, but she understood why Sissy might. "It still runs great, and I love it. When the motor blows up, I'll consider buying a new one. See you two later." She waved and drove away; hoping Tom would have an answer to the ghost lights at lunch.

Sissy stood watching as the little red jeep disappeared through the trees, then turned to Evan. "Some people don't care how they look. I love Carolyn, but sometimes I just don't understand her."

Evan took his mother's arm. "No, Mother, you wouldn't understand at all." He kissed her cheek and walked her back to the house. He fervently hoped if and when he married, it would be a much happier union than his parent's. He was sure he knew what it was that had built such a barrier between them.

Chapter Six

Las Vegas, Nevada

Jenny's knees shook as she sat on the edge of the chair in Dr. Ken Blackwell's plush office. The nurse asked her to wait, telling her the doctor was with another patient, but would be in shortly. Her heart was racing and her mouth felt like she could spit cotton. Why hadn't Diego come in with her instead of waiting outside? Dr. Blackwell was *his* friend, wasn't he? She had never met the man she was about to trust with her life. She took a deep breath. She felt trickles of sweat begin to start down her back. She hoped she wouldn't have to wait much longer.

The minutes ticked by with agonizing slowness and still no doctor. Maybe she would just get up and leave. Damn Diego, he should be in here! Just as she was about to bolt for the door and forget the whole thing, the door opened and a short, bald, kindly looking man with black, horn-rimmed glasses and a trim mustache, walked in. He was wearing black slacks, with a loud, black and yellow checked, sports coat. Underneath the jacket he wore a white turtleneck. No tie, no white doctor's coat. *Very Las Vegas*, she thought, but kept that to herself.

"Hello, Jenny. I'm Ken Blackwell. It's very nice to meet you. Diego told me all about you." He shook her hand with a firm grip, and then going behind his large, burled walnut desk; he sat down and leaned back in his chair.

"Tell me why you are having this procedure? Are you sure you want to terminate the pregnancy? I know Diego wants you to, but how about you?" His eyes were soft and kind and Jenny felt herself relax a little.

"To be honest, Doctor Blackwell, I'm not sure I *am* doing the right thing. I know Diego thinks so, but I can't help thinking there is already a life growing inside me, depending on me to take care of it." She felt her lips tremble, and bit back tears.

"If that's the way you feel, my dear, you should reconsider. An abortion is not a matter to be taken lightly, and I can tell you aren't. Why don't you go home, wait a few days and think it over. Once it's done, it's done, and there is no going back. I would hate for you to regret your decision later on." He watched the lovely, young girl with sympathy. She was in a tough spot. Diego could be very persuasive, and she obviously loved him. He was surprised when he saw her. She wasn't one of the middle aged, wealthy women Diego usually hung out with. This beautiful girl looked vulnerable and innocent. He felt a surge of anger at Diego for putting her in this situation. He wasn't going to hurry her into anything, no matter what Diego had asked him to do. He would make sure she was okay with this.

Relieved at the chance to delay her decision, Jenny stood up. "I think you're right Doctor Blackwell. I was on my way home anyway. Diego and I are going to Lake

Tahoe to visit my parents. I'll have some time to think about this while I'm there. A few days won't make much difference, will it?"

"Not at all, my dear, I think that's very wise. I'll be here for you, whatever you decide. Just give me a call and let me know." The kindly doctor stood up and escorted her to the door. "I'll wait to hear from you."

With a dizzying sense of relief, Jenny thanked him and hurried out. She closed the door behind her and looked around the waiting room for Diego. Where was he? The only occupants of the waiting room were three obviously pregnant women sitting in comfortable chairs. They smiled at the red-haired girl, admiring her slim figure, wishing they still looked like that.

Jenny turned to the receptionist. "Did you see the man I came in with? Did he say where he was going?"

"No, honey, he got up and left when you went in to see Dr. Blackwell. He didn't say where he was going. Can I call a taxi for you?"

Jenny was confused and embarrassed. This was so unlike him. He must have gotten an emergency call – or something. "Yes, I would appreciate that. Thank you."

Her suitcases were still by the chair where Diego had been sitting. They had come directly to the doctor's office, not stopping to get a room at a hotel. Her cheeks on fire, Jenny picked up the suitcases and quickly left the office, but not before she caught the look of pity on the women's faces. She knew what they must be thinking.

Jenny stood outside the medical building and waited for the taxi. She had tried Diego's cell phone three times but it had gone directly to voice mail. The hot Las Vegas sun was already beginning to burn her fair skin. Coming from the rainy weather in Paris, she was unprepared for such serious heat.

By the time the cab pulled up, she felt as though she would melt. I must look a mess, she thought. Her wool skirt and cashmere sweater were creased from the long trip, and completely out of place.

The taxi driver lifted the trunk and tossed her bags inside, then slammed the lid and opened the door for her.

"Where to, miss?" he asked as she slid inside the blissfully air-conditioned cab.

"I'm not sure. I just got off an airplane, and it appears my friend who came with me has disappeared." Even as she said the words, Jenny could not believe what was happening. Where could Diego have gone, and why would he leave her? Was it part of his plan all along? Her stomach churned. She left her cell phone on; he would call her and let her know where he was. She was sure of it. But right now she had to make a decision. The cab driver was waiting.

"I need to find a motel. Can you recommend one that's not too expensive? I'm sure my friend will call me, we're not staying long." She tried to sound confident, hoping the driver didn't hear the waver in her voice.

The cabby nodded. "There's a nice Motel 6, just down the street. Is that okay?" As hard as she was trying to hide her nervousness, he could tell she needed his help.

"I'm sure that will be fine. Thanks." Jenny sat back as the cab pulled quickly away from the loading zone. She was starting to get a headache, and her stomach felt queasy. That was happening a lot lately. If Diego didn't call soon she would be on a plane for Reno tomorrow.

Diego smiled at the cute, blonde flight attendant hovering over his seat. He paid her for the martini she handed him and looked out the window of the 747. Las Vegas was disappearing rapidly in the distance as the plane climbed out over the red walled canyons to the west. He was finally rid of his problem. He felt like a heel deserting Jenny like that, but he didn't have a choice, did he? When Ken Blackwell told him how much the operation was going to cost, he had to get out fast. Even with the discount, he didn't have that kind of money! When he got back to Madrid, he would call to make sure Jenny was okay. Her parents would help her. She would get over him in time, they always did. He felt a twinge of guilt as he remembered the trusting look in her eyes. He wasn't used to dealing with a girl so young and inexperienced. But, a baby! Just what he needed! No, he certainly wasn't ready for that, and, he told himself, neither was Jenny. He picked up his drink and downed it in one gulp, noticing with disgust, that his hands were shaking.

Chapter Seven

J enny stepped into the small but clean motel room and tossed her purse on the bedside table. "Just put my suitcases in the corner, please," she said to the thin, gray haired valet. "Thank you." Handing him her last five-dollar bill, Jenny sat on the edge of the bed and sighed.

"If you need anything else, miss, just ring for me," the man said, as he closed the door and left the room.

Now what? Jenny thought to herself. Where in the world was Diego? She reached for her purse and extracted her cell phone from the side pocket. Flipping it open, she looked at the screen, but there were no messages. She would wait a little longer, and then she would have to acknowledge that he had left her to face their mistake alone. She felt tears of frustration and self-pity begin to well up in her eyes and she jumped off the bed. She would not cry. She was as responsible for her predicament as Diego was. She was not going to let him ruin her life. Getting involved with him had been a mistake from the start, but he had swept her off her feet. He was mysterious, handsome, charming, and fun. Just what she thought she needed after running away from Clear Water Cove – and Evan.

She had been in love with Evan Burney since she was a little girl, but he never seemed to notice. He brought lots of girlfriends to the lake, but the last one had seemed serious. Too proud to grovel at his feet, she finally gave up and fled to Europe with the excuse that she needed to expand her education and paint. Before she left Paris, she had been given a once in a lifetime chance to exhibit her paintings at the Schilling Gallery in New York, but this took precedence over everything. Her naiveté and foolishness might cost her the career she had worked so hard for.

She walked up and down the small room rubbing her forehead and trying to think straight. First she would call the airline and book a flight to Reno. She didn't want to tell her family over the phone that she was pregnant and worse, that the father of her child was a louse who had deserted her! Oh, damn! She was such a fool. She needed a nights rest from the long transatlantic flight before she faced her mother and dad. She knew they would be hurt and puzzled. They were such great parents. They did not deserve this. However, she knew they would support her, no matter what she decided to do, they always had. Maybe the worse part would be Evan finding out! That would surely end her chance of a relationship with her lifelong friend, who was now a successful lawyer. Sitting back down on the bed, she got a credit card out of her purse, picked up the phone, and dialed the number for Southwest Airlines. She would get on their earliest morning flight to Reno.

Jenny awoke to the buzzing of the alarm. She rolled over and reached for the noisy box. Her fingers found the button and pressed hard shutting off the racket. Blazing sun filtered through the thin gauzy curtains. It was going to be another scorcher. Great! There was nothing in her suitcase that would be appropriate for the desert heat. Her flight was in two hours, not enough time to shop for cooler clothes. She yawned and stretched, pushing her mop of curly red hair out of her eyes. If she went directly to the airport and waited there for her flight, she could escape from the heat. Everything in this town was air-conditioned, the room, the cab, and most importantly, the airport terminal.

She kicked off the sheets and stood up, then abruptly sat back down. She felt sick and dizzy. Oh, no, she was going to throw up! She staggered to the small bathroom and lost what little she had left from yesterday's airplane food. She splashed cold water on her face and peered into the mirror. She hardly recognized herself. Her face was pale and drawn, and there were deep blue shadows under her eyes.

"Get it together," she whispered out loud. "This is only the beginning. You'd better get used to it!" From all she had heard and read, morning sickness could last for weeks, if not months! Stepping into the shower, she turned on the hot water and stood for a long time letting the steamy flood pour over her. Finally, with the grime and sweat of the trip washed away, she felt more relaxed. She stepped out onto the blessedly cool tile floor and began to prepare for the next episode in her life. In a few days she would have to make some big decisions. Hopefully, she would choose the right ones.

Diego woke from a short nap and reached for Jenny's familiar soft hand.

"Watch it, mister, "came from a deep, masculine voice.

Startled, Diego turned his head and saw a short, fat man leaning as far from his outstretched hand as possible without falling into the aisle.

"Excuse me!" he stuttered confused. Then it all came flooding back, and he turned quickly to the window. Jenny! He really was a cold-hearted bastard, but what else could he do? He wasn't ready to be a father! First of all, he couldn't afford it, and secondly…well, frankly, he just didn't want to be tied down. Maybe when Jenny got back to Europe they could see each other again. By that time she would have recovered and she would be the charming, sexy girl he had enjoyed being with so much.

He sat back and smiled, having a son might have been interesting. He might have considered owning up to a boy, but of course it was too late for that now. By this time tomorrow it would all be over. He would call his old girlfriend, Francine, when he got to Paris. Getting back in bed with that long legged, French beauty would wipe away his thoughts about Jenny. As the smiling flight attendant came by, he flagged her down and ordered another martini.

Chapter Eight

Reno, Nevada

The sign read, "Reno Tahoe International Airport". Jenny smiled as she made her way down the corridor to the baggage claim area. It was such an impressive name for the relatively small facility. She loved it. It was a welcome change from the overcrowded terminals she had been dealing with. The crush of people at the terminal in Las Vegas had been a nightmare.

She reached the turntables and stood back waiting for the buzzer to announce the arrival of her bags. As she waited, she glanced around, wondering if anyone she knew was here. Turning back to watch for her suitcases, she felt a hand on her shoulder. Startled, she spun around.

"Jenny, isn't it? Jenny Robertson?" The tall, blonde man in the cowboy boots and gray Stetson hat looked at her with a twinkle in his deep blue eyes. Then, seeing the puzzlement on her face, he laughed. "Justin, Justin King, we met a few years ago at a party in Clear Water

Cove. Let me think. Ah yes, you're a friend of Maggie Anderson." His smile made her heart skip a beat, and she remembered. He had been at Nadia Miller's birthday party with a beautiful brunette. It would be hard to forget this handsome cowboy.

She smiled back, her dimples flashing. "Justin, of course I remember. You were with a beautiful, dark haired lady. That was some party! I don't think anyone left before 3:00am!"

"Yep, that was fun. But, as I recall, the bonfire on the beach almost got out of hand, and so did some of the guys. If I remember correctly, you had to beat them off!"

Jenny felt her cheeks burn as she remembered the wild scene on the beach. Some of the partygoers had stripped naked and plunged into the icy water. Hitting the freezing lake had sobered them up quickly. She wanted to change the subject, not sure she cared to go into all the details of that night, the last few hours of which had been fuzzy, but she vaguely remembered Evan taking her arm and leading her home.

"So, are you leaving or arriving?" she asked.

"I'm coming in from New Mexico. We just sold a bunch of cattle in Albuquerque. I'm on my way back to the ranch." He couldn't keep his eyes off the stunningly beautiful, red-haired girl. How had he let this one get away? "And since you are waiting for luggage, I guess you're just arriving from..."

"I'm going up to Tahoe. I've been in Europe for a year, studying and painting."

"You're an artist! I never would have guessed! I would have thought maybe a model, or actress, as lovely as you are!"

He didn't want to leave, but he could tell she was getting nervous. "Listen," he said warmly, "Here's my business card. If you have a free day or two, call me. I'll come up to the Cove, and drive you out to Eagle's View. I'd love to show you around my ranch. Do you ride horses?"

"I've never been on a horse in my life. I'm afraid I would be poor company." Seeing him hesitate, she smiled and added, "But I am always up to a challenge."

"Good girl. I'll be waiting to hear from you." Flashing his own big dimples, the tall rancher tipped his hat and strode out of the terminal.

Before she could dwell on the chance meeting, the buzzer sounded, and the bags began to arrive.

Chapter Nine

Clear Water Cove

The gatekeeper at the entrance to Clear Water Cove stopped the unfamiliar rental car and peered inside. Recognizing the visitor she smiled.

"Why, Jenny Robertson! Where have you been? I haven't seen you in a long time. Are you here for the summer?"

Jenny smiled back at the gray haired lady. Grace had been the gatekeeper for as long as she could remember. "I'm not sure, Grace. Maybe, but first I have to get in the gate."

"Oh my, of course, it's good to see you back, my dear."

Waving her on, the kindly lady stepped back into the gatehouse and pressed the button that would lift the heavy iron gates and allow Jenny to proceed. As she drove through, Jenny waved back out the window and took a deep breath. It was good to be back.

"Surprise!" Jenny called as she opened the door of the charming, old, weathered lakefront house and peered inside. "Is anyone home?"

Footsteps sounded on the staircase and in seconds Carolyn careened around the corner, her arms stretched out to embrace her daughter.

"Jenny! Where did you come from? How did you get here? Why didn't you call us and let us know you were coming?" Tears of joy filled her mother's eyes as she hugged her only daughter's slender shoulders. She pulled back to look closer at her.

"What have you been doing, starving yourself? You look so thin! Come and sit down. Dad's playing golf, but he'll be back soon. Oh, Jenny, we've missed you so much." She hugged her again, and then led her into the living room. Pushing her into a big, overstuffed chair, she sat down opposite her.

"Tell me everything. How was Europe? Where is Diego? Is he bringing in your luggage? Did you get your showing in New York? How long are you staying?"

"Slow down, Mother, it's good to be home, but please give me a few minutes." Jenny looked out the big picture window at the blue water of Lake Tahoe. She had forgotten how amazingly beautiful it was. It seemed like a lifetime since she had sat here with her mother and talked. So much had happened.

"Jenny, is everything alright? Darling, you look so sad? What's happened? Where's Diego?"

"Diego isn't here, Mother. He's not coming. I think he's gone back to Spain."

"But, I thought you said he was coming up to the lake with you? What made him change his mind? I thought you two were pretty serious, or at least it sounded that way." Carolyn took Jenny's hand and saw it was trembling. "Let me get us a cup of tea, and then I want you to tell me exactly what's going on. I'm your mother, and whatever it is, we'll deal with it."

Jenny didn't dare speak. She knew she would start bawling if she did. She would wait for the tea and try to pull herself together.

Carolyn returned shortly, carrying a tray with two cups of steaming green tea and placed it on a small round table between their chairs. "Take a sip, then sit back and tell me all about your trip and why Diego didn't come with you." She patted Jenny's hand.

Jenny picked up the cup, carefully tasting the hot tea. In a moment of clarity, she knew she wasn't going to tell her mother about the baby. Not yet. She didn't want any pressure from anyone. Keeping, or not keeping this baby, would be her choice alone. She put the cup down and smiled at her mother.

"It's a long story, Mom. I'd much rather hear about what's been going on here at Clear Water while I've been away. There must be some interesting news, there always is."

"Darling, I want to hear about Europe! You've been gone for a year! Nothing that's happened here can possibly be as interesting!"

Carolyn frowned. There was something Jenny was hiding, but she wouldn't push her. Eventually she would tell her. "If you don't want to talk about it right now, that's fine. So, let me think. Our life here at the Cove has been pretty relaxed and sane. Not too much excitement, which is fine with us. Actually, a strange thing did happen the other night. Do you remember me telling you about Evan's father? I mean his *real* father?"

"Sure, Mom, I've never said a word to anyone. I know you aren't sure if Evan knows anything about him." Jenny looked at her mother curiously; glad she had changed the subject. Carolyn had a strange, almost scared look on her face. "Does this have anything to do with the famous ghost, Sirena?"

Carolyn looked out the picture window at the serene blue water of the lake. There was nothing scary about it this morning. The bright sunshine and sparkling surface looked peaceful and inviting. "I'm not sure, honey. We haven't seen, or heard anything from Sirena since Evan lost the necklace in the lake. We wanted to believe that when she got it back, she would be content, but the other night..." She didn't know whether to tell Jenny what she had seen, or not. She looked so fragile. Maybe she shouldn't worry her with silly suspicions.

"What, Mom? What about the other night? For goodness sake, you can tell me! I'm a big girl. Ghosts don't scare me anymore."

Jenny smiled, her face lighting up. Carolyn felt her heart fill with love; she was such a beautiful and precious child. If anyone has hurt Jen they would answer to her.

"Well, something woke me up the other night, and when I went to the window, there was a very bright waving light over the part of the cove where we last saw Sirena's ghost. I can't imagine why she would be coming back now. It's been so many years since all that happened."

"I love a good mystery, Mom. I hope if it happens again, you'll wake me up. I remember seeing her ghostly figure under the water the day Evan lost the necklace. Some of what happened during those years was tragic, and some of it was just plain weird!"

"I'll be sure and do that, my darling. That way I won't think I'm going crazy!" Carolyn relaxed. Jenny looked better. The story had caught her interest, and some color had come back into her face. "So, how was the airplane ride? Long, I'm sure. Did you have many layovers?" She saw a shadow cross Jenny's face, and knew there was a lot more to this story.

"I stayed overnight in Las Vegas. It was dreadfully hot. I am so glad to be back here where it's cooler! What a relief, after that furnace. Oh, here's an interesting tidbit for your inquiring mind. You'll never guess who I saw at the airport. Justin King! What a handsome man! He invited me out to his ranch."

"I remember that family. They have a beautiful ranch north of Reno. How nice, sweetie. Are you going?"

"I don't think so, Mom. I have some decisions to make in the next week or so. I won't have time to go running out for a horseback ride."

Seeing the puzzled look on Carolyn's face, she got up and gave her a hug. "Give me a little time, Mom. Soon, I'll tell you everything. It's such a beautiful day, how about getting on our swim suits and going down to the beach?"

Although frustrated by Jenny's secrecy, Carolyn knew she couldn't pry. Jenny would tell her what was troubling her when she was ready.

"Sounds like a great idea. You're father will be so excited to have you home. Just wait till he gets back from golf and sees who's sitting under his favorite umbrella."

The two women headed to their respective rooms to change. Carolyn went upstairs to the big master bedroom, and Jenny went down the hall to her newly appointed bedroom on the first floor.

"Come up when you're changed." Carolyn called from the staircase, "I'll show you where I saw that strange light."

Chapter Ten

Jenny climbed the steep staircase to the second floor. The pine wood banister, worn with age, felt soft under her hand. As she walked down the hall, she passed the newly paneled wall that covered the doorway into what used to be her bedroom. The entire inside of the house was paneled in knotty pine, so the recently covered opening had vanished completely. She felt a pang of sorrow. She had loved that little hobbit hole of a room. It was adjacent to the master suite and only a few steps from her mother and father's big bed. It had two little doors that opened up to cozy hiding places under the roofline. Places she had played in as a child, hiding from make believe monsters. The room had lots of angles and nooks that seemed nonsensical, but were perfect for young imaginations. After she left for college, her parents had torn the wall down and made it into a large walk-in closet and dressing room. The remodel was lovely, but she missed her old bedroom.

Her mother was in the new closet looking for her

beach thongs when Jenny came in. She sat down on the bed and waited for her.

Hearing Jenny enter the bedroom, Carolyn called out, "I'll be right there, honey. Now where have those darn flip-flops gone! Never mind! I'll just walk fast. By midmorning that sand really gets hot."

Carolyn came into the bedroom and Jenny looked at her still lovely slim figure with admiration. The blue flowered, one-piece swimsuit fit her like a second skin. She could have passed for thirty. With her mop of curly red hair so like Jenny's, and her perfect, creamy complexion, she would still attract a lot of attention on the beach. The small sprinkle of freckles across her nose only made her more endearing. Maybe, Jenny thought, if I get out in the sun I can acquire a few of those. She needed to feel the warmth of the sunshine on her pale skin and the hot sand under her feet. Relaxation was good for the soul. Jenny got up off the bed and went to hug her mother.

"Mom, you look spectacular. I don't know how you do it! I hope I look that good when I'm your age. Come to the window and show me where you saw the lights. "

Carolyn moved to the big picture window overlooking the cove. "There, over by the end of the pilings. It's where Jim dove to look for that damn necklace – and where he drowned. It's not a good memory, sweetie. I want the ghost to stay away. I really don't want to revisit that time."

Jenny peered out the window. "Don't think you'll have to, Mom. It looks normal to me."

"Right now it does, but this was the middle of the night. If I see the lights again, I'm coming to get you, asleep or not!" Carolyn shuddered. "I hope to God I don't."

"Enough! Let's go to the beach." Jenny said, "I'm ready."

Carolyn looked at Jenny in the tiny, two-piece bikini, and worry creased her forehead. "Darling, we really have to start feeding you. You're way too thin."

"Don't worry, Mom, I'll put on more weight, now that I'm back home." Now that I'm pregnant, she thought to herself. I'll be getting fat as a pig! Pushing the thought out of her head, she followed Carolyn out of the room, down the stairs and out the back door.

They crossed the well tended green lawn and followed the path down the stone steps to the place where beach chairs were set up under a colorful umbrella. The red and white beach umbrella shaded the two women as they sat back against their chairs and surveyed the scene. Families with children and young and old couples sat under similar umbrellas enjoying the late August sunshine. Most sported a deep tan, painted on by the high mountain sun, but some had peeling noses and sun burnt skin, showing their failure to apply enough sunscreen. Probably their first time at the lake, Jenny thought. They would learn soon enough. Even under the protection of the umbrella, she had made sure they were covered in number 50 sunscreen. At this altitude the sun's reflection off the water could burn, even in the shade. She closed her eyes, feeling the heat of the sand begin to relax all the muscles of her body. She had forgotten how wonderful it was to be here.

"Well, well, look what the cat drug in!" A teasing deep voice made Jenny open her eyes. "Ah, now I see. It's a very beautiful, enticing young lady who looks very familiar."

The darkly tanned, muscular figure loomed over Jenny and she felt her heart flip flop. The warm brown eyes, with their impossibly long lashes, smiled down at her. She sat up and shaded her eyes with one hand.

"Evan! I didn't know you were here. Sit down and visit. It's been a long time."

Her heart still racing, Jenny reached out and took Evan's hand, pulling him down beside her. He looked wonderful. So American! Not like the pale, almost effeminate European men she had met in Paris. Even Diego, as good looking as he was, wasn't a hunk like Evan.

He sat down beside Jenny and kissed her on the cheek. "I'm not sure Europe did you any favors, my love. You look like you could use some sun. Still beautiful, just pale and skinny!" he teased, then instantly regretted it, she looked so fragile, not like the sun kissed, healthy girl who left here a year ago.

"Well, you look wonderful, Evan. Being a lawyer must agree with you." Noticing his rippling muscles, she added, "How often do you go to the gym? I don't remember you being in such great shape?"

"I go at least twice a week, my dear. Being a defense attorney takes it out of you. It's the way I relax. It also helps with the ladies." He flashed his dazzling white smile at her. "I tried to wait for you, but I hear you found someone else. You've broken my heart!" He peered into her face, looking crushed.

Jenny blushed. "I thought I had too, but it seems like all the men in my life that I care about, run off and leave me. Tell me, Evan. What am I doing wrong?" She said it with a laugh, but it hurt nonetheless, first Evan, then Diego. Maybe she should give up and be content with being a single mom. Raising a child wouldn't be the worst thing she could do with her life.

"Wrong?" Evan sighed. "You, my love could never do anything wrong. You just have to stay put a little longer. You might be surprised at what could happen." He saw Carolyn smiling at him and leaning over Jenny, he grasped her hand. "And how have you been, Mrs. Robertson. You look smashing, as usual. See Jenny, you'll always look twenty-one as long as you stay at the Cove. It's all the fresh mountain air and sunshine."

Carolyn shook Evan's strong hand. He was so like his father. Even his mannerisms were just like Jim's.

"I'm going to run up to the house and get something cool to drink. Do you two want anything?" She wanted to give the two young people time alone, still hoping somehow they would connect again. From the look on Jennie's face, she could tell she was glad Evan was here. She had often wondered if he was the reason Jenny had gone away.

"No thanks, Mom. Actually, I've had enough sun. Thirty minutes out here with my, too white skin, is about all I better risk."

Evan stood up and helped Jenny to her feet. "Maybe we could have dinner before I go back to San Francisco where I now fight to protect the innocent. There aren't a lot of eligible females up here. I've been craving the company of a beautiful woman. Are you up for that?"

Jenny paused. There couldn't be any harm in having dinner with Evan. They had been friends forever. She could use a friend right now. "Sure, call me. I'm not going anywhere for a while."

Giving him a brotherly hug, Jenny gathered up her beach towel and went up the stairs after her mother.

Evan stared after her. Something had happened to Jenny. He had known her all his life. He wasn't wrong; he could read her like a book. Whatever it was, he would find out when he took her to dinner. He loved her like a sister. If he could help, he would.

Chapter Eleven

Paris, France

Screams echoed in the shabbily furnished room, unheard by anyone. The rest of the run down duplex was deserted. The man slapped the voluptuous woman across her ample bare behind. "You love it and you know it. Don't be so noisy. You'll wake up the neighbors."

Francine screamed again. "Don't, Diego, please! You told me you wouldn't hurt me!" She fought against the powerful arms holding her down on the bed.

"I said you would enjoy it, I never said it wouldn't hurt." Diego forced her legs farther apart and entered her again, slamming against her with brutal force. He was too powerful for her to resist and she continued to cry out.

"Shut up!" he growled and with one final forceful thrust, he fell on top of her. "You have to quit being such a pussy, Francine. This was your idea." He bit her neck cruelly, leaving a bright red mark.

Tears ran down her cheeks. "Why are you so mean, Diego? What's happened to you?"

Diego got off the bed and tossed a robe to the naked woman. "Cover up. I don't want to look at you anymore. You disgust me. All you do is shriek and complain. I'm going out. Maybe I can find a more willing partner."

Diego dressed quickly and without glancing back at the sobbing woman, he left the bedroom, slamming the door behind him. He sat down in a shabby chair in the tiny living room of his cheap, rented flat. What was the matter with him anyway? He had been in a foul mood ever since he had returned to Europe. Mistreating Francine was not like him. It was the same with the other women he had slept with since he had been back. In Paris, Madrid, it was always the same. Was he trying to hurt them, or was *he* hurting so much himself that he took it out on them? Damn it! He had called Jenny every day since he returned, but she refused to talk to him. What was going on? He should call Ken Blackwell and make sure she was all right. If he missed her this much, maybe he should think about trying to get her back to Europe to be with him again. But then who would pay the bills?

Rummaging through a drawer in the kitchenette that shared the living room space, he found his address book. He flipped quickly through the pages until he found Ken Blackwell's telephone number. Looking at his watch, he quickly calculated the time difference. It was nine hours earlier in Las Vegas. The clock on the wall said 11:30 pm, that would make it 2:30 in the afternoon; the office would still be open. He picked up the telephone and dialed.

"Dr. Blackwell's office," the sweet voice of his young secretary came over the line.

"This is Diego Rivera calling for Ken Blackwell. I'm in Paris, France. Could you please put him on the line?"

He wanted the girl to know this call was expensive. He couldn't afford to hold very long. Francine was another mistake. He had wasted time with her thinking she had money. But, after servicing her for two weeks, she had finally admitted she didn't have a pot to piss in. He was angry with himself and felt betrayed, he needed to get rid of her and move on. He was startled from his self-pitying moment by the deep voice of his friend.

"Hey there, Diego, how are you?"

"Great, Ken, just great. I was wondering how the operation went for Jenny?" He felt a small twinge of guilt, knowing he had left without helping pay for the procedure. Ken also knew he had left Jen to deal with everything, alone.

"I haven't heard from her; don't know what she's decided to do. I told her to call me when she made up her mind, but so far she hasn't." the doctor said.

Diego felt his stomach turn over. "Are you saying she didn't get the abortion? What happened? Where is she? What did you say to her?" He knew he sounded mildly panicked, but he couldn't believe what he was hearing.

"I didn't tell her anything, my friend. First of all, if you had stuck around instead of running off like you did, you would have known the answer to all those questions. This was a decision she made on her own."

Diego could hear the accusation in Ken's voice and realized he had made a big mistake. He should have stayed and made sure this went as he had planned. What the hell was she thinking? Did she really plan on keeping this kid? His kid? He groaned out loud.

"Sorry, Diego, it's her right. Next time you get a girl knocked up make sure she's not one with a conscience."

Diego felt his face burn. "Yeah, well, that won't be happening again, Doc. Anyway, do you know where she is?" He needed to talk some sense into her. He was not going to be held responsible for this kid. What if she asked for child support? He clenched his teeth so hard his jaw ached.

"I believe she was going up to Tahoe to visit her parents. You can probably reach her there."

"Thanks, Ken. I'll try that." Diego hung up, shaken. So that's why Jenny hadn't answered any of his calls! Damn! Now what was he going to do?

Kicking the wall hard, he went to the sagging cupboard and pulled out a bottle of vodka, then looked around for a glass. There were no clean ones only a stack of dirty dishes in the sink. Shrugging his shoulders, he grabbed the bottle and took a deep drink. He wiped his mouth with the back of his hand and went back into the bedroom where the frightened woman lay huddled in his bed, the covers pulled up tightly around her neck.

"Quit looking like I'm going to kill you," he said in a low voice and took another big swallow from the bottle. Then he flung the bottle against the wall where it shattered. Walking over to the bed, he yanked the sheets off Francine and jerked her to her feet.

"Get dressed, and then get the hell out of here," he growled.

Francine scrambled to her feet and reached for her clothes that lay flung across the floor. Diego sat on the bed and watched as she bent over to put on her string bikini underwear. Maybe it was the vodka or the sight of her soft, pink bottom, but he felt himself grow hard again. He sprang to his feet and grabbed her from behind. Ignoring her shrieks, he pushed her face against the wall and with sadistic pleasure ripped off the tiny piece of underwear. He kicked her legs apart and thrust into her. With one hand he held her still and with his other hand he reached around and grabbed one lush breast, pinching the nipple hard. She screamed with pain and tried to struggle, but he was not about to stop now. He'd teach the bitch not to try to fool with him. She lied to him about having a rich old man because she wanted to get laid. He would make sure she got her wish.

Chapter Twelve

Clear Water Cove

The bright red Corvette drew up in front of the house. Jenny's family had owned the place for decades. Evan liked it much better than his parent's home. It fit in with the surrounding meadows and trees. Unlike the glass and steel mansion he had just left, this house felt like a home.

Jenny was waiting for him at the back door. His heart caught in his throat as he watched her run towards the car. Her bright red curls were caught back by a blue ribbon, and the sky blue shift she wore revealed how thin she had become. He saw her mouth curve in a smile, showing the big dimples in her cheeks. She was as beautiful a woman as he had ever known, and it hurt him inside to see her like this.

He got out of the car and caught her in his arms, swinging her around easily. She laughed out loud. He loved the sound of her laughter. Putting her back down, he looked into her wide blue eyes and smiled. "You don't weigh anything, pup. Let's go get you a big steak!"

Jenny shrugged out of his arms. "If you don't quit telling me how skinny I am, I'm not going! You're making me feel self conscious." She frowned at him and made a face, secretly loving that he was concerned.

Evan's face fell. "I never want you to feel that way. I'm sorry. Look, I dressed up especially for you. I'd be devastated if you turned me down." He looked at her pleadingly.

Jenny saw that he had indeed cleaned up nicely. He had on a black silk dress shirt, open at the throat and black slacks. It made him look sexy and mysterious and her heart beat faster. Afraid to let her feelings show, she turned away and started for the passenger's side of the low slung car, but Evan was there first, holding the door for her.

"My lady," he gestured with a sweep of his arm, bending over at the waist in a low bow.

"Oh, brother!" she laughed, knowing that no matter what she had said, she was not about to turn down a dinner date with the man she had always loved.

Evan helped her into the seatbelt and leaned over her, kissing her lightly on the lips. "Oh fairest maiden, come away with me." His long lashes brushed her cheek.

"You're such a clown! Get in the car and quit being so weird. By the way, have you ever considered trimming those lashes? Honestly, it's just not fair!" Jenny said, pushing him away, hoping he didn't notice the flush on her cheeks, or the rapid beating of her heart.

"Nope, it's part of my charm. It appears I will need every bit, if I am going to win the heart of my dinner date." He pinched her lightly on her ear and then went around to the driver's side and got in the car. Turning on the key, he revved up the powerful motor and with a grin in her direction, spun the tires and roared off down the dirt road, ignoring the 15 mph speed limit. Jenny threw her head back and laughed. It was so good to be back home – and wonderful to be with Evan again.

The waiter stopped by the small, candlelit table, and hesitated. He didn't want to interrupt the handsome couple, but they appeared to be finished with their dinner. The posh North Shore restaurant sat on the top floor of Harrah's Hotel and management had a strict code for their waiters. They were to keep a close eye on the customers, but were never to be intrusive. Basically, they were to be invisible until needed. The well-trained waiters learned to read people well.

"Excuse me, sir. Can I get you a dessert menu?" the waiter asked softly. It was obvious the two young people were in deep conversation.

Evan looked up, then over to Jenny. "Dessert?" he asked.

"Oh, no thanks, I have had more than enough. In Paris the servings are never this large. I can't remember when I ate so much at one time, but thank you anyway," she smiled up at the polite face of the waiter, and then looked over at Evan." You go ahead."

"Nope, not me, I have to watch my figure, but Jen you could use…" he stopped as he saw the warning look in Jenny's eyes. "Sorry, babe." He looked at the waiter. "Guess we're good." Then asked, "How about an after dinner drink, maybe a Grand Marnier, or something?"

Jenny wasn't sure she was going to keep this baby, but if she did she wasn't going to do anything that might harm it either. "Evan, please, you have one. I'm on the wagon for awhile." She looked away, afraid the tremble in her voice might betray her feelings.

Evan heard the quiver in her answer and waved away the waiter.

"Jen, please, I know there's something you're not telling me. I've felt it from the moment I sat down by you on the beach. You can trust me with whatever it is. We've been friends forever. There's a reason you came home looking like you've been on a starvation diet. I want to help. Whatever it is, tell me." He reached over and took her small, cold hand. Looking into her eyes, he was not surprised to see big tears trailing down her cheeks.

"Okay, that's it. We're getting out of here. We'll go somewhere more private. You're going to spill the beans."

Evan paid the waiter, who had been carefully monitoring the two, and got up from the table. He helped Jenny to her feet, and taking her by the hand, led her out across the thick, deep blue carpet and out the door. When they got outside the hotel, he handed the valet the ticket for his car. As they waited for it to appear, he put his arm around her and drew her closely to him.

"Don't worry Jen. Your buddy, Evan, is here."

Jenny leaned against his lean, strong body and took a deep breath. Should she tell Evan about the baby? And, would she ever be able to tell him she wanted him to be more than "her buddy?"

In a few minutes, the valet appeared with the Corvette, pulled up to the curb and jumped out. He opened both doors and waited for his tip.

"Thank you, sir. Nice car," the young man said admiringly, as Evan handed him a five-dollar bill.

"Thanks. I worked hard for it!" Evan looked at Jenny

and winked. She giggled. She knew the car was a birthday present from his parents. They gave him a new one each year. Just because he was a grown man and a successful attorney didn't mean Sissy was going to quit spoiling him.

Chapter Thirteen

The full moon laid a path of silver across the night-darkened water of the lake, and a cool evening breeze stirred Jenny's hair. They had stopped at a tiny, hidden cove and walked down to the beach, where they sat down on a rough log. The moon cast a glow on Jenny's red curls and her pale skin looked translucent.

Evan felt a stab of pain in his chest. She was so beautiful. Why was she always just out of reach? He felt for her hand. "It's truth time, Jen. I'm waiting. Start from the beginning. I promise not to interrupt."

Jenny looked at his dearly familiar face, and her lips trembled. Before she could stop them, the words began to tumble out.

"I'm pregnant, Evan. I came home to get an abortion, but I couldn't go through with it. I guess in his own way, Diego couldn't either. He left me in the doctor's office in Las Vegas. He went back to Paris." She saw the stunned look on Evan's face and quickly continued. "I don't know what to do, Evan. Please, don't get angry with me. I haven't told anyone else. Maybe I should do it. I don't know. What do you think?"

"Jen, you can't ask me to give you an answer about something like this. It has to be your decision. I'll help you any way I can, but don't ask me to tell you what to do."

"I'm sorry, of course you can't, but I need you to help me make a decision. Tell me if I am doing the right thing for my family, for me, for the baby."

Evan sat back and stared up into the star filled sky. Nowhere else were the stars this bright and clear. He wished he could reach up and grab one and give it to Jenny. He took a deep breath.

"There's something I have never told you, Jen. I never thought I would tell anyone, but now it may be important for you to know." He looked across the lake at the distant mountains. "I don't know how much your parents have told you about the time when - now don't laugh - a ghost appeared at the cove. It's a long story. Seems my grandfather stole an exquisite necklace from the Clear Water graveyard. It belonged to a dance hall girl that lived in Virginia City way back in the days of the big silver strike. She died at Clear Water Cove when it was a lumber camp. She was caught in a snowstorm wearing the last thing of value she owned, this famous blue diamond necklace.

My grandparents were getting ready for Mom's wedding, and Grandfather wanted to give her something special. He robbed the grave and took the necklace. But, his bodyguard stole it before he could give it to her. The bodyguard was drowned taking the necklace to North Shore in Grandfather's speedboat and it went to the bottom of the cove, inside the boat. Grandfather hired a diver to try to recover it, but he drowned trying. Your father did recover it, with the apparent help of the ghost,

Sirena. Later, when I was seven years old, I stole if from your parent's house, and then lost it again when I was showing off for you diving off the pilings. As far as I know, it's still down there."

Jenny looked at him curiously. She had heard the tale of the diamonds and vividly remembered the day Evan had lost them in the lake. She also remembered seeing Sirena's ghost under the water. Apparently Evan had forgotten she had been there.

"I know a little about the story, Evan, but what has that got to do with me?"

Evan dug in the sand with his shoe. Should he tell Jenny the whole story? Why not? She needed to hear it all.

"Jen, at the time, my mom was engaged to your dad." He heard the gasp of surprise and saw Jenny's eyes fly open. "Let me finish, please. *Your* mother and dad had been in love since high school, but somehow lost touch. Your dad never thought he would see Carolyn again, and so my mom, you know her Jen, snapped him up. She was very pretty back then. Grandfather promised your dad the world if he would marry her, because that's what she wanted, and Mother always got what she wanted, at least up until then. When your mom appeared back here at the Cove, your dad fell in love with her all over again and dumped my mother."

"Oh, Evan, that must have been awful for Sissy!" Jenny could hardly believe she hadn't known all this before.

"No, don't feel sorry for her, Jen. It was at that time the diver Grandfather hired, was looking for the necklace. Mom met him, and immediately fell back in love with, in her words, the most handsome man she had ever seen. He had black hair and brown eyes with the most unbelievably long eyelashes she had ever seen."

Jenny sucked in her breath. Was this going where she thought it was? She sat very still, not daring to interrupt.

"Before he drowned they had an affair. A month after the drowning, she and my dad were married. Everyone thought I was a month early, but the truth was, my real father was the diver, Jim Evans."

"Oh, Evan, I never knew! What did your father think when Sissy named you Evan? Did he know she was pregnant when they got married?"

"I don't know, Jen, but as I grew older he had to know. Apparently I look exactly like my real dad. I always wondered if Mom told him. I think that might be the cause of all the problems in their marriage. Dad was madly in love with Mom his whole life, kind of like your mom and dad, so when she agreed to marry him in such a hurry he didn't question anything but his good fortune. After I was born and didn't remotely resemble him, or my mother, he must have questioned Mom. She only told me a year or so ago. Don't know what prompted her to tell me, but she made me swear not to let Dad know she had."

Jenny could only stare at Evan, trying hard to absorb all she was hearing.

"I'm telling you this, Jen, because as much of a bitch as I know Sissy can be, she didn't have an abortion. Lord knows she could have. My grandparents had plenty of money, and Grandfather had plenty of shady friends that could have arranged it, even though it was illegal back then. She risked her marriage by keeping it a secret. She was afraid if she told Dad, he would reject me, or worse yet, leave her."

"Evan, I'm so sorry! I don't know what to say!"

"You don't have to feel sorry for me, Jen. I think Dad knew, but he has always treated me like his own blood.

I know he loves me. Anyway, there you have it. If Mom had done what you are considering, I wouldn't be here. Not that I'm anything special, but I would have missed growing up here at Tahoe and would not have had the opportunity to know you."

Jenny put her arms around Evan's broad shoulders and hugged him.

"Thank you for telling me, Evan. I know how hard it was for you. It certainly gives me something to think about. I can't imagine not having you in my life. Are you mad at me for being so stupid?"

"Of course not, I'm just jealous of the guy you thought so much of, you allowed him to do this to you."

"I thought I was in love, but I was on the rebound from a love I felt was hopeless." Jenny turned her face away; she didn't want Evan to see the look in her eyes.

"Whoever *that* fellow was he must be crazy. Hopefully you're over that."

"Maybe, maybe not, time will tell," Jenny said softly

"Well, that's enough confession for tonight. Come on; let's get out of here. You need your sleep. If you decide to go through with this you are going to have to take better care of yourself." Pulling her to her feet, Evan walked her slowly back to his car, her stunning revelation echoing in his head. Jenny, his Jenny, was carrying another man's child and he had spent the last half hour telling her she should keep it. He sincerely hoped history was not repeating itself, or maybe he was hoping it would!

Chapter Fourteen

Evan zipped up his hoodie as he walked along the shoreline. The morning sun had yet to warm the air. He had come out for an early walk, unable to sleep. Thinking about Jenny's situation had kept him awake all night. He wasn't sure how he felt about it. At one time, he thought he was in love with her, but their relationship was always more like brother and sister. Maybe that was the problem. They were too close to see how much they really cared for each other, if that was possible. He looked out beyond the old railroad pilings at the deep place in the lake where his father had drowned long ago. Their conversation the night before had reminded him about the promise he had made to himself when he was a boy, about finding the necklace when he grew up. Well, he was grown up now. He was financially successful, and could well afford the equipment he needed to look for it. He had never done anything so dangerous. His mother wouldn't have tolerated it. But, he was not under her control anymore. Frankly, he could use some excitement in his life. Jenny was taking a big risk if she had this baby, maybe he should take one of his own. Besides, he still felt guilty about losing it; it was a piece of jewelry that could have been incredibly valuable to Jenny.

He walked faster, his nose was cold and his eyes were tearing from the nippy, morning breeze. Looking up he saw he had come to the bank where Jenny's house stood. He jammed his hands into his sweatshirt and stared up at the imposing old lady of the cove. Jenny's great grandparents had built the house in the 30's. It was one of the few that fronted the lake. It was old, but wonderful. He loved the fact that the house had never been remodeled and still held all the charm of the early days of Clear Water Cove.

"Hey there, come up and have some coffee." The clear, high voice shook him from his thoughts, and he turned his head to see Jenny standing at the top of the stone steps. With her halo of red curls, blue bathrobe and fresh scrubbed face, she looked like a pale, but beautiful angel. Evan felt a ripple of pleasure. He would tell her his idea of going after the necklace and see what she thought about it.

'Hey there yourself, I'm on my way." Ducking his head against the breeze, he ran across the sand and up the stairs, taking Jenny into his arms in a bear hug.

Caught by surprise, Jenny instinctively snuggled against him; loving the feeling of security he gave her. Being in Evan's arms felt so natural.

"Umm, you smell great, sweetie," Evan said against her cheek. Then he pulled back, surprised by the surge of emotion he felt, certainly not brotherly. He lifted her chin and kissed her soft mouth. Surprised as he was at the unexpected urge, he was even more surprised when she returned the kiss.

"Well, my little friend has grown up!" Evan looked

into her half closed, blue eyes. "I believe that's the first time I've ever kissed you. I didn't realize what I've been missing all these years."

Jenny felt her heart pounding. She felt dizzy. How many times in her life had she wanted this to happen? She couldn't even count how often she had dreamed about kissing Evan. Was this just a whim? Did it mean anything? Shaken, she stepped back quickly, turning to lead the way to the big, warm kitchen, where coffee and breakfast were waiting.

"Wait up, Jenny. Don't run away. I'm sorry. I didn't mean to startle you. You looked so tempting standing there – sorry." He caught up with her and took her hand. "Come on! It's me, Evan. You know we're just buds. Didn't mean a thing, okay? Can I still have that cup of coffee, even if I was out of line?"

At the back door, Jenny turned to face him. His heart stopped as he saw the tears sliding down her face. "Evan, do you have any idea how many years I have waited and wished for you to do that? Didn't you have any idea how I felt about you?"

Evan felt confused, and then a flash of insight crossed his mind. There was a reason why Jenny had stayed so close all these years, but the reason was one he had never guessed. What a dope he was. He had let this lovely girl slip out of his hands. She had run away because of him! All this was his fault. He had been too stupid to realize what he had right in front of his nose.

He stood there looking at her, his face a study in sadness. "Ah, my little Jenny. I never knew. You never said a word. I would go to the ends of the earth for you. You know that. We were always such good friends. I never looked beyond how great it was just to have that much.

Sometimes you can be too close to someone to really see them."

Jenny brushed the tears from her cheeks and a sad smile stole across her face. "It's a little late for tears, isn't it? I took the wrong fork in the road and now I have to pay the price. Losing you may be the worst of it."

"You haven't lost me, Jen. Now that I know how you feel maybe we can take it a step or two further and see what happens."

"I don't think that's possible now. After talking to you last night and hearing your story, I've made up my mind. I'm keeping the baby, Evan. I couldn't live with myself if I didn't give it the chance your mother gave to you."

Evan took a deep breath. "I'm not sorry I told you about my past and I'm glad you've decided to go through with this. And, Jen, I want you to know, I'm with you every step of the way. Now come on, we'll talk more, later. I'm freezing and that coffee sounds better every minute." He gave her a quick kiss on the cheek as she opened the kitchen door and she felt a glimmer of hope. Perhaps the future wouldn't be so bleak after all.

"Evan! Come in and sit down. I didn't know you were coming for breakfast."

Carolyn hugged the tall engaging man. She marveled, as always, at how handsome he was – and how much he looked like Jim!

"Would you like some bacon and eggs? I'm cooking for my skinny little girl; you might as well join her. Tom has already eaten and gone to the office so make yourself at home." She pulled out a chair at the weathered oak kitchen table. Evan grinned and sat down. As always, he felt more at home here in Carolyn and Tom's large warm kitchen, than he did at his own home.

"Thanks, I'll take you up on the offer. The cold air

and long walk on the beach made me hungry. Maybe if I down a hearty breakfast your starving child will follow suit." He looked across the table and winked. "Between you and me, Carolyn, we'll take care of her and put some meat back on those bones."

"Okay, okay, you guys. That's enough!" Jenny tried to sound angry, but failed. It was wonderful to know these two special people cared so much about her. Soon, she was going to have to tell her mother about the baby. Jenny hoped she wouldn't mind being a grandmother. She certainly didn't look like one yet!

Chapter Fifteen

Evan sat back and mopped up the last little puddle of egg yoke with a piece of buttered toast. Groaning, he pushed away from the table. "Wow! I haven't eaten that much since I was in high school. Thanks, Carolyn that was great." He pointed at the plate in front of Jenny. "I'm sitting here until every bit of what's on that plate has disappeared." Seeing Jenny start to protest, he added, "I'm a patient man." Then taking his cup to the counter, he poured more coffee and sat back down. "While you're eating the rest of your breakfast, tell me what you think of my next new adventure here at the Cove."

Jenny smiled. This would be good. Evan wasn't the adventurous type. He was probably going to tell her about a new type of golf club he was going to try. But his next sentence caused her fork to stop in midair, and she almost dropped it.

"I've decided to look for the blue diamond necklace."

Carolyn had been standing by the sink cleaning up the frying pan when Evan made his announcement. She felt her skin crawl. She put the pan down and turned around slowly. He couldn't do that! There was no way she would let him try to do the same thing that had killed his father. But, she thought, he doesn't know that, or does he? She was afraid to say anything about Jim until she found out what, if anything, Evan had been told. Still, she had to say something.

"That's the most preposterous idea I have ever heard of, Evan. Those diamonds belong right where they are. Do you have any idea what you could stir up by trying to find them again? And heaven help us all if you were to be successful!" She picked the pan back up and wiped it furiously, then shoved in into a cupboard. Her heart was racing. Was this why she had seen the lights on the water? Could Sirena possibly have known what Evan was going to do?

"Now Carolyn, don't tell me you really think that old ghost story is true!" He leaned back in his chair; his deep vibrant laugh chilled her even further.

"Do I think it's true? I know it's true, Evan. You weren't even born when all the trouble started. Tom saw her, I saw her, and Jim Evans saw her. None of us wanted to believe what we had seen, but we should have. If we hadn't gotten involved in trying to recover the necklace, lots of very bad things would never have happened."

Jenny pushed her still unfinished plate aside. "I don't think it's a very good idea either, Evan. Even if Sirena hasn't been seen or heard from for years, there is no reason to provoke her again."

Evan looked at Jenny with wonder. "You believe in all this ghost stuff, too?"

"If Mom and Dad say they saw her, then I believe them. Stranger things than that have happened. Even if there were no ghost, diving as deep as you would have to in this lake would be a crazy idea. Please, don't try it.

Nothing is worth risking another life. Please, don't let history repeat itself!"

Carolyn looked up quickly. Jenny knew the story, but did Evan know Jim was his father? When Evan left, she and Jenny would have a talk. She would find out what Jenny knew.

"Look" Evan said. "I didn't mean to upset both of you. I'll admit it's a pretty wild idea, but it is intriguing. Maybe I'll succeed where my dad didn't!"

Carolyn caught her breath. He did know and he didn't seem to care if they did too! Or was it a slip of the tongue? She saw Jenny frown, not in surprise or puzzlement, but in disagreement. Jenny knew, too! When had he told her, and why?

"I still see food on that plate, Jen." Evan said, trying to change the subject. "If you eat it all, I'll promise to put the idea away – for now."

"I can't eat another bite. I think my stomach has shrunk. I never eat breakfast. I promise I'll try to stretch it, but it will take time." She gave him a secret smile. "It won't be hard."

Evan got up and stretched. " I have to go. Thanks again for the great breakfast, Carolyn. Think I'll go up to the club and see if I can get in a round of golf. I only have a week or so before I have to go back to the grind. I'll see you later, freckles." He tugged a strand of Jenny's curls. "Just one day on the beach made those little beauties pop right out. Now you look more like your mom than ever."

Jenny touched her nose self-consciously. He must be teasing. She couldn't have acquired freckles this quickly. "Will I see you again before you leave?"

"You can count on it. We still have a lot of catching up to do"

After Evan left, Carolyn sat down at the table and

looked at her daughter closely. "Is there anything going on between the two of you that I should know about?"

Jenny's wide blue eyes looked innocently at her mother. "I don't think so, Mom. You know we've always been good friends. We haven't seen each other in a long time. Its fun catching up on everything, that's all."

Carolyn knew there was more to it than that, but she also knew Jenny would tell her what she was keeping to herself in her own good time. She could wait a little longer. The ringing of the telephone brought her to her feet. A deep masculine voice was on the other end asking for Jenny.

"Who's calling? Carolyn asked.

"It's Justin King. I saw Jenny at the airport and I was calling to see if she got home okay."

"Ask her yourself, my dear," and Carolyn handed the phone to Jenny. "It's your airport friend, Justin King."

Jenny reached for the phone. "Justin, it's nice to hear from you. Are you at the ranch?" she asked.

"Yes, I'm home. I couldn't get you out of my mind this morning. I've been thinking about you ever since we met at the airport. I thought I would call and see if you were up to a riding lesson?"

Jenny remembered the handsome blonde man with the big dimples and the charming smile who had surprised her at the airport. "I really appreciate the offer, Justin, but I don't think so. There are a lot of things I have to take care of here. But, if you have some free time why don't you come up to the cove for the day? Do you play golf?" No horseback riding this year, fellow. Jenny thought to herself, but she felt bad turning him down completely, he was such a nice man.

"No, I haven't had time to take up the game, but I might be able to come up in a week or so to visit with you.

We're busy right now cutting hay. Dad isn't doing much work anymore, so it's up to me to oversee the operation of the ranch. Wish you could come, but I understand," he felt a stab of disappointment. He had set his heart on showing Jenny the ranch. "I'll call you again later, if that's alright?"

Jenny heard the disappointment in his voice. She could hardly tell him why she couldn't risk getting tossed off a horse. She didn't know the first thing about riding and this wasn't a good time to learn. "Call anytime, Justin. Let us know when you can come up and we'll plan a day at the beach. If you don't play golf maybe we can go for a sail?"

"Sounds like a plan. Take care now, I'll call you." Justin hung up the phone and left the spacious wood paneled den of the architectural wonder that was his family's ranch house. He walked down to the barn and saddled his horse. Plans for the enchanting Jenny would have to be put on hold. Probably just as well, he was still seeing an older woman. Ruth was the sister of a girl he had been madly in love with a long time ago. It was pretty much one-sided, a rebound type of affair. He knew she was in love with him. He had enjoyed her company for the past few years, but maybe it was time to break it off. He wasn't good at handling two women at once and he was determined to find a way to see more of Jenny.

Chapter Sixteen

Diego heard the phone ring for the tenth time but there was still no answer. Damn it! Where was Jenny? There had to be someone at the house sometime during the day. Slamming down the useless instrument, he grabbed a jacket and left his apartment.

Minutes later he stood in the doorway of a tall elegant townhouse. It was pouring rain and his expensive leather coat was getting soaked. He stamped his foot in annoyance. Where was Claire? She usually left her key under the shutter for him, but it wasn't there today. Paris had never seemed so uninviting, nor had the townhouse of his latest wealthy conquest. He needed money. He had to go to Nevada and find Jenny. He hadn't had a peaceful night's sleep since he left her in Las Vegas. What was it about her? Taking money from rich lonely women had never bothered his conscience but it was different with Jenny. Maybe it was because she was carrying his child, he didn't know. He couldn't figure it out. It wasn't like him to care deeply or at length about a woman.

The rain started coming down harder and he jammed

his finger against the doorbell again. Just as he was about to give up, he heard footsteps and the door opened. A tall burly man in a bathrobe stood there with an unpleasant look on his face. He looked annoyed and quite at home.

"Yes? What do you want?" he asked sharply.

Diego was puzzled. As far as he knew Claire lived alone. Who was this guy? Even with water dripping off his hair down his face and into his eyes, Diego tried to be polite.

"Is Claire at home?" he asked, wishing the big oaf would at least invite him in out of the downpour.

"Claire has gone to the south of France for a week. I'm looking after her place until she returns. Would you care to leave your card?" The unfriendly house sitter didn't move from the entryway.

"No, that's alright. I'll see her when she gets back." Diego turned around and walked quickly down the wet sidewalk, trying to avoid the puddles that were rapidly forming. He cursed silently. Claire was his last resort. She hadn't told him she was leaving town. What was up with that? Was he losing his touch? It would take some time to cultivate a new profitable alliance but he had no choice. Maybe he would have better luck in Madrid. At least he could stay with his parents until he snared a gullible divorcee. Nevertheless soon, very soon, he would buy a plane ticket to Nevada and have a meeting with Jenny.

Jenny stared at the telephone and took a deep breath. She saw Diego's number on the readout. It was hard to keep from picking up the call. She had been home for three months now. At first he had called every night, but now the calls were not as frequent. Still, he called at least once a week.

"Why don't you just give up, you rat," Jenny whispered out loud to the telephone. She glanced at the kitchen clock. It was 10:00pm. She hoped the ringing of the phone hadn't awakened her parents. Finally the ringing stopped and she gave a sigh of relief. He had lost all right to talk to her, or see her, when he left her to face this unwanted pregnancy on her own. Unwanted at first, she mused, but not now. Yesterday, she had felt the first faint movements from the tiny life she was carrying. Even if she had entertained the idea of an abortion, it was out of the question now. There was a real little person inside her, a child already formed. It was her responsibility, her duty, to see this to the end.

She had been half asleep dozing in front of the blazing fireplace when the call came. Now she was wide-awake, and knew she wouldn't be able to sleep. Diego's calls always upset her. Grabbing a coat, she stepped outside into the cold November night. The sky was dark and moonless, the stars bright as headlights in the velvety black sky. She stared out over the water to the end of the pilings and shivered. It was still creepy to think about the ghost, Sirena, and how she had lured Jim to his death. Her mother had told her how she had tried to dissuade him from going back for that last dive to find the necklace. Poor Evan, Jenny thought. He never knew his real father. She couldn't imagine that. She was so close to her own dad.

She had been spending more time with Evan these past few months. He had been coming up to the lake almost every weekend, acting so protective, watching over her like a big brother. Her focus now was on having a healthy baby. She didn't need or want any emotional involvement, at least for now. When the baby was born, Evan would probably fade out of the picture. He wouldn't be interested in raising another man's child. Or would he? After all, that's what his dad had done. Well, that was a long way off; she would deal with all that later.

As she turned to go back inside, her eyes caught a shimmer of brightness over the pothole. She sucked in her breath. What was that? As she watched, the light pulsed and brightened. Her heart raced. Fascinated, she couldn't turn away. For a few long minutes the lights played over the water, then as suddenly as they appeared, they vanished. It must be what Mom saw before I came home, she thought. It was the strangest thing she had ever witnessed. Her mother was probably sound asleep, but Jenny had to wake her up right now and tell her she hadn't imagined the lights.

She tiptoed up the stairs and down the hall to her parent's bedroom, and knocked gently on the door. Hearing only Tom's rumbling snore, she pushed open the door and peered in. A smile curved around her lips as she saw her mom and dad cuddled together. She marveled at how much in love they still were. She felt a pang of envy. Would she ever find a partner in life she would love that much, and more important, who would return her love equally? She hesitated; they both looked so comfortable, and *so sound asleep*. Turning around, she left the room, closing the door softly behind her. She would tell them both in the morning. It would be interesting to get her father's take on the lights.

Chapter Seventeen

Jenny lay in bed feeling the small flutters in her stomach that told her the baby was also awake. She rolled over on her side and crooked her right arm into a V. Grasping the upper half with her left thumb and first finger, she measured how much weight she had gained. If she could still touch the sheet on both sides, she was doing all right. With a sigh of relief, she found she could. She felt like she had already put on a lot of weight, but in reality the scales told her she had only gained ten pounds. Ten pounds Evan said she had needed without being pregnant.

She put one hand on her stomach and patted it gently. She was getting excited about this baby. It would be beautiful if it was a girl, handsome if it was a boy. With a father as smoky eyed and darkly handsome as Diego, it had to be. Somewhere she had heard that a blonde and a dark brunette would always produce a redhead. Idly, she wondered what a redhead and a dark brunette would produce. Silly thoughts ran through her head. She would be content to just have a healthy baby. Sighing, she rolled onto her side. The baby kicked harder. How was she supposed to sleep with all that going on?

A strange noise made Jenny sit up. She pushed aside the covers. Slipping out of bed, she walked to the window wondering if the lights might return, but the lake lay black and smooth under the starlit night. Picking up her cell phone off the end table, she flipped it open and checked her messages. Diego had called again. Would he never give up? If she had her way, he would never see this baby. He hadn't wanted it before; she wasn't about to give him a chance now. She had taken on all the responsibility and challenges, not to mention the expenses. As far as she was concerned he was out of their lives forever.

She pulled on a warm wool robe and wandered out into the living room. The fireplace was still glowing with the dying embers of the fire they had lit that evening. It cast flickering shadows around the room. Out of the corner of her eye, she caught a movement in the kitchen. With her heart racing, she slipped behind the door to listen. The house was dead quiet. It must have been an ember popping in the hearth, she told herself, and moved back out into the room. She walked cautiously toward the open kitchen door.

As Jenny entered the kitchen, she gave a gasp and felt the blood drain from her face. Seated at the table on one of the low benches was the shadowy figure of a beautiful woman. Her long black hair fell down her back in waves and her dark eyes were fixed on Jenny. The scent of heady perfume filled the air.

Frozen to the spot, Jenny could only stare at the intruder. The woman lifted a hand and beckoned her closer.

"Please, sit down." The woman's whispery voice fell on

Jenny's ears like the brush of a bird's wing. It was as if she was hearing the words in her head, not with her ears.

"Who are you?" Jenny stammered, too frightened to move.

"Sit and I will tell you why I am here." A smile flitted across the woman's face and once again she lifted a graceful hand and beckoned to Jenny.

As if drawn forward by an invisible cord, Jenny walked to the table and sat down across from the apparition. Although she seemed real, Jenny could see the pine boards of the walls through her body. What was this thing, she asked herself? Jenny felt as cold as ice as she stared hard at the specter, trying to see if the woman was real.

"You are having a daughter, Jennifer, and also a son. They will be well and healthy, but only if you help me."

The woman's intense eyes burned into her and Jenny felt her heart stop. What was she talking about? Could she really be having twins? She hadn't had an ultrasound yet, but… She thought of all the movement she had felt So much, so early. Could it be true? If so, what could this apparition want with her? How was she going to help a ghost? Under the table she pinched her thigh hard, digging her fingernails in and winced at the ensuing pain. No, she wasn't dreaming.

"Help you? How can I help you, I don't even know who you are?"

The whispery voice sounded sad. "Oh, I think you know, Jennifer. You saw me in the lake when you were a little girl, a long time ago."

Jenny sucked in her breath. "Sirena?" she breathed.

The apparition seemed to fade a bit and then looked more solid. Her dark eyes bore into Jenny's. "Yes."

"What do you mean my baby will be healthy, *IF* I help you? You won't harm it will you?" Jenny was close to tears. She shook her head, trying to see if the nightmarish figure would go away.

The woman ignored the question. "I need your help. If you do what I ask, when the time comes, I will help you find your daughter."

Oh my God! Jenny felt a scream rise from somewhere deep inside her but she shut it down. She had to keep control. Shaking with terror, she asked. "Tell me what you want. I will do anything to keep my child safe."

The woman tilted her head, suddenly looking as impish as she was fey. "It's a simple thing, Jennifer. You must keep that young man from trying to take my necklace from the lake. His father died trying to get it away from me. His son might be successful. If he were, it would prove to be disastrous. That's all, my dear. It's my necklace. You must stop him. It will prove to be of great importance to you." When she finished talking, Sirena's ghostly figure began to fade and then disappeared completely and Jenny was left looking at an empty room. She looked around wildly, her heart thumping so hard it felt like it would leap out of her chest. She felt the baby kicking so hard it hurt.

"What's happening?" Jenny whispered out loud as she sat stunned, then staggering to her feet she returned to her bedroom and collapsed on the edge of the bed. She looked out of the window. To her astonishment she saw the hazy figure of a woman floating across the lake in an aura of light only to disappear over the deep hole, exactly where Jim Evans had drowned.

Jenny lay down on the bed and buried herself under the covers. She didn't seem able to stop shivering. She reached for the extra down comforter and pulled it up on top of the blankets. Tomorrow she would go to see her doctor. She would insist on an ultrasound. She had to find out if the ghost was telling the truth. She bit her lip, how would she be able to handle twins? She shook her head to clear it. How could a ghost know she was having twins? On the other hand, if she had just seen a ghost then anything might be possible. Evan had not said anymore about trying to recover the necklace, at least not to her. He might not tell her though. He knew she didn't approve. In the morning she would tell her parents about the sighting of Sirena. This weird ghost seemed to be a part of their family history. They would know what she should do. If what Sirena said was true, it might be very important to make sure Evan left the necklace right where it was. Finally, the kicking of the baby quieted and exhausted, Jenny fell into a deep sleep.

Chapter Eighteen

"Tom, would you run upstairs and wake up Jenny? Her breakfast is getting cold." Carolyn glanced up at the kitchen clock. "She never sleeps this late. Maybe I should go up." But Tom was already on his way up the stairs.

He and Carolyn had been keeping a close watch on their daughter. She had finally told them about the baby. Carolyn had been torn between shock, bewilderment and delight at the thought of having a baby in the house again. She and Tom had wanted more children, but after Jenny was born, she failed to conceive again. Jenny was their life and their joy. Now she needed them more than ever and there was no way they would let her down. Evan had been a saint, managing to come home every weekend to take Jenny out for dinner and give her life a little spark. Carolyn sighed, if only they could see how perfect they were for each other.

"Here's the sleepy head." Tom said, coming into the kitchen, followed closely by a pajama clad, sleepy eyed Jenny.

"Sorry I slept so late, Mom. I had a terrible dream last night. At least I think it was a dream. And, I saw your lights, – or I think I did." She shook her head and sat down. "It's all a jumble now. It was so clear last night. Our friend Sirena was back. Wait 'til I tell you what she said."

Tom and Carolyn looked at each other. This wasn't good news. Jenny didn't need to be getting visits from the Lady of the Lake. What could she possibly want with their daughter?

Tom spoke gently. "Tell us what you saw, baby. Don't worry, we are well acquainted with the old gal, you can't surprise us with anything she might say, or do."

"Then you think she's real, Dad? I mean, it could have been a dream." Jenny's wide eyes searched their faces for an answer.

"Well, real or not, this family and Evan's family have been affected by her appearances. Let us decide whether or not you had a dream, or if it sounds like the ghost we all know and love." Tom tried to lighten the mood, but he saw Jenny's face grow pale. "No matter what, Jen, she can't hurt you, you can only be affected by her, if you let her. She's just a ghost. She's not capable of real harm."

Jenny took a deep breath. "Of course, Dad, you're right. But, the thing is, she warned me not to let Evan go back to look for the necklace. How did she know he was planning anything like that? And Mom, Dad, she said I was going to have twins and it was important for their safety that I keep Evan away from her diamonds. It was just too weird. She was sitting right here last night. Right here at this table. She was talking to me just like I am talking to you now, clear as day, except I could see right through her!" Jenny paused and ran her hand through her tousled curls. "Boy does that sound freaky! Maybe I was just dreaming."

"Tell you what, darling," Carolyn put her arm around her daughter, "just so you don't worry about anything so silly, we'll call Dr. Avery after breakfast and make an appointment. You're at least four months along, certainly by now they can tell if there is more than one little person inside that tummy." She smoothed the hair back from Jenny's forehead. "If by some remote chance you *are* carrying twins, think how much fun it would be!"

Jenny tried to smile. Having twins would be a unique challenge. She was an only child and didn't want to have an only child, but she would prefer to have one at a time. She would have much preferred the second one to be Evan's.

"Turn around now and eat your breakfast. I'll go make the appointment. If we're going to have two babies, you'll have to eat more!"

Jenny's heart thumped. Her mother was acting like the visit from Sirena had actually happened, but she wasn't convinced. She would wait and see what the doctor found out. Then, if the ghost was telling the truth, she would have to have a very serious talk with Evan. Had he ever had an encounter with Sirena himself? Jenny didn't think so. She wondered if he knew about her at all. How much had Sissy told him about how Jim had died? Had she told him about the encounters Jim had with the ghost? If not, Evan might not believe her. She would just have to cross that bridge when she came to it. The sharp kicking of the baby made her straighten up and hold her breath. It was beginning to feel like a whole nursery school in her belly.

Chapter Nineteen

Snow lay deep and frozen over the roads that wound through the winter pasture. It caused the big, Dodge truck with its long trailer load of hay, to slide and weave precariously.

"Damn." Justin swore out loud. "I don't know why I don't hire someone else to do this! It's not like we can't afford to!"

"Guess you just can't trust anyone else, Boss." Mike smiled over at his boss. He had been working at Eagle's View for fifteen years and he knew Justin as well as anyone. "If you didn't love this place, you would have left all this to hired help a long time ago."

Justin pushed down gently on the brake pedal as they skidded around a corner, hoping to keep the truck on the road. "Yeah, you're right, Mike, it's in my blood. But, there are definitely times when I wish I was on a beach in Hawaii."

They slowed to a stop as a large herd of hungry cattle came into view. The animals began a chorus of low bellows when they smelled the hay truck. The two men got out and waded through the deep crusty snow to the trailer. They picked up big tined forks off the back of the trailer and began to toss the hay to the hungry cattle.

After the trailer was unloaded, the men got back in the truck and turned around, heading back to the ranch house. Mike settled down and dozed as they began the slow, cautious drive. Justin looked over at his faithful employee and sighed. It looked like it would be a long, quiet drive home, but Mike deserved the rest. No one worked harder.

As he drove, Justin's mind wandered. He wished he had someone important in his life. The love of his life, Maggie, had married someone else, and her sister, Ruth, who he had dated for some time, was teaching school in Washoe Valley, a long drive away. It seemed he was always busy here at the ranch, and Ruth was always busy with her school kids, which made dating a seldom occurrence. His dad depended on him now that he was getting on in years. Justin's father had sold all his companies, so now his parents had all the money they needed to live a luxurious life. So could he, if he didn't love getting his hands into everything having to do with running the ranch. His twin sister, Julie, was happily married to a lawyer. They lived in San Francisco with their two children. He rarely saw them. Any interest she had in the ranch had faded when her children were born. Now her time was devoted to her family. And so it should be, he thought.

He thought about Jenny, the stunning, red haired girl he had met at the airport a few months ago. He had been too busy as usual, to take her up on the offer to come to Clear Water Cove. He hadn't gotten around to calling, either. He brushed his blonde hair back with one work-hardened hand. Holding up his hand, he stared at it for a moment, seeing all the cuts and calluses. Not a hand a girl would appreciate, he thought. Maybe he should take a vacation in the spring. No, not a good time he mused, the cows would be calving and he would need to be here. Was there ever a good time? Maybe he could go in the summer when the hands could pretty much take care of everything. The cattle would be moved to the higher pastures and on their own. Only the horses and farm animals would have to be looked after. He slowed as a lone coyote loped across the road. It stopped for a minute and gave the truck a furtive look, then disappeared into a stand of aspen trees. He sighed. As much as he loved this place, he really needed to take a break.

Jenny pulled on her heavy winter parka and opened the door to an icy February morning. The blast of cold air made her catch her breath. The doctor had told her to take a walk every day, but as she grew bigger, the once pleasant stroll around the golf course was becoming more of a chore. Just as Jenny stepped outside the telephone rang. Her parents had left on various errands, so she should answer it. As usual, her heart skipped a beat fearing it might be Diego, even though he hadn't called for months. Not since last fall. Every time the phone rang she prayed it wasn't him. She never picked up his calls, but still, ignoring him made her feel uncomfortable. After all, the two babies she was carrying were his children. Clumsily, she stepped back inside and made her way to the kitchen phone. The unfamiliar number on the readout told her it was not Diego.

"Hello?" she answered, slightly out of breath.

"Hi, Jenny, remember me? Justin King. We met at

the party at the lake last summer, and again last fall at the airport."

"Hello, Justin. Of course I remember you. You were going to come up and visit last fall." Jenny pictured the tall, blonde, cowboy with the stunning blue eyes. Too bad horses weren't one of her favorite things.

"I know, and I apologize. It's not that I didn't want to come, but I've been very busy here on the ranch and haven't had a moment for myself. All that aside, I was thinking about you yesterday, and I wondered if you would like to have dinner some night if I drove up to Clear Water."

Jenny thought quickly. She should tell him about the babies. He had no idea she was pregnant, and even worse, pregnant and unmarried. For reasons she couldn't quite put a finger on, she didn't want to tell him, at least not over the phone. But, if he came up and saw her overblown figure there was no telling what his reaction would be.

"That would be very nice, but to tell you the truth," (*Yeah, right Jen,*) she thought to herself, "I am sort of involved with things here at the lake. I would love to take you up on your offer, but I'm afraid it will have to wait 'till spring." (*What I really mean is after I have the babies, and know what the heck I am going to do!*)

Justin heard the hesitation in her voice. Maybe he hadn't made a very good impression, or maybe, like his luck in the past, she was involved with someone else and didn't want to say so.

"Sure, that's fine. When things get uninvolved give me a call. The offer is open whenever you're free."

"I'll do that, and thanks again for calling and inviting me. I would love to see you again, but the timing isn't good right now." (*Boy that sounds great,*) Jenny thought. She hated not being upfront with her predicament, but she knew she was holding back for fear it would end whatever chance she might have to see Justin again. She was surprised that it mattered!

Justin hung up the phone, and took a deep breath. Ever since his sister, Julie, was kidnapped years ago, he had become somewhat of a recluse. He had almost lost his life during that event, and almost lost his sister. Since then he only left the ranch to deal with cattle buyers, and buyers for their small number of well bred quarter horses they sold each year. He really needed to get out. If he was ever going to find a life partner he couldn't keep hiding out at the ranch, no matter how beautiful and safe it was. He was, after all, a grown man, not a vulnerable child, and the millions his family had no longer made him an easy target for ransom.

Chapter Twenty

Winter passed slowly for Jenny. The doctor had confirmed she was having twins. When she looked at the ultrasound, she was excited but scared, not quite able to wrap her head around raising two children by herself. Today, not unlike the other days this long winter, she felt alone and confined in the house. Although the lake and mountains was the perfect subject for her paintings, she had not felt like picking up a paintbrush since she had come home. Her mind was too occupied with how she was going to cope with being a mother of twins.

The snow was too deep now for her morning walks and the babies were getting more active, making it hard to sleep and uncomfortable to stand. Most of her days were spent lounging on the couch looking out at the lake wondering what was going to happen when she had to take care of two infants on her own. Of course, her mom and dad would be here to help, but without a father the family would be incomplete. Evan's visits had become more infrequent and he only dropped by on the rare occasions when he was home for the weekend. His business kept him busy and the winter weather made the passes slow and risky. Her only break in the monotony was when, once a week, she would slough through the snow along the plowed roads to her grandparent's house behind the golf course. When her dad had decided to move into the lakefront house her mother had inherited, they had rented his parent's old home to summer visitors. In the winter the house was closed, but even so someone needed to check on it while it was empty. Tom had given her that chore to get her out of the house.

Morning sun streaming through her window awoke her, and she yawned and stretched. It was going to be a cold, but nice day. It was March, just one month away from when the babies were due. She felt enormous. Lowering her legs over the side of the bed, she looked at her ankles. Always slender and lovely, they were now swollen and fat. She made a face. Hopefully, she wouldn't regret not going through with Diego's plan. She wondered if she would ever look normal again.

After taking a shower and drying her hair, she pulled on a pair of large, gray sweat pants and a gray oversized sweatshirt. She didn't bother with makeup, who would care? She could smell breakfast cooking and wandered out to the kitchen where Carolyn was frying bacon. She glanced up as Jenny came in.

"Hi, sweetie, sit down. Breakfast is almost ready. How do you feel today?" she said, smiling at her.

"Fat, that's how I feel, Mom. Did you feel fat and ugly when you were carrying me?"

"No, sweetie, I was so thrilled to be having a baby I never thought about what I must look like. All I cared about was having you." Carolyn came over and sat down beside her daughter. "Actually, darling, you have never looked lovelier. You skin just glows. I can't wait to be a grandma and hold those precious little ones. It has been a long time since I cared for a baby."

Jenny smiled and shifted her body. "I'm glad you are excited about this, Mom. I just want it to be over with. I am so uncomfortable. It feels like a there are a dozen rambunctious kids in my belly."

Carolyn hugged her and went back to the stove. "It will be over before you know it. You will forget how hard it was when you are holding your babies in your arms. It's a feeling like nothing else in the world."

A sharp pain stabbed Jenny and she gasped. "Oh, wow! That hurt! I haven't had a pain like that before." Then almost immediately she felt another, harder cramp. "Mom! I'm not sure, but I think I'm having contractions!"

Carolyn dropped the spatula she was turning the bacon with and ran to Jenny's side. She put her hand on Jenny's distended belly and waited. She felt it harden as Jenny gasped in pain.

"Just sit still. I'll call the doctor. I think maybe these little ones are going to make an early appearance!"

Tom and Carolyn paced the hall of the Carson Tahoe hospital. On their doctor's advice they had loaded Jenny into Tom's Cadillac Escalade and raced down the mountain to Carson City. By the time they arrived at the hospital the labor pains were coming every five minutes, and it was obvious the babies were not waiting for their due date.

"Mr. and Mrs. Robertson?" asked the tall, dark haired doctor as he walked toward the two anxiously waiting parents.

"Dr. Phillips! How is Jenny doing? How much longer do you think it will be?"

"Actually, it's over. You are the grandparents of a very active and healthy set of twin girls! They are a little small, so they are in the Neonatal Intensive Care Unit, but that will only be temporary. They are doing great, and so is Jenny. She had a fast, uncomplicated delivery. She's in her room waiting to see you.

"Thank God!" Tom breathed a sigh of relief and hugged Carolyn.

Carolyn tried unsuccessfully to hold back her tears. "Thank you so much, doctor. We were very worried about them coming so early."

"Worry no more, my dear. They are as healthy as any preemies I have seen. Now, go in and see your daughter. After that, you can see the girls. The nurses will let you in the N.I.C.U. Just make sure you stop and wash your hands according to the directions, and put on the gown they'll give you. Congratulations, by the way!" The doctor shook Tom's hand and hugged Carolyn. "Come on, I'll show you to Jenny's room."

Jenny was sitting up in bed when Tom and Carolyn entered the room. Seeing them, she gave a tired smile and raised her hand, signaling them to come in.

"Darling, that's such good news! Two little girls, we couldn't be happier." Both parents leaned over and kissed Jenny soundly.

"Have you seen them yet?" Jenny sounded anxious.

"We had to come see you first. Now we'll head right down the hall and see our granddaughters," Carolyn said, glowing with pride.

Jenny pulled her closer. "Mom, the ghost was wrong about my babies. She told me I was going to have a boy and a girl. So maybe she was wrong about everything. Do you think so?"

"Jenny darling, stop worrying about that stupid apparition. You can see now that she was wrong. You have nothing to worry about. I believe she was trying to frighten you into keeping Evan from looking for her damn necklace. Now forget about all that nonsense. Do you feel like getting up and coming with us to see your daughters?"

"You and Dad go, Mom. They will bring them in to nurse in a little while. I think I would like to rest right now. I am so tired." Jenny dropped her arms to her sides and closed her eyes.

"Of course, sweetie, we'll report back to you later. Tom brought his cell phone so he could take a video of them." Carolyn smoothed the pillows and stepped back, looking worriedly at Tom. He pressed her arm and led her out of the room.

As soon as they were in the hall Carolyn stopped walking and turned to Tom. "Can you believe she's been worried about Sirena's prediction all these months?"

"Well, the old ghostly apparition was off target on this one." Tom said. "I think it would be best if we didn't mention anything more about her, or what she told Jenny. Let's just forget it. Come on, I want to see those babies." Taking Carolyn's arm, Tom walked down the hall to the nursery.

Carolyn wanted to forget everything about the ghost but a nagging fear kept digging at her, telling her they hadn't heard the last of Sirena.

"Oh, Tom, look at them! They are the most beautiful babies I have ever seen!" Carolyn leaned in closer as the two nurses held up the tiny pink infants. They were tightly wrapped in blankets, but their perfect little features were clearly visible.

"You're not prejudiced are you, my darling?" Tom said teasingly, but as he stared at the two minute little girls, he had to admit for such tiny newborns, they were amazingly beautiful and perfect.

The nurses put the babies back in their incubators but Carolyn remained, staring at the two soundly sleeping infants. "Look how different they are, Tom! No one will ever mistake them for twins. The one with the dark hair must look like her father, but the other one looks just like you, darling!"

Tom grinned. It was true, he thought. The baby in front of him had a brush of pale white hair that would probably turn into her grandfather's thick, golden mop. Even as tiny as they were, Tom could see the long pale lashes against her pink cheeks. He felt an immediate burst of love for this helpless bit of humanity.

"Probably going to be my favorite," he joked. "You can spoil the other one."

"Tom!" Carolyn chided. "That's the most ridiculous thing I have ever heard you say. I know you too well. You will spoil them both beyond any redemption."

Tom hugged his wife. "We are really blessed. They are both beautiful. Let's go tell Jenny she's produced two amazing grandbabies for us."

Chapter Twenty-One

Carson City, Nevada

The Escalade pulled up in front of Carson City's impressive new hospital just in time to see the nurse wheel out Jenny and the two well covered infants.

Tom raced to the passenger's side and opened the rear door, then helped Jenny to her feet. Carolyn got out and stood next to her, anxious to help.

"Do you have the car seats in the back, Dad? I hope they showed you how to install them properly." Jenny looked worriedly at the car.

Tom pinched her cheek and gently lifted one small bundle from her arms. He was glad to see how quickly Jenny had become a caring, protective little mother.

"Everything has been checked and double checked. I'll put little Ava in first. You sit back down until I have her safely buttoned up, then your mother can help you get Alexis in her little safety seat."

Jenny watched Ava being strapped into her car seat,

unaware that the scene was being watched with great interest from a few feet away by a tall, blonde man in a Stetson hat, his forehead covered with a thick bandage.

When Tom finished and turned to help with Alexis, his eyes met Justin King's curious stare. Aware that Tom had seen him watching the group, he came forward.

"Jenny? It is you! So, this is what has been keeping you so occupied all winter. If I had known you were married…"

Jenny's face flushed with embarrassment. "That's not exactly… the thing is…"

"Hey, you don't have to explain. I'm very happy for you. Two babies! That's quite an accomplishment. Where's the proud papa?"

Justin tried to keep an upbeat attitude, but his heart sank. He had been hoping all winter that when spring came he would have a chance to get to know this lovely girl better. Now he could see that was just a pipedream. She was obviously married – and now has a family.

"Uh, he's not here right now," Jenny stammered. "He's in Europe." She felt terrible not telling the truth, but this was neither the time, nor the place to explain. She had to get the newborns home and settled. She was in no condition to think about Justin, or what problems hiding the truth from him might cause.

"What a shame! He must feel terrible missing the birth of his two – girls or boys?"

Jenny managed a small, proud smile. "They're both girls, just not identical."

"Well, congratulations. Wish I had known sooner, I would have had a birthday present for them. Tell your husband he is a very lucky man."

Justin tipped his hat and turned to leave.

"Wait, Justin. What happened to your head? Did you get in an accident?"

As much as Jenny wanted to leave, she felt concern for this very attractive man. She had thought about him many times after his phone calls, wondering what it would be like to actually have a date with him. Now, here he was, in the most awkward situation she could have imagined. She was probably ruining her chances of ever seeing him again.

"It's nothing. I was loping my horse through the pine trees and got attacked by a big branch that knocked me right on my rear end. I'll be fine. Just a few stitches"

"Oh, I'm so sorry." Jenny felt Alexis stir in her arms and a faint cry came from the little bundle. "Guess I'd better get my little girls home. It was nice seeing you Justin."

"Good to see you too, Jenny. Good luck with your new family." He winked and quickly walked away.

"Come on, Jen." Tom said gently. "We have to get these babies home. You need to get home and rest, too." Tom handed the second child to Carolyn, who carefully carried her to the car and settled her in. Then Tom helped Jenny in beside them and the big car drove slowly away for the short drive back up the mountain to Clear Water Cove.

As the car pulled away, Jenny glanced out the window and saw Justin climb into his Dodge pickup. She had way too much on her plate right now to think about a romantic attachment, but seeing him again made her wonder why her pulse had quickened. She looked down at her two, wonderful twins, tucked securely in their seats. They were so tiny and helpless. She wondered what it might have been like if Justin had been their father.

Chapter Twenty-Two

Clear Water Cove

The weeks slid by quickly and before Jenny knew it, spring had arrived. The girls had bloomed like little rosebuds opening to the world. Smiling and gurgling; they were the center of attention in the comfortable, old house. The second downstairs bedroom had been converted to a nursery, so Jenny was close enough to hear the slightest whimper.

When Jenny wasn't nursing the twins, Carolyn was holding them or rocking them. When Tom came home, he took them both in his arms and walked around the house acting, he said, like a goofy grandpa

Despite all the joy of watching her children grow and thrive, there were days when Jenny felt left out. She missed Evan's visits. He had not been to Clear Water since she had given birth. Watching her parents made her feel lonely. They were so happy together. She had the babies, but she needed more.

Sometimes Jenny wondered if she should call Diego and tell him about the twins. Ava looked so much like him it was amazing. Then she remembered the awful day he deserted her in Las Vegas, and her determination to never let him near them grew stronger.

June arrived with mild weather and sunshine. The snow had almost completely melted, and golfers were already out on the course wearing only light windbreakers. Robins were industriously pulling up worms on the front lawn to feed their new babies and the pesky woodpeckers were rattling the pine boughs to search for bugs and insects. Tiny delicate flowers bloomed in the meadow and the creeks ran full and cold. Spring was here and Jenny was restless.

"Why don't you take Ava and Alexis for a walk to the clubhouse?" Carolyn suggested. " I'll clean up a bit and meet you for lunch. It will be good for you to get out of here. You don't get out enough. A little fresh air and sunshine will do you good."

Jenny glanced up from the couch where she was folding some baby clothes. It was true, she had seen herself in the mirror. She was as white as the little t-shirt she had in her hands. "Maybe I will, Mom. Will you get the girls ready while I get dressed?"

"Of course, you go put on a nice outfit. And comb that unruly mop of hair! Oh, yes, put on some lipstick too, you're as pale as the moon last night."

"Thanks, Mom. I won't be long. They have just been fed, so they should be good for at least a couple of hours." She hugged Carolyn, and pushing aside the laundry basket, retreated into her room.

Jenny pushed the double stroller through the door of the clubhouse. The walk in the cool mountain air and sunshine had worked its spell, and the two chubby girls were fast asleep. When the waiter saw her come in, he rushed to help seat her and moved several chairs away from a table near the window to accommodate the stroller.

"Thanks, Antonio." Jennie smiled at the familiar employee. His once black hair was graying at the temples, but it only made him more attractive. He had been a waiter at the club for as long as she could remember. He was a fixture here. He knew everyone and everything that went on at the cove. There were few family secrets he didn't know, but kept them discretely to himself.

"You're looking beautiful this morning, my dear," Antonio beamed at her, noticing the healthy glow of her skin. She was as beautiful as her mother, he thought. This family had good genes. "And how are Ava and Alexis today?" He peered down into the stroller to peek at the sleeping babies. "They're getting big, and almost as pretty as their mother." He straightened back up. "What can I get for you this morning? Will you be having breakfast, or lunch?"

"Since there seems to be peace right now, I'll try a grilled cheese and a root beer float, please. I'll try to eat before they wake up and raise the roof. They can get very loud!"

Antonio laughed. "I'll bet they can. But right now they look like two little angels. I'll hurry the order for you. We want you to be able to enjoy your lunch," He winked and hurriedly left to place the order.

Jenny sat back in her chair and pushed her red curls behind her ears. It was a treat to get out of the house, even though she had the babies along. Maybe they would sleep long enough for her to enjoy herself for an hour.

As she waited for her lunch a group of golfers came in the door. They were laughing and joking about their game. When they spotted Jenny they nudged each other and looked appreciatively at the lovely, young woman. She was wearing a pair of tan slacks and a green cashmere sweater that emphasized her flaming hair and perfectly recovered figure. The babies were still nursing, which made her breasts much larger and fuller. It was enough to turn the men's heads, almost causing them to bump into another golfer coming into the room after them.

"Hey, Justin!" one of the men called out. "Over here. Come have a seat, we're about to order lunch."

Jenny's head swiveled around. What on earth? She recognized the tall, blonde man instantly. What was Justin doing here? She grabbed a menu and tried to hide behind it, but the men had already made Justin aware of her presence. Before she could run and hide, Justin's long legs were standing next to her.

"Jenny! We seem to keep running into each other. How are the kids?" He glanced down at the still sleeping twins and smiled. "Wow, they sure don't look like twins, do they?" Then as he sensed Jenny bristle, he added, "I mean, one is blonde and beautiful, and one is a brunette and also beautiful. I see you in both of them. Beautiful mouths, skin, hair…"

"Okay, okay. It's all right. I'm used to that. I think they are the prettiest children in the world. I love that they don't look alike, but then I *am* their mother." She relaxed and when she smiled up at him, his blue eyes were twinkling.

"So, did your husband get back from Europe? I'll bet he's very proud."

Jenny hesitated; maybe it was time to tell the truth.

This charade couldn't go on forever. "Do you have a minute, Justin? There's something I need to explain."

"Sure, let me tell the guys I'll be a minute or two." He headed to the table where the men were casting envious stares in their direction.

"Who's the glamour girl, Justin? How do you know her?" said, Kevin, a pudgy lawyer who lived in the cove. He couldn't keep his eyes off Jenny.

"Ask your questions later, guys. I'm going to visit with her for a few, hold my order 'till I get back." He patted Kevin on the shoulder. "And quit staring. It's not polite, besides, if you'll notice, she has two little babies in that stroller and they aren't mine!"

Even more curious, the men watched as Justin sat down beside Jenny.

"So, what do you have to explain, Jenny? As he looked into her enormous, dark lashed, blue eyes, Justin felt his pulse race. She could excite him just sitting there, like no girl he had ever met.

"To put it right up front, Justin, I'm not married, nor divorced. I'm a single mom raising two babies by myself, with the help of my mom and dad, of course." As she saw the look of shock on his face, she almost laughed. It wasn't like she said she was a terrorist or something, just a single mom like so many others! "You can close your mouth now. It's a long story. I'm sure you don't have time to hear it all right now. I can see your friends are waiting for you at your table." She smiled over at the leering group of men. She waved and they turned away, embarrassed. "Tell your friends I'm just an old acquaintance." Jenny stopped talking and looked up at Justin, waiting for a response.

Justin seemed frozen to his chair. His mind was spinning. Jenny wasn't married! She was single, and that meant… *Whoa there, cowboy*, he told himself. *Slow down.*

She's not exactly free and clear, but damn, she is still single. He reached over and took her small, soft hand.

"Well, well. That took courage. I'm proud of you. I'm sure you had choices. It makes a big difference to me that you made the right one." He paused and cleared his throat. "I came up for a round of golf. Just business, I'm really not good at it." I'd like to come back and see you sometime soon. Maybe we could have dinner?" He grinned, but his heart raced. He prayed she would say yes. To be truthful, golf was not one of his favorite sports, but when he got the invitation to come up to the Cove, he had hoped he might run into Jenny again.

Jenny thought fast. There was no denying the electricity that shot between them when she was close to Justin, and she definitely got goose bumps when his blue eyes met hers. But was it smart to get involved with anyone while the children were so little? She still had to resolve the problem of Diego, in her own mind at least. However, a visit shouldn't involve much risk. After all, Mom and Dad would be at the house, she would make sure of that.

"I would like that, Justin. I'm almost always home now. These two keep me pretty busy and tied to the house." Ava stirred and her long lashed, brown eyes opened wide. She stared up at Justin and a big smile broke out over her little face. She waved one tiny hand in the air and Justin caught it in his two long fingers.

"Hey there, little girl," he said, and smiled over at Jenny. "I think she likes me, Jen. What's her name?"

"You are holding hands with Ava. She does seem to like you; she's not always so friendly with strangers."

The wonder on Justin's face tugged at her heart. What a great father he would make for some lucky girl, she thought.

The peaceful scene was interrupted by a wailing cry

from the second stroller seat. Alexis's blue eyes were open and quickly filling with tears.

Jenny made a face. "Times up, got to go. Guess I'll eat my lunch at home. Do me a favor, Justin and tell Antonio I'm sorry, but I can't stay for lunch today. Call me, and we can decide on a day for us to visit."

By now both babies were wailing loudly, Ava taking the cue from Alexis.

"I'm off. I'd better go before I get thrown out." Jenny grabbed the stroller handle and before Justin could object, she had wheeled the two crying babies out the door and down the path toward her parent's house.

Justin looked after them. His hands were sweating and he wiped them on his slacks. Watching her cute behind bent over the stroller as she exited the door, he felt a rush of desire. He had forgotten he could feel so strongly about a woman. Babies, or no babies, he was absolutely going to take her up on the offer. He would call her in a day or two. He wasn't sure he could even wait that long.

When he returned to the group at the table he was inundated with questions, none of which he answered. He only smiled and reached for the menu.

Chapter Twenty-Three

Paris, France

Diego ran his tongue over the dark-haired woman's bare stomach. She writhed, and pulled his naked body closer. The satin sheets were stained and wrinkled from their previous joining.

"You are such an animal, Diego. I would do anything for you. Let's do it again, please? I can't get enough of you."

Margarite grabbed for his manhood, squeezing it gently, stroking and rubbing, trying to get a response. Not having much luck, she slid down his body and took him in her mouth, bobbing her head rapidly. Feeling him harden, she spread her legs and pushed his half hard erection between her heavy thighs. Her ample rear end humped up against him.

Diego entered her again, any real feeling of desire fading fast. He had to make her climax while he still could. He tried to imagine Jenny beneath him, but it was impossible. The flabby body that slapped against him had no similarity to Jenny's high, perfect breasts and youthful, firmness. He closed his eyes and tried harder. He had to make Margarite happy; happy enough to cough up the twenty thousand he was going to ask her for, enough to get him to Nevada to see his children – and Jen. This woman was rich, very rich. She wouldn't even miss the money. He had to make her want him, – a lot.

Taking a deep breath, he pushed away and lowered his head between her legs. She moaned with pleasure as his tongue drove into her. He felt her breathing become more rapid, and rising back up over her, he caught her nipple in his teeth and rolled it around, grinding softly. As his right hand slid between her legs, he felt himself begin to soften. He gritted his teeth. This had never happened before. Damn, he was losing his touch! It was all Jenny's fault. He couldn't get her out of his mind. He shouldn't have any trouble getting it up with this rich, old bag. Money had always acted like an aphrodisiac for him. The more money his conquests had the harder his cock became, but it didn't seem to work any more.

"Oh God, Diego, I'm coming, Now, now, Yes, Yes!" She screamed with pleasure, seemingly unaware that it was his probing fingers doing the job his limp member could not. He kept his fingers stroking and moving until she stopped squirming, and with a cry, fell back against the pillows.

"How was that, baby? Good enough for you?" He nipped her large, brown nipple again, making her cry out.

"Don't ever leave me, Diego. I'll do anything if you'll just stay with me."

He rolled off her damp body and stroked her breasts. "Well, there is one thing…"

Chapter Twenty-Four

Eagle's View Ranch

Driving back down the mountain toward Reno, Justin kept thinking about his meeting with Jenny. She looked fantastic for a woman who had just had twins. They must be about three or four months old now. He tried to count the weeks since he had seen her at the hospital. Unconsciously, he touched his forehead, feeling the narrow red scar where the branch had hit him, knocking him off his horse. The babies were really cute. Seeing the twins had brought back memories of his childhood with his twin sister, Julie. He would like to have kids of his own someday. His parents nagged him constantly. They reminded him they were not getting any younger and wanted more grandchildren even though his sister, Julie, had two beautiful children, Elijah, who was three, and Stephanie, who had just turned five. Daydreaming as he drove, he wondered if he could love two children that weren't his. When he was with Jenny anything seemed possible. *Guess I'm just a crazy, love struck cowboy*, he thought.

Two hours later he pulled up to the massive iron gates that kept strangers out of his ranch. Reaching above his visor he pressed the remote and the heavy panels swung inward allowing him to drive through. He drove down the hill through a forest of ponderosa pine trees, down to the lush, grass filled valley below. The architectural marvel that his father had built years ago stood high above the valley overlooking the ranch and pastures. The house sat on a hilltop like a giant bird's nest. From a distance, you could see why his father had named it Eagle's View. Wide decks surrounded the circular structure and its walls of glass reflected the picturesque valley below. The grey slate roof flared up on both sides, resembling the wide spread wings of a massive bird.

As usual he felt a sense of pride as he approached the massive house. It never failed to lift his spirits. He parked the truck down at the barn and ran up the long set of fieldstone steps that led to the front door.

"Justin's home," Laura called to Jordan, who was busy cleaning his gun collection in the spacious, paneled den he called his sanctuary.

"Good! I need to talk to him. Send him in here when he gets in the house."

Laura smiled. She loved her two wonderful men so much. She was grateful that Justin had stayed to help with the ranch after graduating from college. If it wasn't for him, they would have probably sold the ranch and moved into town. It would have broken their hearts, but they were both getting too old to manage the large spread by themselves. The front doors flew open and Justin walked into his mother's arms.

"Darling, your father wants to talk to you," she said, giving him a big hug. "And when you finish talking, I have a batch of fudge brownies just waiting for a hungry son."

"Hey, thanks, Mom. It's been at least an hour since I had lunch!" he teased.

"Fine, then just leave them there. Your dad will be happy to eat them all."

"Not a chance. I'll be back as soon as I talk to him."

Kissing Laura on the cheek, Justin went down the long, curving hall and into the den.

"Justin. Just the man I want to talk to. Sit down for a minute." Jordan said, pleased that his son had appeared so promptly.

More curious than concerned, Justin sat down in one of the comfortable leather chairs that surrounded the wall to ceiling fireplace. He leaned back and closed his eyes, loving the smell of leather and gun oil that permeated the room.

Jordan put the lovely, hand carved Weatherby 300 down on the bar and turned to look at his son. "I've been thinking," he began.

"Oh oh, Dad, that can be dangerous," Justin joked.

"Seriously, son, I think it's time your mother and I took a long overdue, vacation."

Justin straightened up in his chair and looked curiously at his father, waiting for him to continue.

"You know we have been hibernating on this ranch for years. Not that we have minded. You know how much I love this place."

Justin smiled. This was going to be interesting.

"Don't laugh, but we were thinking about taking a

private guide and going on safari in the Ngorogoru game reserve. I've never been to Africa. Your mother and I have talked about it a lot, but never thought we could leave the ranch that long. However, since you have been running the place for several years now, basically single handedly, I think we can safely leave and not worry."

Justin stood up and put his hand on his father's shoulder. "I think it's a terrific idea, Dad. How long would you be gone?"

"I'm not sure. I haven't firmed it up yet, but probably about three or four weeks. I would like to come back through Europe and give your mother a whirlwind tour of Spain, France and England."

"It sounds great. It's about time you two got away from here. You know I'll take good care of everything. When are you leaving?"

"I have tentatively set it up to fly out of here in two weeks. We'll be back well before the fall roundup."

"Even if you stay longer, don't worry, Dad. With the great ranch hands we have, you can take your time."

"I know I can count on you, Justin. I wish you had a wife to help with the house, though," he smiled at his tall, handsome son. "Can't figure out what's taking you so long."

"Guess I'm just waiting for the right girl." Justin smiled, thinking to himself. Maybe he had already found her.

Chapter Twenty-Five

Clear Water Cove

Jenny pushed the stroller slowly along the dirt road that curved around the golf course. The twins had fallen asleep in the cool morning air and she was enjoying the relative quiet.

A loud squawk from an alarmed Jay caused her to look around. She stopped and put her hands on her hips. Following closely behind her was Evan, his brown eyes twinkling. He had on cream colored cords and a red golf shirt. He looked so handsome she felt her breath catch in her throat.

"Evan! Where did you come from? I didn't know you were up here. It's Tuesday. Don't you have to be in San Francisco at your office?"

"I'm taking a couple of weeks off," he said, stooping over to peek at the sleeping children. He bent and kissed her lightly on her cheek. "Plus, I needed to check on my little family."

The kiss caught Jenny off guard and it took her a minute to recover.

"Seriously, you're just going to play golf for a couple of weeks? Must be nice."

"Well, not quite," he grinned. "I've decided to try and fulfill my childhood promise to myself to find that darned old necklace."

Jenny felt her heart skip a beat as she remembered Sirena's warning. "No, you're not really going to do that, are you? It's too dangerous, Evan."

Evan smiled. He loved that Jenny cared enough to be concerned.

"Yep. I bought all the equipment I need yesterday at South Shore. I even bought a boat!"

"But, Evan, you know what happened to your dad!"

"That was an accident, Jenny. I'll be careful, I promise.'"

Jenny thought quickly. Evan didn't know anything about Sirena's ghostly appearances. He might not believe a word she told him, but it was time for him to hear the whole story about what happened that summer and the part the ghostly owner of the necklace had played in the death of his father.

"While the twins are still asleep walk with me to the park, Evan, we can sit down and talk. I have a ghost story to tell you."

"Now, that's quite an invitation! It sounds weird, but interesting. What does it have to do with my dive?"

Jenny looked at him, her blue eyes serious. "Everything."

On a cool pine shaded bench at the edge of the park,

Jenny told of the sightings of Sirena she had heard about. She told him about Jim, his real father, seeing the woman in the dance hall costume in Virginia City, the visit her father had from the ghost one night years past in his bedroom and the fatal sighting in the depths of the lake's deep pot hole where Jim had tried to reach out for the necklace. The appearance of Sirena in the deep water had caused him to become so disoriented he lost his air supply and drowned. Lastly, she related seeing Sirena under the water when he was eight years old. The day he dove in with the stolen necklace in his pocket and his trunks came off. She couldn't help laughing a bit remembering the naked little red-faced boy, as he swam to shore and fled down the beach.

When she was finished, Evan put his arm around her. Taking her chin in his hand, he pulled her face up and looked into her eyes.

"Do you honestly believe all that stuff, Jen? There has to be a rational explanation for every thing you told me. Now listen to me. The lady my father saw in the Virginia City bar was without a doubt a paid employee, costumed to entertain the customers. The visit your father had in his bedroom was probably just a nightmare. And, what you saw under the water the day I lost my pants," he paused and made a face remembering how embarrassed he had been, "was probably a floating log, or a big Mackinaw trout. Children have vivid imaginations. You probably heard your parents talking about Sirena and you wanted to think you saw her, too."

"You're wrong, Evan, I never heard anything about the ghost before the day I saw her under the water. Mom and Dad never talked about her around me until I was a grown up. I know what I saw. I was scared out of my wits for days."

Evan stood up and stretched. "It makes a good story, my love, however I am not a believer in ghost stories, just the story my grandfather told about the necklace. I know that part is true. He had it in his possession. By the way, how did your parents come to have it? I remember stealing it from their bedroom," he shook his head. "I was a real little thief, wasn't I? At least I reformed. Now it's up to me to find them again. Fate has a twisted sense of humor."

"It was Sirena's visit to my father's bedroom, Evan. When she appeared she told Dad exactly where to find the necklace you lost in the lake. He was so convinced, that even though Mom begged him not to, he dove into the lake and found it, exactly where she had said it would be!"

Evan rubbed his chin, "That is pretty strange, but I still can't believe a ghost was involved in anything that happened."

"Alright then, here's the last and most frightening message from her. She was in our kitchen before the twins were born and warned me that if you, or anyone else, tried to get her necklace, my babies would be in danger. And yes, she said babies. She told me I was going to have twins. She did make a mistake about them both being girls, but, Evan, I saw her with my own eyes and it scares me. I wouldn't have anything to live for if something happened to my girls."

A horn honked on the road and both Ava and Alexis woke up. Startled by the loud noise, they both started to cry at once.

"Guess we'll have to talk about this later," Jenny said, disappointment shadowing her face, "One thing about having twins, when one cries the other one has to cry, too." She stood up and rocked the stroller, trying to quiet the babies, hoping they would go back to sleep so she could continue the discussion, but they only howled louder.

": Alright, alright, we're going. I'll call you later, Evan. Please don't do anything before we have a chance to talk about this again." Without waiting for an answer, which she couldn't have heard anyway, Jenny wheeled the two squalling infants down the road and back to the house.

Evan watched her go. He shook his head. Women, they had some wild ideas. If Tom, an inexperienced diver, found the necklace, he should be able to, even without the help of their, so-called, *ghost*. He walked back to where he had left his Corvette and vaulted over the door into the drivers seat. As he drove off, he felt more excited about the dive than he had before. Somehow, hearing the ghost stories had made it much more intriguing. As far as anything happening to Ava and Alexis, that was just foolish. They lived in Clear Water Cove for crying out loud. It was as safe and secure as anywhere on earth.

Chapter Twenty-Six

South Lake Tahoe

Diego stopped the rented Ford Taurus beside the steep embankment and opened the door. The day was a typical August day at Lake Tahoe. Afternoon breezes had sprung up and ripples were stroking the surface of Clear Water Cove. From the highway he could see down into the small community. He noted the large iron gates that blocked any unauthorized access to the million dollar homes. He stretched and smiled. He didn't need to drive through the gates, all he had to do was hike down the hill, make his way through the forest and find Jenny's house. He had gone on Zillow, the home finder website and had the directions as well as a site map of the property. It wouldn't be hard to locate. There were few beachfront homes in the cove.

He had to plan what he was going to say to Jenny when he saw her. Margarite had been very cooperative. He had promised to move into her villa in the south of France as soon as he returned from his "business trip" to America. She was unattractive, middle aged and previously sexually frustrated, a perfect combination for him. He had fulfilled her every fantasy and made her feel like a queen. When he asked her for a twenty five thousand dollar loan, she had not only given it to him, she had forked over an additional five thousand just because, as she told him with a sigh, she loved him *so much*.

A gust of wind brought the smell of pine, newly mowed lawns and flowers from the verdant valley below. He breathed in deeply. No doubt this was one of the most beautiful spots on earth. Maybe he would think seriously about asking Jen to marry him and come here to live! As fast as the thought entered his head, it fled on winged feet. He laughed out loud. Marry? Not a chance. But he did want to see his children. Maybe he could get Jenny to let him take them back to the villa for a month or two, just to let her think he was interested. And then perhaps when he grew tired of them he would ask for compensation if she wanted them back! He was no fool; he knew the price a mother would pay to ransom her offspring. He felt a tinge of remorse, remembering how kind and gentle a person Jenny was. It would be easy to take advantage of those very traits.

He turned back to the car, got in and started the motor. He was staying at a luxurious suite at Harrah's on the south shore of the lake. He would think more about what he was going to do in the next few days. He had plenty of time and plenty of money. He had gambled many times in the past at the tables in Europe. He was excited about trying his skill here at the lake. Gunning the motor, he shot out into the traffic, keeping within the speed limit. He cruised along, being careful not to attract a cop. It was imperative to keep a low profile until he knew what he was going to do.

That night, after losing five thousand dollars at a blackjack table, Diego decided he had better forget the gambling and get down to the cove to meet Jenny and his kids.

Jenny sat on the front lawn with the twins who were happily playing with a box full of baby toys. They were starting to crawl and the playpen was the safest place for them to be while she relaxed. She watched with pleasure as they played. Ava's dark beauty contrasted so vividly with Alexis' bright red curls. Even thought they weren't identical, they were closely bonded and seldom quarreled over anything.

The breezy afternoon had attracted sailors in their tall-masted sailboats. With their full white sheets billowing in the wind, they fled like exotic birds across the blue water. Across the mouth of the cove water skiers were creating crystalline sprays that shattered with bursts of color in the bright sunlight. The skiers soared up and over the tall wakes created by the propeller driven motor boats, some making it back down safely, others taking a hard dive into the icy cold lake. Jenny never tired of sitting out on the lawn looking at the beautiful scenery and activity on the water.

As she gazed out at the old railroad pilings she could see young children bobbing up and down on big inflatable rafts, screaming and yelling with delight as the boat wakes caught and rocked their floats. Further out over the deep blue pothole, her eyes caught sight of the new boat Evan had recently purchased. The bright turquoise and white hull of the SeaRay made it easy to spot. She reached for her binoculars and lifted them to her eyes. As her eyes focused on the boat, her breathing stopped, the figure standing on the open bow of the boat was in a full dive suit.

"Oh, no," she gasped out loud. "He wouldn't. He – I … we were supposed to talk more about this before he decided to try and find that damn necklace!" Her heart began to pound as she remembered the ghost's warning. She fumbled around her chair for her cell phone and punched in Evan's number. "Come on, Evan, pick up before you cause all of us a whole lot of trouble," she murmured under her breath.

The call went to voice mail and she tossed the phone down. "Damn it!" she swore softly. Maybe he would see her if she ran down to the beach and waved a beach towel at him. The twins were happy and safe right where they were. She would only be a minute. Getting up quickly from the lounge chair, Jenny ran down the steps to the beach. She grabbed a red and white towel from the boathouse and continued on down the shoreline until she was even with where Evan's boat was anchored.

Diego had made a decision. He was going to take the children away with him to Margarite's villa in the south of France. When they were safely home with him, he would be in a great position to become very rich, very quick. He had come to the cove well prepared for the kidnapping. A small bottle of ether, rags and a large duffle bag would get them to his car. He had been watching and waiting for two days for the opportunity and now, amazingly, here it was. It was stunningly easy.

Dressed in a light blue Izod golf shirt and gray slacks, he looked like any other Clearwater resident. The gym bag could be for any sport available here at the lake.

As soon as he saw Jenny leave the twins alone on the front lawn, he made his way quickly up the stairs from his observation point on the beach. His heart pounded as he saw the two little girls playing happily in their playpen. As he drew closer, he smiled. No denying one of them was his! The little dark haired child was the image of his baby pictures. He frowned, the information the doctor in Las Vegas had given him was that Jenny had borne twins, but there was no resemblance between these two! Maybe there had only been one baby. Maybe the child with the red hair was a neighbor's child who had come over to play.

He thought quickly, he could take no chances. Kidnapping his own little girl was one thing, taking someone else's, was a whole different story. Approaching the girls, he put the duffle bag down and leaned over the playpen. When Ava saw the man smiling at her, she put her chubby little arms up and gurgled at him.

"Ah, you know your father, don't you, little one! Come now, we're going for a ride." He bent down and picked up Ava. She squirmed and cooed, patting his face with her tiny hands. "No need to put you to sleep right away, my pet. I think you will go with me without a peep. Come now, we must hurry." Alexis had pulled herself to her feet and was hanging onto the railing of the playpen watching the strange man. Without a glance at the puzzled little, golden haired baby, Diego picked up the duffle bag and with Ava in his arms, disappeared back down the stairs.

Chapter Twenty-Seven

Clear Water Cove

Waving the towel wildly, Jenny ran along the beach, hoping to get Evan's attention before he dove into the lake. Just as she was about to give up, she saw him walk to the railing of the boat and glance towards shore. Spotting Jenny, he smiled, waved, and pushed off backward into the water.

"Oh, no, damn it, Evan!" Frustrated, Jenny threw down the towel and put her hands on her hips. "Don't you dare find that necklace today, Evan! Not before I have a chance to put a stop to this."

As she stood there glaring out across the water, Jenny heard wailing coming from the house. The twins! She shouldn't have left them, no telling what trouble they had gotten into now. Stomping her foot in the hot sand, she turned and trudged back to the bank and up the stairs to the front lawn.

It only took a fast glance for Jenny to realize Ava

was missing. Alexis was lying on her stomach sobbing. Jenny ran to the playpen and grabbed her up in her arms. "Where is Ava, Alexis?" She looked around the front yard, her heart racing. Maybe her mother had come home and taken her into the house to change a dirty diaper or something. She ran to the back of the house and tore open the door, Alexis was still sobbing in her arms, scared by the actions of her mother.

"Mom, Mom!" Jenny shouted out as she ran from room to room, but there was no answer. "Oh, my God, where is my baby?" By now Jenny was frantic. She flew out the door once more and began to circle the house. As she ran up the driveway, she saw her father's golf cart coming down the road.

"Dad! I can't find Ava!"

Tom leapt from the cart and ran to where Jenny was standing. He took one look at her and knew something terrible had happened.

"What do you mean, you can't find her? Where did you leave her?" Seeing the terror on Jenny's face, his heart began to race.

"I, I left them in the playpen on the front lawn!" she stammered, "I went down to the beach for just a minute, and when I came back up, she was gone!" Overwhelmed by guilt, Jenny started to cry along with Alexis whose little face was almost as red as her hair.

"Go in the house and call the police. I'll start looking around the area. Someone must have seen something. She couldn't have gotten out of the playpen by herself. Maybe someone heard her cry and took her for a little walk to quiet her. She might be just around the corner, but just in case someone…, never mind, go call the police, and Jenny, calm down, you're scaring Alexis. See if you can quiet her down before she gets too upset. It's not going to help anything if you lose control." He made sure Jenny went back to the house, and then he began to run as fast as he had ever run in his life, hoping to catch up with whoever had taken his precious granddaughter.

By six o'clock in the evening, the entire community of Clear Water Cove had been alerted. Carolyn and Tom were in the kitchen with Jenny, along with Sissy, her husband, Allen and two sheriff officers.

"We've questioned every resident in the cove, and it appears no one saw or heard anything,"

One of the officers looked over at Jenny. "Is there anyone you can think of who might have any reason to take the child?" *Other than raking in a sweet ransom*, he thought to himself.

"No, officer, I can't think of anyone! They're just babies. Who would want to harm them?" Jenny's eyes had deep blue shadows under them and her hands were trembling. The officer felt sorry for the young woman, but there had to be something she wasn't telling him, or else her baby had fallen victim to a kidnapper. So far, no phone call and no ransom note. There had to be something else.

"Right now everything is important. Where's the baby's father?" the officer said.

At this question Jenny looked up with surprise, could Diego possibly have something to do with this? No, it wasn't possible. He was in Paris, or Spain, or where ever, besides he had never seen the children. He had no idea what they looked like.

"The baby's father, Miss?" the officer asked again.

"Well, ah, they don't really have one, I mean, well…" she was stuttering and knew it, but didn't know how much she was required to tell the young man.

"Please, ma'am, do you know who their father is?"

Jenny reddened. "Don't be ridiculous, of course I know who he is!" she retorted.

Carolyn put her arms around her daughters trembling shoulders. "Darling, he's just trying to help. Could Diego possibly be behind this? Have you heard from him lately?" She glanced up at the officer. "Do we really have to get into this now?"

"Yes, Mrs. Robertson, I'm afraid we do. It's important to know about anyone who might have the slightest connection to the baby."

"It's alright, Mom." Jenny stood up and began to pace the kitchen floor, then stopped in front of the officer. "The truth is the twin's father and I were never married. I met him while I was in Paris over a year ago. He has never seen them. As far as I know he doesn't know I had twins or any baby at all. He left me in Las Vegas to get an abortion, which I obviously decided not to do. Even if he somehow knows about the girls he would never want to be bothered with them." She sat back down at the table and put her head in her hands. Both Sissy and Carolyn went to her side and put their arms around her.

"Do you know how to get in touch with him?" the deputy asked gently.

"He calls here once in awhile, but I never answer the calls. I think he is still in Paris. He lives off different women who have money. I have no idea where, or who he might be living with right now." She raised her head and gave the officer a beseeching look. "Please, find my baby."

"That's just what we're trying to do. If you will give me his full name and last address, we'll take it from there. There's a slight chance he might be involved. Any lead is important at this point in time. If it's the father and he's headed back to Europe, we need to stop him before he leaves the country. Tell me everything you know and we'll head back to the station. We'll need to alert all the port authorities. Do you happen to have a recent picture of Ava?"

"Let me get it, Jenny." Carolyn insisted. "You sit here and give the deputy all the information you can about Diego. I'll be right back. Finding a picture won't be hard, we only have about a million," she gave a slight smile and left the room.

Jenny told the officers all she could about Diego and where he might be. When she was finished, Carolyn gave the officer a handful of 8x10 photographs of the twins.

"Ava is the one with the dark hair," she told them, as they took one of the pictures and put it into a folder.

"Does she look anything like her father?" the officer asked. "That might help with his description.

Jenny took a deep breath. "Actually she looks very much like Diego, but she's just a baby, and a girl. How's that going to help?"

"Don't worry; we have ways to computerize an image. We'll leave an officer here tonight outside the house, just in case. Jeff and I are going back to the station. I'll get started on the father angle. I hope my hunch is right. If it is, we could have Ava back to you by morning." He smiled, and the two men left.

After the officers left Jenny broke down sobbing, "Oh, Mom! My baby, where is my baby? Who would do something so awful?"

"I don't know, my darling, but in a way I hope Diego is involved. At least it gives us a place to start looking."

"If you are going to be alright, I think Allen and I will go back home." Sissy said.. "I just can't stand seeing Jenny so upset. Thinking about poor little Ava has me sick,"

"Of course, you and Allen go home." Carolyn said.

"We'll be okay. Jenny should get to bed anyway. She's about to collapse."

"You don't look so good yourself, Carolyn," Sissy said, staring at her friend.

"I'll be fine. You and Allen run along. If we hear anything I'll call you."

"Alright then, I am a bit tired. See you tomorrow. Don't worry darlin, they'll find your little Ava." Sissy kissed Jenny lightly on her cheek and taking Allen by the arm they left.

Jenny shook her head. "Does Allen ever get to say anything? Or does he just think it's easier to be quiet? Sometimes I want to smack that woman, but I know she means well. I'm tired, too, Mom. I think I'll get Alexis and take her to bed with me. Somehow, I know I won't be able to sleep if she's not right beside me."

Jenny hugged her parents and went to gather her remaining child. With tears streaming down her face, she took the sleeping baby in her arms. She bent and kissed her red gold curls. "Don't worry Alexie, sweetie, we'll find your sister." Then with a sob, she wrapped the soft, white crib blanket around her little child. Holding her close, Jenny went into her bedroom, locking the door securely behind her.

Tom watched her go into her bedroom, then without a word he walked upstairs to his bedroom where he kept his Glock handgun locked in a closet safe. He unlocked the safe and took the gun out, making sure it was loaded. As he was checking it, Carolyn came in.

"Do you think we'll need that?" she asked a frightened look on her face.

"I don't know, sweetheart, but the officer can't guard every door and window in this house. If that bastard even thinks about coming back, I'll blow his damned head off."

Chapter Twenty-Eight

South Lake Tahoe

"Oh, shut up!" Diego shouted, as he paced the floor of the hotel room, the screaming baby held tightly in his arms. "What the hell have I gotten into?" he asked out loud. Was he crazy? Just because he wanted to get back at Jenny, he had a hysterical baby on his hands. Worse yet, he didn't have the faintest idea what to do about it.

He laid the sobbing child down on the bed and looked down at her. Her little face was puffy and red from crying, her little fists balled up tightly. Looking at the baby, his stomach rolled. He could see how much she resembled his baby pictures. He was putting his own child in jeopardy. He had to find someone to help him care for her until he could get her a fake passport and get on a plane for Spain. Once home, his mother could take over. The immediate problem was to stop the awful noise she was making. He had to find out how to deal with a small baby long enough to get her out of the country.

A knock on the door startled him. He picked up Ava and took her into the bathroom. Laying her on the floor, he closed the door. She was still crying but the sound was a bit muffled now. Whoever was at the door might think it was coming from the next room.

He cracked open the door a few inches and was surprised to see a pretty dark haired young girl standing there. "Yes, what do you want?" he said gruffly.

"The concierge sent me up to see if I could help. The occupants of the room next to yours have complained about a crying baby. I'm a baby sitter for the hotel."

Nerves still on end, Diego managed a smile. Maybe this was the answer to his prayers. She could shut the kid up and take care of her until he found someone to produce the passport he needed. Those people were everywhere. It should be even easier here with all the gambling and weird people, he just had to find the right person to ask.

"Ah, what an angel." Diego said to the girl as she waited for an answer. "My wife just walked out on me and left me with our little baby. I'm afraid I'm not very adept at taking care of her. Please come in. I have a few errands to run. Would you be so kind as to care for her while I'm gone? I won't be long. When I get back, you can show me how to do the diaper thing."

"What a terrible mother! I don't understand how anyone could do that!" The girl smiled at him. "My name is, Alicia. I would be happy to watch her until you get back. Where is she?" The young girl looked around the room, the sound of muffled cries still coming from somewhere.

"Just a minute, I'll get her. I was in the bathroom trying to figure out how to change, you know the wet pants, but I don't have a clue!" He smiled charmingly at the girl, and going to the bathroom returned with the baby. With a sigh of relief, he thrust her into the girl's arms.

"Shush, little one," Alicia crooned to the sobbing Ava, rocking her gently in her arms. Calmed by the rocking and soft female voice, the baby stopped crying. Her little hiccupping sobs, finally subsiding. "Oh, she's just beautiful! She looks just like you." Alicia smiled up at the handsome, dark haired man. "Now, where's her bottle and diaper bag?"

"Her mother didn't leave anything with me. Tell me what she needs and while I'm out, I'll get it for you." He swallowed hard. He really had not thought this through at all.

Alicia frowned. "You had better not take too long. She looks like she's hungry. How long since she's had anything to eat?"

"Ah, well, here's the thing. Her mom just left her and took off. I don't really know! Do you think she will be alright for a few hours?" he asked hopefully. He had no clue how often a baby had to eat.

"I doubt it. Do you even know what kind of formula she's on? "Before he could answer she saw the puzzled look on his face and sighed. "I'm going to call down to the "in house" nurse and have her suggest something. She will know. I'll explain the situation to her. It's pretty unusual, but we have to feed her. Maybe the nurse will have a diaper or two we can use. As soon as I find out exactly what kind of formula the nurse recommends, I'll call you so you can buy some. Do you have a cell phone?"

Diego wiped his hand across his forehead where beads of sweat were beginning to form. Maybe he should just take off and forget this whole business. Even if he got the baby to the airport, wouldn't the authorities be looking for her by now? *Do a reality check man,* he told himself. How the hell was he going to pull this off?

"Look, Alicia. Do whatever you can to quiet her. Call me with the list of things she needs when you have it put together. I should be back in an hour."

"Alright," she answered, jiggling the baby on her shoulder, "I charge $20.00 an hour, is that okay?"

"You bet. I'm just very happy you showed up. I was really at my wit's end." Trying to show concern, he patted Ava on the back. Her little head bobbed, and he could see she was closing her eyes and was about to fall asleep. "I think she likes you," he smiled at Alicia. "Take care of her. I'll be back soon."

Alicia sat down in a big, comfortable chair and held Ava close. Something just didn't seem right, but for now the important thing was to take care of this baby. It was obvious the father didn't have a clue. She waved to Diego as he left the room, then reached over to the end table and picked up the phone to call the hotel's nurse.

Diego waited out front for the valet to bring his rented Ford Mustang around. He took a deep breath, sighing with relief. He got into the car and began driving around the lake. He had to take a few minutes to think. Did he want to continue with this? It wasn't really a kidnapping, was it? How did the law in the U.S. look at it? He had no idea. As the child's father, didn't he have a right to take her home for a visit? So what if he hadn't asked permission. He wasn't used to having to ask permission to do anything he wanted. But, did he really want to deal with this? He didn't even know what his child's name was! What was he going to call her? He'd have to think of something. Even with his story about the mother walking out on them, he would know her name. Maybe he would rename her Jessica; he had always liked that name. Yes, that would do. Jessica. He rolled it around on his tongue. It was a good name.

He pulled the car over to a rest stop where the lake was in full view. It was a beautiful sight. Too bad he had to leave. He opened the door and walked down to the shoreline. The snowcapped Sierras soared upwards to form a magnificent frame for the sparkling crystal blue water of the deep alpine lake.

Spying a bench beneath a pine tree, he sat down to think. The waves lapped gently at the sandy beach, the soft rhythmic sounds calming his nerves. He took a deep breath and tried to relax. He'd only had the baby a few hours but he knew the hue and cry would already be in full swing. He had to decide quickly if he wanted to go back to the hotel or just go back home. So far no one knew he was anywhere near Lake Tahoe. As far as Jenny knew he was still in Europe. He walked back to the car and got in. It might be too hard to sneak her out of the country. After he got a quick lesson on childcare, maybe they would just drive to Sacramento. He could rent a motel room and get in touch with Jenny. He knew she would do anything, pay anything, to get her baby back. He would have to make sure she didn't take any legal action. He wasn't going to jail for any kid.

As he started the car and backed out of the rest stop, his cell phone rang. It was Alicia with a list of items he needed to buy. He grabbed a pencil and paper from the glove box. Taking careful note, he wrote down the things Jessica would need.

Chapter Twenty-Nine

Clear Water Cove

Jenny sat curled in an easy chair in the living room. Dawn was just breaking over the glassy waters of the lake. The high clouds reflected the morning sun, throwing a pink haze over the sky. Her eyes felt like they had the whole beach full of sand under her lids and her stomach was in a hard knot. She hadn't slept at all. There had been one call from the sheriff, but it wasn't encouraging. So far, there were no leads on the whereabouts of Ava.

She heard the phone ringing, but her mother beat her to it. Trembling, Jenny stood beside her trying to hear. Carolyn handed her the receiver. "It's for you, sweetie. It's Justin King."

Jenny frowned; she didn't want to talk to anyone right now. If the phone was tied up they might miss a call from the sheriff's office. Seeing her hesitate, her mother nudged her. "Take the call. He doesn't even know about Ava. Perhaps you should tell him. After all, he is a friend."

Reluctantly, Jenny picked up the phone. "Hi, Justin," her voice was barely audible. "Sorry, but this isn't a good time to talk. Someone has kidnapped one of the twins." Her voice broke as she uttered the words and try as she might tears began to leak down her face.

"Oh, my God, when did this happen? What can I do to help, Jenny? Please let me help."

Jenny heard the compassion in his voice and a sob escaped her lips. "I don't think there is anything anyone can do. The sheriff has no leads. We have no idea who could have done this unless…"

"Unless what? What do you know that you aren't saying, Jenny?"

She could hear the anxiety in his voice.

"I don't know. There is a possibility Diego could be behind this. It's the only thing that makes any sense. They were playing out front in their playpen. I went down to the beach for only a minute or two and when I came back to the house Ava was gone!" Jenny tried hard to hold back the tears, but it was impossible.

"Okay, I'm on my way. I don't know what I can do to help, but there must be something."

Jenny started to protest, but Justin interrupted her.

"I'm not taking no for an answer. I'm on my way." He hung up without another word.

Jenny turned to her mother, "He's coming up here! I barely know the man and he is willing to drop everything to help. I didn't know what to say to stop him."

"No need, darling. Maybe there is something he can do. The sheriff isn't exactly making great progress. We'll take it one step at a time."

The sound of Alexis waking up from her nap got Jenny's attention and she went into her room to pick her up. Without her twin sister, Alexis had been cranky and not sleeping well.

Chapter Thirty

Eagle's Nest

"Jake, get Mitch and Larry. Let them know I'll be leaving for the day. I may not be back until tomorrow. I've got an emergency I have to take care of. I'll have to leave the ranch work to you guys until I get back. If you need anything, call me on my cell phone. I'll be up at Tahoe." Justin patted the small, tough cowboy on the shoulder. "It's nothing for you to worry about. A friend's in trouble. I have to try and help."

"You bet, boss. Don't worry about anything. You know we can handle whatever comes up. We'll call if we need you. Go help your friend." Jake watched as Justin loped off to his truck. He shook his heard. He had never known anyone as loyal or compassionate as his boss. He would do anything for a friend. He trusted this man with his life.

As he watched Justin roar out of the driveway, he waved. "Take care. Don't let the trouble rub off on you!" He knew Justin couldn't hear him, but felt the need to say it anyway. Helping someone in big trouble was sometimes dangerous. And the way Justin had taken off in such a hurry; it had to be big trouble.

Keeping an eye on his rear view mirror, Justin ramped up the speed on the truck. He wasn't sure why this was affecting him so strongly. From the minute he had set eyes on Jenny at the airport, he knew she was going to be an important part of his life. He hadn't been able to get her out of his mind since. Even seeing her at the Clearwater clubhouse with her two beautiful children in tow had not discouraged him, nor lessened his attraction to her. Hearing about the kidnapping was going to give him a golden opportunity to see her again and show her how much he cared.

He made it to Carson City in record time, and then the traffic got congested and he had to slow down. He pounded on his steering wheel; frustrated by the time it was taking to make it through the small town's main street.

Back on the main highway again, clear of the town, he pressed down on the gas pedal and the truck sped up. He heard the beeping of his radar detector and grimaced. He hated to slow down, but getting a ticket wouldn't help either. Easing up on the gas, he ran his fingers through his blonde hair and frowned. If Jenny's boyfriend, who was unfortunately the father of her twins, had taken Ava, was it because he wanted the baby, or money? From what he had observed, it didn't appear as if he was too interested in the twins. Jenny said he had never even seen them. If it was he, it showed what a bastard he was. He needed to talk to Jenny and have her tell him the whole story about this guy, Diego.

As he pulled into the driveway of the Robertson's house, Justin could see a small group of people standing by the back door. A tall, dark haired man in a wet suit was talking to them, agitation showing in his face. He parked the truck and got out quickly. His heart was racing; maybe they had found the baby.

As Justin got out of his truck and approached the house the back door opened. His heart skipped a beat as he recognized Jenny's bright red-gold curls. What was it about this young woman that grabbed his attention and caused his belly to burn with yearning? He wanted to take her in his arms and tell her everything would be all right. He noticed the blue shadows under her eyes. If there was anyway he could help he would.

Justin put out his hand and grasped her arm lightly.

"Jenny, I am so sorry. When I heard about the kidnapping I had to come and see if there was anything I can do to help you find your baby girl. How long has she been gone? Are all these people looking for her?" His stomach lurched as he looked back at the man in the wet suit. "They don't think she could have fallen into the lake do they?"

Jenny saw his eyes lock onto Evan and sighed. "No, we don't think that's possible. She could not have climbed out of the playpen by herself. Evan was scuba diving and came running up when he heard. I would give anything if he hadn't been."

"You don't like scuba diving?" Justin was puzzled. The look she was giving Evan was almost as if she thought he was responsible for what had happened.

"That's not it. It's what he was looking for that matters." Seeing the questions on Justin's face she sighed. "It's a long story, Justin, and I don't have time to go into it right now. To be honest, I have no idea how you can help, unless you happen to know where my ex-boyfriend, Diego is at this moment. I have an awful feeling he's the one who took Ava. He could have taken either twin, but she looks just like him. I have no idea why he would do this. He never wanted anything to do with the children. All he ever wanted was for me to get rid of them before they were born."

"Have you heard from him at all since you came home? Is it possible he could have taken Ava to get you to come back?"

"I don't know. I just want my baby back." Jenny's eyes filled with tears and Justin stepped forward and took her in his arms. It felt natural and right to have her against his chest. He smoothed her hair and lifted her chin up, looking into her clear blue eyes.

"We'll find her, Jenny. Let's hope it was Diego. At least her own father won't harm her."

Jenny looked at him and her eyes widened. "I hadn't thought of that. Diego is a lot of things, but I know he wouldn't hurt one of his own. He is very protective of his family."

"See, there are some positives here after all. Come on, let's see if any of these people have heard anything," Justin dropped his arms and took her hand, leading her over to the little assembly of neighbors who had spent the night searching.

As they approached, Evan looked up. Seeing Jenny holding hands with the tall blonde stranger, he frowned. Who was this guy? Whoever it was, he seemed to know Jenny pretty well. He eyed Justin suspiciously, noting the jeans and cowboy boots. Where the hell did this man come from? Not from around here, that was for sure.

"Who's your friend, Jen?" he asked, frowning at Justin.

"This is Justin King, Justin, this is Evan Burney, his family lives here at the cove." The two men shook hands, taking stock of each other. It was apparent to Justin that Evan had more than a neighborly interest in Jenny, but he couldn't worry about that. They had to come up with a plan to find little Ava quickly while she might still be in the area.

"I'm not one for standing around," Justin said. "If you'll tell me where the sheriff's office is, I'll head over there and see if they can use some help."

"I'm going in that direction, myself." Evan offered, "If you can wait a few minutes for me to get out of this wet suit, I'll drive you over." He wanted to get to know this guy better to see why he was really here. Had he made a special trip? Or was he playing golf and heard from the grapevine about Ava's disappearance? By now the word had spread like wildfire. If he had designs on Jenny he would find out.

"Sure," Justin said politely. "I'll go sit in my truck and wait for you. I don't know anyone here, so I'll just chill out till you're ready."

"There's no need to wait in your truck, Justin," Jenny said. "Come on into the house. I'll get you a soda or coffee. I can show you some pictures of Ava in case you need to…," she paused, terrified at what she was thinking.

Seeing the frightened look on her face, Evan put his arm around her. "Jen, stop it. Ava is fine. I just know it. We're going to find her."

Jenny glared at him, shrugging off his arm. "If you had listened to me, this might never have happened!"

Shocked, Evan started to speak, and then thinking better of what he might say about the ridiculous idea she had about a ghostly prophecy, he turned and walked to his Corvette. "I'll be back in about ten minutes, Justin. Wait for me."

Justin was more puzzled than ever. What did she

mean; if Evan had listened to her this might not have happened? How was he involved? He felt Jenny take his arm and pull him toward the house. He definitely needed to ask some questions.

Chapter Thirty-One

South Lake Tahoe

Alicia paced the floor of the hotel room. The baby had long since given up crying and fallen asleep. Since there was no crib in the room Alicia had placed her in the middle of the big bed, but at six months she could still wake up and roll off, so she stayed close by making sure she didn't wake up. That man should have been back by now, she thought to herself. She had called him on the cell phone number he had given her and he had answered. That was encouraging. At least he hadn't just run out on his baby like the mom did. She had given him a list of items he needed to bring back as soon as possible. No telling how long the baby had been without food and she certainly needed her diaper changed.

The sound of a key card being swiped in the door made her jump. As she turned around, Diego stepped into the room loaded down with packages. With a sigh of relief Alicia hurried over to help him with his purchases.

"I hope you brought the formula," she said a bit crossly. "This baby has cried herself to sleep, probably because she was hungry. Her mother must be some kind of person to leave her like this. And how come you don't know anything about taking care of her?" Alicia realized she had no right to be angry. After all, this fellow seemed to be doing his best, considering the situation he had been left in.

"We were separated before the baby was born. Not that it's any of your business. This is the first time I have seen my daughter. Now that bitch comes here and just dumps her in my lap," he growled. "If you think I'm enjoying hearing the kid cry for hours, think again." Then realizing he needed this girl to help him, he calmed down and spoke softer. "Sorry, I have a lot on my mind. Please stay a little longer and show me what to do. I've never fed, or changed a baby in my life."

Alicia looked at the obviously unhappy man, and sat down in an armchair.

"I told you I charge twenty dollars an hour. You already owe me eighty dollars. If you want to pay for the time, I'll be glad to stay and help you out."

"Thank you. I'm a fast learner. Just show me the basics. I can deal with the rest."

Alicia cocked her head and looked closely at Diego. He was a very handsome man, but something didn't seem quite right. Why would a hunk with money get into a situation like this? Oh well, she mused. Just be smart and take advantage of the situation.

"Okay, then. I'll have to wake her up so you can learn how to feed and change her. But, before we do that, let's get all this stuff out and fix her formula. She'll be hungry when we wake her up, and I've heard about all the crying I want to for awhile."

Diego took a deep breath. This girl might be his salvation. When he was ready to leave here with Jessica, he would try to convince her to come along. He could not deal with the baby by himself. If she didn't want to come along – well, there were ways to persuade her. She seemed to be attracted to him, and she was pretty enough. Getting pretty woman to do what he wanted was what he did for a living, wasn't it? He gave her a brilliant smile. "So, what are we waiting for? Let's get started! By the way, the baby's name is Jessica."

An hour later, formula made and supplies neatly packed into the duffle bag Diego had bought, the two stood over the sleeping baby. Diego looked at the young helper and smiled. "You are a very pretty girl. I'll bet you have lots of boyfriends."

Alicia blushed as the smoldering dark eyes took in her face and wandered over her slender body knowingly. "I don't have a boyfriend. I just moved to the lake a year ago. Luckily, I got this job right away, or I would have been out on the street." His hand touched her cheek and she moved away. "We had better wake her up now. I have to be at another baby sitting job in a bit."

Diego took her hand and rubbed her fingers lightly. "Do we have to hurry? She's still sound asleep," he murmured, gesturing at the sleeping baby. Jessica's long, dark lashes were feathered on her pink cheeks and her breathing was even and deep. "I could use some company. Come and sit down over here," he gestured to the second queen bed. "She'll wake up shortly, but while we wait, we can get to know each other. Back in Spain I knew a beautiful girl that looks like you. I miss her a lot. But, she is gone now. She left me for another man, just like my wife."

Alicia felt her pulse pounding. He was very good

looking and had a great body. She loved his dark, curly hair. She took a deep breath. His black eyes seemed to set her on fire. He could be dangerous though, she should be careful. But, how dangerous could a man be who was taking such good care of his baby daughter? Against her better judgment, she followed him to the bed and sat down beside him.

"You see my life has been a sad tale so far." Diego said with a sigh. "Maybe you are the one to cheer me up?" He tilted her chin up and kissed her lightly on her lips.

Shocked Alicia jumped up from the bed. "I'm not that kind of girl! I'm leaving. Just pay me what you owe me please." Her heart was pounding and she felt panic begin to take hold of her

"Well, let's see," Diego began softly. "By now I owe you about a hundred dollars, but it could get a lot better." He reached for her and pulled her back down on the bed. "Don't struggle, my little one. You will be treated better than you can imagine. You are about to have the best time of your life."

Alicia slapped Diego as hard as she could across his handsome smiling face. "Get away from me, you pervert." She began to cry. "Just give me the money you owe me. What are you, some kind of maniac?"

Realizing his charm was not having the desired affect, Diego stood up. "Ah, I can see you are a lady." He bowed deeply from his waist. "I apologize, dear girl. Please forgive me. I made a huge mistake. I will get your money."

Alicia straightened her blouse and swallowed hard. Maybe she had misjudged him. After all, she *was* in his hotel room, and men sort of expected a maid to do anything that was asked of them in these high roller rooms, weren't they?

"Sorry I yelled, but you scared me."

"Don't worry about it. Here's two hundred. It has been worth it to know I can take good care of Jessica now - thanks to you. You've been wonderful." He walked to the door, holding it open for her.

She hesitated. Perhaps she had been too hasty. She didn't really have another job to go to. What did men pay for a sleep over? Too new to the fast paced. gambling town, Alicia could only guess. Maybe it was thousands! She could use a chunk of money to get a better apartment. She thought quickly. It was only one time and he was a hunk, he smelled good too. That was nice.

Diego saw her hesitation, and smiled to himself. Money was the best aphrodisiac ever invented. "Are you sure you don't want to stay? It will be very lucrative for you, I promise."

"How much is it worth to you?" she said boldly, but her insides were shaking.

"That depends on what we are going to do with the time you spend here. If you stay all night, I think we could agree it would be worth a couple thousand dollars." He knew his money was running low, but he was starting to get caught up in the idea of taking this scared, young woman to bed, for what appeared to be her first time. The idea was interesting. Most all the women he bedded were older and well used. This one was different. He could feel the heat begin to burn in his belly.

Alicia swallowed hard. The maids probably did this all the time. If she was going to work here, she might as well take advantage of the extra money she could make by being "available".

"I'm not sure, I've never done this before, but I could use the money."

Diego closed the door softly and took the trembling girl in his arms. "Don't worry, I won't hurt you. I'll take you where you have never been. Just come lie on the bed with me. I want to undress you."

Alicia lay stiff and frightened as Diego began to remove her shoes, and then slid off her skirt. As he unbuttoned her blouse, she turned to him, "You'll be careful, won't you?"

"Of course I will, just lay still." His fingers began to shake as he unhooked the frilly bra and pulled it away. Her small pink tipped breasts thrust up at him innocently and erotically. He licked his lips and then fell forward taking her nipples in his mouth. His hands moved downward, stripping off her pantyhose and his knees pushed her legs apart. He settled between them, waiting, wanting the pleasure of feeling her untouched body to last.

"Act as if you want me, girl," he growled softly.

"I don't know what to do," her faint voice was muffled by his body.

"Just move against me. It's not difficult. Don't you want me?" he was almost beyond control now as he felt her soft smooth skin against his.

He began stroking places on her body that had never known the touch of a man's hands. It was beginning to excite her. He felt her thighs tighten and wetness flood her. She began to breathe faster, matching Diego's heavy panting.

"There, that's right. Put your hand on me," he said his voice hoarse and raspy. Then opening her with his fingers, he entered her. He began thrusting. Gently at first, then feeling the resistance of her virginity his control failed and breaking the delicate tissue, he rammed into her.

The muffled screams from the bed stayed in the room, but they were enough to wake up Jessica, who started a high-pitched wail. Alicia struggled to rise.

"Lie still, I'm not done with you." Diego thrust harder

and faster, driven crazy by the tightness of Alicia's young body.

"Stop, you're hurting me! Please, stop!" Alicia begged.

"I'll stop when I'm done. Now move faster when I tell you to."

He was in frenzy, not caring that the baby was howling louder than ever.

Finally, with one last crushing thrust, he finished. He rolled off the sobbing girl onto his back and put his hands over his ears.

"Make that noise stop! Enough!" he yelled, the pleasure of the coupling forgotten as the baby's loud wailing assailed his ears.

"I'm bleeding!" Alicia sobbed her eyes wide with fright as she looked down at the stained sheets.

"Oh, for crying out loud, how old are you? Don't you know that always happens the first time you get laid? Go clean up, and then take care of that screaming baby. And, by the way, her name is Jessica."

Stunned and hurting, Alicia hobbled to the bathroom and closed the door. She looked at herself in the mirror. Seeing a purple bruise beginning to form on her cheek, she bent her head. What had she done? Was this what love was like, this awful, hurtful act? No, this was why she was getting paid two thousand dollars. She took a deep breath. She had asked for it, now she would have to suffer the consequences. Splashing water on her face, she cleaned herself up and smoothed her hair. She thought quickly. If he was willing to pay that much for one time, maybe she could make more money for a second time, *if* she could stand it. She felt like a different person. Something inside her had changed. Maybe what they said about losing your innocence was true. The harm was done. She might as well make the best of it. Taking a deep breath, she turned and walked back out into the bedroom and picked up the crying baby.

"I'll feed Jessica for you, "she said, smiling at Diego. He smiled back. He had no doubt she would do more than that for him after they left here and found a safer place to hide "Jessica". He had no doubt her greed would buy her services for as long as he needed her.

Chapter Thirty-Two

Clear Water Cove

Alexis was napping again, and the house seemed unnaturally quiet after the hubbub that was going on outside. Justin sat down next to the big picture windows that afforded a panoramic view of the lake. He could have sat and taken it in for hours, but his attention was diverted by a cold drink dripping onto his arm.

"Sorry, it's just lemonade. Do you need a napkin?" Jenny apologized as she saw the drops land on the fine gold hair on Justin's tanned arm.

"I'm fine. Thanks for the drink. Please, sit down. I don't want to be nosy, but I'm a little confused about how your friend, Evan, is involved with this."

"It's a long story. You probably won't believe me if I tell you. It happened before Evan was born. I'm not even sure I *should* tell you, since it involves something Evan probably doesn't want everyone to know."

"Can you tell me a bit, leaving him out of it?"

"Maybe, but I know you'll think me and my whole family are crazy."

Justin laughed a hearty laugh. "I don't think that's possible. From what I've seen, your family is a very normal one, like my own parents. They seem loving and comfortable around each other. Mostly, I've noticed how much they care about you. Can't say that I blame them. It's not hard to see why." He flashed his dimples at her drawn face, hoping to elicit a small smile, but she just nodded.

"They are wonderful." She said solemnly, "I'll tell you a little, just not everything."

"Whatever you want, it might help us find Ava."

A tear trailed its way down her cheek as Jenny began the edited tale of the blue diamond necklace and the ghost of Sirena.

"So you see. She warned me about anyone trying to recover it again. I told Evan not to try to find it, but he thinks I am just dreaming up this ghost." She leaned forward and put her small hand on Justin's.

"I'm telling you, Justin. The only person in this story who hasn't seen the ghost is Evan. Guess I can't blame him for not believing. It is a pretty wild story."

"Yes, I have to say it is, but if you say you and your parents have seen this ghost, then I have to take it seriously. Having said that, if it's true that she's causing this, we have to make Evan promise to stop looking for it. If she hears him say he'll leave it alone, maybe she will give us a clue that will help find Ava. Just speculation, I know, but it's worth a try."

Jenny looked at him searchingly, trying to find any falseness in his response. Seeing none, she stood up. "In that case, we have to convince him quickly. I have a feeling if we don't find my baby soon, we never will."

They got up and walked back out of the house, Justin following Jenny's slender backside. He thought her shoulders looked a bit straighter now, her walk a bit more focused. As he left the house, he stopped for a minute on the doorstep. He shook his head slightly. A ghost! Wow. He had to believe her if she was going to trust him, but what a story.

He should be at Eagle's View. His parents weren't going to be very happy to find out he had left their foreman in charge of the ranch, but the powerful attraction he felt for Jenny far outweighed anything as sensible as staying out of the trouble she was facing.

As Justin walked out of the back door, he spotted Evan coming down the drive. His jaw tightened as he watched him give Jenny a kiss on her check. He was too good looking. Those long eyelashes belong on a girl, he thought to himself as jealousy pushed its ugly specter into his mind. He saw Evan wave him over to his Corvette.

Justin shook his head. "Let's take my truck; it's a four wheel drive. We might need that."

"Fine, let's go." Evan got into the passenger's side of the big truck and looked around. "Nice wheels," he remarked, as Justin settled into the driver's seat and started the powerful engine.

"Thanks," Justin answered gruffly, still not sure how friendly he wanted to be with this guy. "Can you show me how to get to the Sheriff's office? I'm sure you know your way around here far better than I do."

"Yep, been here all my life, Jen and I grew up here." He smiled. It didn't hurt to let this cowboy know how close he and Jenny were.

"The sooner we get some idea of where we should start looking, the better. The more hours that slip by, the less chance we'll have to find the baby," said Evan as he settled into the soft leather seat."

Jenny watched as the truck sped off down the dirt road toward South Shore. She had to find a way to let Sirena know she was not going to let Evan recover the necklace. How she was going to do that, she had no idea.

Chapter Thirty-Three

South Shore, Lake Tahoe

After the newly named, Jessica, was fed. Alicia took a blanket off one of the beds and put it on the floor. She lifted the sleepy little girl up and laid her on the blanket. "Now we don't have to worry about her rolling off the bed," she said. She looked over at Diego, who was staring at her again. She felt the heat rise in her cheeks. "Would you mind if I went to get us some take out?" she asked politely. "You were gone so long I haven't had lunch, or dinner. I'm really hungry."

Diego thought about the request for a minute before he answered. It was too risky; she might tell someone about the baby or her newly lost virginity. No, he couldn't risk it.

"You stay here with Jessica. I'll go and bring you something to eat. What would you like? McDonalds? Chinese?"

Alicia stood up from where she had been sitting by

the baby. "I don't care, just don't take too long. I feel like I have been in this room for days. Are you sure I can't go?"

Diego took her in his arms and crushed his lips on hers. "No, my dear, I am your servant now. I'll be back soon, I promise. The night has only begun for us. By morning you will be a rich girl!"

Alicia's heart raced. Rich? What did he mean? Maybe the stories about men paying thousands for favors were true! She shrugged her shoulders and pushed away from him.

"Okay, but don't be long."

"Don't worry. I'll be back before you know it. Keep the kid quiet."

Diego pinched her on her small behind, eliciting a yelp of pain. He laughed and quickly left the room, closing the door behind him.

Alicia frowned. He hadn't paid any attention to the baby at all. Was it really his? And why had he taken his bag when he left the room? He surely wouldn't leave without his little girl. What was going on here? She hoped she wasn't getting herself into a whole lot of trouble. To make things worse, she still hadn't seen the two hundred dollars he had promised.

Diego wondered if Alicia had noticed he had taken his bag when he left the room. Even if she had, she wasn't the brightest penny in the jar. She probably thought all his money was in it. Actually, along with the few clothes he had brought, it was! The sex hadn't been nearly as satisfying as he had expected. Experience was what counted. She hadn't had a clue. It had left him unsatisfied and disappointed. Afterwards, while Alicia was caring for Jessica, he'd thought about his situation. Did he really want to try and leave with the baby and this young girl? He began to doubt his sanity. What a fool he had been. What had he been thinking? Everything was getting out of hand. The best thing for him to do was dump the brat and go home. It had been a stupid idea from the beginning. Rich and lustier women awaited him back home. As far as Jenny went, he would have to forget about her. Alicia had given him the perfect escape he needed.

Without a glance back at the hotel, he hailed a cab. As the driver opened the door, he threw his bag in the back seat and got in.

"Where to, buddy?" the cabby asked politely.

"San Francisco International Airport"

"That'll cost you a bundle, mister," the cabby said looking back at the tall, well-dressed man.

"Whatever it costs, its well worth it," Diego smiled, and settled back for the long ride, happy he hadn't paid the stupid babysitter any more money.

Alicia held Jessica over her shoulder. The baby had started to cry again. She glanced at the clock. Eight o'clock! She looked out the window. It was dark outside, and there was no sign of Diego. It had been hours since he left, and he had not called. She had no idea what to do. She jiggled the small child to quiet her and felt her relax. When she looked sideways at Jessica's face, she could see her eyes were closed. She tiptoed to the bed and laid her down. Her heart went out to this child. As the baby lay sleeping on the bed, Alicia stared down at her. Jessica's dark hair curled damply around her pudgy, pink face. Her long, dark lashes swept her cheeks. She was such a beautiful baby, Alicia thought. She gently stroked the fat little arms and legs. Someone had taken very good care of her. The one piece pink coverall, embroidered with lace, was clean and expensive. Why had her mother deserted her?

Alicia had no friends here at the lake, no one she could call to ask what to do. If she called the police, she might get in trouble. Anyway, they would just take this precious little girl and give her to a foster family. She was starting to feel a strong bond with Jessie. The baby would be better off with someone who really cared about her.

As Alicia paced the room, she began to form a plan. She would leave a note for Diego, no, that wouldn't work; someone else would find it and know she had taken the baby... She made a quick decision. Loading up the formula and diapers Diego had left for Jessie, she bundled them into a sheet and tied it securely. She wrapped Jessie in a large bath towel, and then slinging the baby's small bundle of belongings over her shoulder, she gathered the sleeping child in her arms and left the room.

At this hour most of the maids had gone home and the hallways were relatively empty. The guests were either still at dinner, or gambling. No one took notice of the slender young maid with a bundle of sheets and towels as she crept down the back stairs and exited the hotel.

The night was frigid. All she had on was her light uniform. She shivered with cold and fear. Was she doing the right thing? What if Diego came back? She really doubted he would. He didn't act like he cared about the baby. He didn't even know how to take care of her. Between her and her mother, Jessie would get a good home. She would tell her mother Jessie was hers. She had been away from home long enough that it was possible. She still had the money Diego had given her. It would pay for the cab fare home. Raising this beautiful little girl on a cattle ranch was far better than a cold, uncaring foster home. Alicia's dark hair was a match with Jessie's dark curls. No one would ever guess she didn't belong to her.

Alicia did not go back to her apartment but went straight to the taxi stand. Her room was a month to month rental and she was paid up for the current month. She could come back for her things later. It was important to get Jessica to a safe place as soon as possible. As far as the hotel was concerned, they would barely miss her. No shows were common. She felt no guilt about leaving unannounced. They would fill her position immediately.

As the cab carrying Alicia and the sleeping baby pulled away from the curb, Alicia thought she saw a shadowy figure standing by the roadside watching them. A faint smile lit the lovely face of the dark haired woman and then she seemed to just disappear. Alicia felt a chill run down her back. "That was weird," she said out loud. "I must be seeing things", she muttered.

Outside in the darkness, the echo of Sirena's laughter could have been heard, if someone was listening closely.

Chapter Thirty-Four

Clear Water Cove

It had been two weeks since Ava had been taken. Jenny was sitting in a yellow lounge chair on the front lawn of the house watching Alexis playing on a blanket she had laid down on the grass. Jenny had lost weight and her eyes were huge in her face. Her fingers drummed nervously on the arms of the chair. She couldn't seem to sit still; she kept thinking there must be something she could be doing to help with the search for Ava. How could it be possible she had just disappeared into thin air? Evan had kept her posted on the search, but so far, neither the FBI, nor the local authorities, had any leads. Justin had left a few days after the disappearance of Jessica to go back and take care of things at the ranch.

To her dismay, Evan was still diving in the cove, trying to locate that haunted necklace. There had been no more warnings or appearances from Sirena, but in her heart,

Jenny knew that somehow the warning she had been given had something to do with Ava's disappearance.

She sighed heavily and stood up. It was time for Alexis's nap. She must not let her despair over Ava keep her from being a good mother to Alexis. She might be the only child she had left. She picked up the fat, wiggly baby, and holding her tightly, took her into the house.

The phone was ringing as she entered the kitchen and she reached over the baby to answer it. When she picked up the receiver she heard Justin's deep voice.

"Jenny? How are you, sweetie? I'm on my way up there, should be at your place in about fifteen minutes. I have a proposition for you"

Curious, she cradled the phone on her shoulder. Jenny could hear the concern in Justin's voice. She shifted the baby to her other hip. Nothing Justin could propose could possibly lift her anger and sadness.

"Okay, Justin .I'm just putting Alexis down for her nap. I'll be in the kitchen. I'll make some coffee."

"See you in a few," he said and hung up.

He sounded excited, and Jenny's heart soared for a split second, and then she realized he would have told her immediately if he had any news of Ava. She put the phone back on the receiver and carried Alexis into her room. However she was not ready to go to sleep, so Jenny sat beside the crib and sang her an ancient lullaby her mother had sung to her. "Tura lura lura, Lura, lura li"

As she sang the familiar old tune to the fussing baby, she looked over at the empty crib and her voice cracked. Tears flooded her eyes and she struggled to finish the song. She couldn't let this tragedy affect Alexis. She already showed signs of distress at the absence of Ava. She reached down and patted her small, warm back and kept singing, getting her voice under control. At last Alexis's eyes closed and she slept. Jenny wished it were that easy for her to sleep at night.

A knock on the back door signaled Justin's arrival, and Jenny hurried to answer before the loud knocking woke up Alexis.

Jenny and Justin sat facing each other in the big warm kitchen. Jenny had made coffee for both of them. Justin reached across the table and took her hand.

"Jen, I just had a long talk with Mom and Dad. We want you and Alexis to come and stay at the ranch. Being here isn't doing you any good. You need to get away from all the constant reminders of what has happened. The ranch will be good for you. The house is enormous, and Mom is excited about having a pseudo granddaughter to enjoy." He stopped for a minute as he saw the shocked look on Jenny's pale face. "Please, take a day or two and think about it. There's nothing you can do here. If there is any news, you will hear it just as quickly at the ranch as you will here. It will be something different to take your mind off the search."

Jenny stared at him, a look of disbelief on her face. "Do you honestly think I could forget about Ava by going to your ranch? Not a chance. I have to be as close to the search as possible. She might still be at the lake somewhere."

"Of course I don't think you will forget about Ava. Nothing like that! I am only thinking of you, Jen. You need to get away from here, away from the constant reminders, and the ghost stories. Every day you see Evan diving for that crazy diamond necklace and you sit here thinking it's the cause of Ava's disappearance. Don't you see? If you come to the ranch, you can step back and take some time to regroup." He gave her a lopsided grin, "Besides, I want you to come."

"You don't believe any of us ever saw Sirena or heard her warnings, do you?"

"Baby, I don't know what to believe, I only know it's making you sick."

"It's Evan's grandfather's fault. If he hadn't dug up Sirena's grave and stolen that necklace years ago, everything would be different. I have to stay here and try to stop him or I may never see my baby again!"

"Evan's a grown man, Jen. You aren't going to stop him from doing what he thinks is his birthright. He believes he is meant to have that necklace. Nothing, or anyone, is going to stop him from trying to find it. Evidently, he hasn't seen this ghost of yours and isn't worried at all about the consequences."

Jenny put her hand on Justin's arm. She felt the strong muscles under his cotton shirt. "You can stop him, Justin. He will listen to you."

"No, Jen. He won't. I don't think he'll stop until he finds it, or drowns trying. He appears to be on some sort of mission. Anyway, take a few days and think about what I've said. Come and stay with us for a little while. I'm not saying a long stay, just a few weeks, until you can get a better perspective."

Jenny's heart was torn. She was falling for this handsome cowboy who was so earnestly trying to help her, but how could she possibly leave the scene of the abduction? What if Ava was nearby?

"I'll think about it, Justin. Really, I will."

Justin felt a flicker of hope. Maybe this could work. Jenny was so frail and thin. She needed a change. The ranch was just the ticket. He knew she would love it, and

155

he and his mom and dad would love having her and Alexis more than she knew.

After Justin left, Jenny wandered out onto the front lawn and stood looking out over the lake. She watched as the sun began its slide behind the mountains to the west. The cloud-streaked sky took on all the colors of the rainbow which deepened as the night descended. There surely was no place on earth as beautiful as this, she thought. And yet, she knew something strange lurked out in the deep water of the cove. Something she had seen. A vengeful ghost she was sure had caused Ava's disappearance.

She shivered, remembering the visions of Sirena. As the sun disappeared, the air grew cold and she turned to go back inside. Just as she reached the door, she heard her name called. As she turned around, she saw Evan bounding up the stairs. He was all smiles and grabbed her in a big bear hug.

"Hey, little one, what are you doing out here in the cold? You don't have enough fat on you to last five minutes in this night air. Come on; come up to Mom's with me. Cook will have dinner ready by now. I'm sure she'll be delighted to have a chance to feed you."

"No thanks, Evan. I'm too tired. But since you're here, I have to ask you to do something for me. Please stop diving for the diamonds."

Jenny's mind had been racing to think of a way to convince him to give up the search ever since Justin had left. Now was as good a time as any. "I know you don't believe in ghosts, or ghostly prophesies, but I do. If you care at all for me, you'll give up this ridiculous hunt. That damn necklace has done nothing but cause trouble since your grandfather turned grave robber and stole it. Whether you believe the ghost of Sirena is real or not, you have to admit that's when all the trouble started." Her eyes looked at him pleadingly.

"Okay, so there has been trouble, but it was all man made, not the work of some ethereal creature. I made a promise to myself when I was a little boy that someday I would recover what my father wanted so badly. Besides", he grinned down at her, "I am having the time of my life looking."

"Then I guess there is nothing I can do but hope you will change your mind." Jenny struggled out of his grasp and stood back away from him. "I thought you cared about me, Evan, but I see now that your "fun" is more important than our friendship."

Suddenly, she knew what she had to do. "I'm going to take Alexis and stay with Justin at Eagle's View for awhile. While I'm gone be careful. I know what kind of trouble Sirena can cause to keep anyone from taking that necklace again. I would hate to see anything happen to you."

"What the hell! Why would you run away, Jenny? You can't be serious? What can you do at Eagle's View that you can't accomplish here?"

"For one thing, I won't have to watch you risk your life every day trying to make a dive that is way too deep to be safe. I also won't have to wonder when Sirena is going to show up again to punish us. Just be very careful, Evan, I mean it."

Evan laughed, but somewhere deep inside him, a warning bell rang. Jenny was no fool. She was convinced this ghost was real. Could she possibly be right?

He would find out soon enough.

Chapter Thirty-Five

Eagle's View Ranch

"Marry me, Jenny." Justin leaned down from his big bay quarter horse and took a lock of her hair in his fingers. They had ridden miles from the ranch up into the hills, farther than usual. His heart swelled with happiness as he looked at the change the month at the ranch had made in her. She had gained weight and her cheeks glowed with a healthy blush of pink. She looked beautiful. Fortunately, she had taken to riding quickly. She was a natural rider and had fallen in love with the stocky little palomino mare he pulled from the pasture for her to learn on. He leaned closer and his leg brushed hers.

Jenny looked up at him and sighed. "Justin, I wish I could say yes, but my mind is too full of what I can do to find Ava to think of anything else."

Justin sat back up in his saddle and looked off into the distance. "It's been almost two months, Jen. No one will ever give up looking for her, but I think you have to realize the chances of finding her are becoming less every day. Life has to go on. You have a beautiful little girl to take care of and a life to continue with. Hard as it is to accept, we may never find Ava." He swallowed hard. He seldom talked this frankly to Jenny. She was still too broken. He looked around to see if he had upset her, and saw she had stopped her horse and was way behind him.

Expertly spinning his horse around, he urged him into a lope and skidded to a halt beside her. She was bent over her mare's neck, her face buried in the mare's long silver mane. He heard her sobbing.

"Damn it, Jen. I didn't mean to make you cry. I know how hard this must be, but sometimes I have to tell it like it is."

Jenny looked at him, tears streaming down her face. "No you don't, Justin, you have no idea how hard this is. I will never believe that I won't see Ava again. I know she is still alive, we just have to keep looking until we find her."

"And we will, darling. But in the meantime, we still have a life to live."

"I'm trying, Justin. Alexis is a godsend, but every time I look at her my heart is ripped out of my chest thinking about what could be happening to her sister. Who has her? What are they doing to her? I keep having these terrible thoughts that won't stop going through my head."

Justin got off his horse and took the reins of the little palomino away from Jenny. "Get off your horse. Sometimes walking helps clear your mind."

Jenny did as she was told, and Justin took her in his arms. He kissed the top of her head and held her tightly. "I want you to know, I will do everything in my power to find Ava. I will make sure no one ever stops looking." He lifted her tear-streaked face and kissed her tenderly. "Now, let's walk and talk about you and me for a change."

Jenny tried to smile. Justin was such a good man. She was so lucky he cared for her. Maybe someday the ache would stop and she would find room in her heart to love him.

They walked for an hour, almost reaching the house before they remounted their horses. Justin had directed the conversation to the coming horse sale the ranch had every year. Eagle's View quarter horses were highly prized, and the few yearlings they sold each year commanded a high dollar amount. The ranch had an open house during the sale, with a picnic and barn dance, complete with a bonfire and cowboy poetry readers. The family looked forward to it, and he thought it might be something Jenny would enjoy. It might even take her mind off the search for her missing child.

Jenny listened as Justin went on about the event, but her mind was not on the party. Soon, she would have to return to Clear Water Cove. She prayed she would find that Evan had given up his search. A glimmer of hope filled her as she thought what that would mean. As strange as it might sound to anyone else, she felt sure Sirena would give her a sign and let her know where Ava was if Evan gave up his quest. The more she thought about it, the more her hopes rose. She tuned back into Justin's conversation just in time to hear him ask her if she would like to read some poetry at the bonfire.

"Justin, I have to go home. I've been here too long as it is. It's not helping me find Ava. You have been terribly kind, and I do feel better. I have to go back and see if Evan has stopped diving for the necklace. I have to do something to get Sirena to make another appearance. She has to know where my baby is."

Justin looked at her face, so full of hope. It broke his heart. There was no credible evidence that anyone but a kidnapper had taken Ava. The longer Jenny kept hoping some ghost was going to lead her to the baby, the longer it would take for her to come back to him – and the real world.

"I know you believe this, Jenny, but please don't pin your hopes on a visit from a ghost. If you feel you and Alexis have to go home, then that's your decision, but if you make this about seeing ghosts, I'm afraid you're in for a big let down."

Jenny patted his cheek. "I'll miss you and your folks. They have been so good to Alexis and me. I feel like part of your family, but this is something I have to do. You might not understand because you have never seen Sirena. I have."

"Whatever you want, but you'll miss a great party, and Mom and Dad are going to miss Alexis like crazy. I think Mom feels like she is her own granddaughter. She adores that baby, and who wouldn't. She's beautiful. Just like her mother." He smiled at the golden haired girl on her golden horse. Somehow, he would have her for his own. He wasn't sure how he would make it happen, but he knew he had to try. Letting her go home was hard, but he was aware that keeping her here any longer would be impossible.

Chapter Thirty-Six

Clear Water Cove

The big motor boat belonging to Evan, slowly made its way out to the deep hole in the cove where, supposedly, the diamond necklace had been lost. *Why couldn't he just give it up*, Jenny thought, with growing anger. She had been home for less than a week, and each day she had watched as Evan spent hours diving in the lake. It seemed he didn't tire of the endless search.

She was sitting on the beach under a wide green and white striped umbrella, watching as Alexis dug small holes in the sand, her curls blowing gently in the breeze like a crown of gold. She was such a beautiful child. Jenny thought how lucky she was. The kidnapper could have snatched both children. She often wondered why he had chosen Ava.

An hour later, she picked up her small pair of binoculars she had been bringing to the beach to keep track of any progress Evan might make. She raised them to her eyes and saw him climb out of the lake into the boat. His hair had bleached almost white from the sun, and his skin was darkly tanned. Jenny couldn't help but admire the muscular body as he stripped off his dive suit. She wasn't sure they were even friends anymore. He had completely ignored her request to stop this nonsensical search. For some time they had hardly spoken.

Small cries from Alexis made her drop the glasses. The baby had tried to brush the hair out of her eyes, but had instead filled them with sand.

"Oh sweetie, come here. Let mommy see." Jenny picked up the wailing infant and tried to brush the granules off her face. Seeing she wasn't doing much good, Jenny gathered Alexis in her arms and slipping on sandals, made her way across the hot sand, up the stairs and into the house. As she entered the kitchen, Carolyn came running.

"What's wrong with my darling?" she cooed, removing Alexis from Jenny's arms.

"She has sand in her eyes, Mom. I'm not sure how to get it out."

"Let me take care of it, dear. I had a lot of experience when you were this age." And without any more explanation, Carolyn took the wailing child into the upstairs bathroom to do what - Jenny wasn't sure.

Carolyn had become overprotective of Alexis and so, Jenny thought, had all her family. Grabbing a sweater, she wandered back outside. She decided to take a walk along the golf course. She could use the exercise and that way she didn't have to listen to her baby cry.

Without realizing it, she had walked past the golf course around the meadow and up to the century old graveyard. The residents of Clear Water Cove had kept the small plot of land intact, but the old wooden grave markers were tilted, grey with age and worn. Even though the markers were weathered, you could still read the names and dates on most.

Carolyn hesitated, and then opened a small, iron gate that led into the graveyard. A chill breeze had sprung up and she shivered. She knew that somewhere in here lay the remains of the dance hall girl who had shadowed her family's lives. If Evan's grandfather was telling the truth, her grave had no headstone. They had found it from a map, hidden in the walls of an old hunting lodge he owned. She pulled the sweater tighter around her slender shoulders. Why hadn't they just left it alone? Greed was the cause of most of the world's woes. Greed had cost Evan's father his life. Now, Evan was on course to follow in his footsteps.

She stepped carefully around the old graves. Evening was falling and the light was fading, but she could still see. Many of the markers showed a child was buried beneath. Some who died at an early age here in Clear Water Cove when it was an old logging camp. Life must have been very hard back then. She felt sadness come over her as she looked at the pathetic old markers, knowing how it hard it was to lose a child.

Taking a seat on a weathered wooden bench that had been placed at the back of the graveyard, Jenny closed her eyes. If only Sirena would come back. She had so many questions to ask her.

When she opened her eyes, Jenny was startled to see a figure walking up the path through the graves. She wasn't too surprised. It wasn't exactly a popular spot, but it was of some interest to the local population.

As she watched the figure approach, she realized it was a woman wearing a long black skirt and red sweater. Her heart began to pound. Surely this had to be her ghost. The woman's hair was long and dark, but she couldn't make out any features. Rising quickly, she approached the woman, and then stopped as she recognized Maggie Carlyle, one of the residents who lived a few houses down from her parents. Relieved, but vaguely disappointed, Jenny raised her hand and waved.

"Hi, Maggie." Jenny said, her voice shaky, thinking she had been about to face, Sirena. "

"Hello, Jenny. What are you doing up here alone?"

"I'm just out for an evening walk, how about you?"

"Believe it or not, I have never been in here. It's a very interesting place. However, I don't have much time to look around. I have to get home before it gets colder and so dark I can't see the path."

"I'll walk back with you," Jenny offered.

"Thanks, but I think I'll wander around a little more, see if I can find any lost relatives," Maggie said, trying to make a joke out of being in a graveyard after dark.

Jenny looked at her worriedly. "Are you sure you'll be alright? Walking home alone after dark isn't the best idea."

"Anywhere but Clear Water Cove you would probably be right. I don't worry here. I think it's probably the safest place I know."

Jenny's face took on a strange look and Maggie knew what she must be thinking. "Ava's abduction was the only crime ever committed here in Clear Water Cove, Jenny. I believe it will be the last. Don't worry about me, I'll be fine."

"Well anyway - be safe. I'll call your house in an hour to make sure you made it home okay." Jenny turned and slowly began to pick her way through the graves, to the little gate.

As she walked down the road to the house, she looked back at the graveyard, now shrouded in darkness and shadows. Maybe Maggie would get to meet Sirena, she thought wickedly.

Chapter Thirty-Seven

Yerington, Nevada

"Take the child off that old burro, Alicia. She'll get burrs in her diapers."

The old woman's sharp tone belied the laughter in her eyes. This new grandchild had become her pride and joy. She knew they were spoiling her rotten, but she didn't care. She had bought the tiny Levis Jessica had on, and although she had tried to buy her little cowboy boots, they were too hard to put on her fat little feet, so she was sporting baby Nikes. Her checkered cowboy shirt was also a gift from Martha, as was the child's, red cowboy hat that hung off her head. She loved to wear it, but had trouble keeping it on. Martha didn't care how much she spent on this precious baby, "That's what grandma's are supposed to do," is what she always said.

When Alicia had shown up at the remote ranch with a baby in tow, everyone had been shocked, but now, Martha and Pete Cunningham, Alicia's parents, had fallen in love with the beautiful baby. Alicia took a job at the Foster ranch, some fifteen miles away, cleaning and cooking for the ranch hands and Martha had become Jessica's caregiver. She loved every minute of it.

The Cunningham's C Bar III was a working ranch. It had been in the family for generations. Pete Cunningham, Alicia's father, ran a herd of 200 head of cattle and a small band of quarter horses. They led a simple life on their 3000-acre ranch. No T.V. or computer graced the household, but they had each other. Their simple, hardworking life-style suited them just fine. They only went to town for supplies once a month and with no newspaper delivery, they were blissfully unaware of the tumult of the outside world. Had they been in the twenty-first century of communication, they would have learned soon after Alicia returned home, that half the country was looking for a stolen baby named Ava that looked exactly like Jessica.

Today was Sunday and Alicia was at home spending as much time with her toddler as she could. Being raised on the ranch, Alicia was an accomplished horsewoman. She had brought the old burro Peanut up to the barn a few days earlier. He was the wild burro her father captured on the range ten years ago and he had become the family pet. He was perfect for Jessie. He was sweet and calm, and his fat, soft, furry back was a cushion for the little girl's small behind. The only burrs were in his tail, picked up in his rambling tours of the desert.

Jessica's eyes danced and her tiny hands grasped at the short, fuzzy mane of the patient animal. Alicia held the lead rope tightly with one hand, while the other held onto Jessica's arm.

At two, Jessica was a lovely child. Her dark eyes and black curls sharply contrasted to her milky pink and white complexion. She was tall for her age and her body was solid and slender. Smart and gregarious, she had been walking since she was ten months old, and at eighteen months could put words together to form short sentences. It puzzled her grandmother to see that as the baby grew, she looked less and less like her mother, but figured she had taken after her father, whoever that might be. Alicia had never said anything about the man who was the other half of this charming little girl, only that he had treated her badly and had walked out on both of them.

Tired of the game, the burro stopped dead. He lowered his head and appeared to fall asleep. Jessica's little heels dug into its side.

"Go, go," she chirped, but Peanut had had enough.

"Come on, Jess, time for a nap." Alicia said. She lifted her off the burro, and settling her on her hip, started toward the ranch house where her mother waited for them on the worn, wooden front steps. Peanut happily wandered off to graze on the unkempt patch of grass that made up the front lawn.

"I think she is going to be a rider just like me, don't you, Mom?"

"That will take awhile. You been ridin since you were no bigger than a grass hopper." Her mother smiled at the two. "How's that boy over at Foster's you're so keen on? Seems he's always sniffin around here on weekends. He's takin a likin to Jess, too."

"Oh, Mom, Steve's nice, but I don't think he's serious. Don't know many guys that want to be saddled with a baby, startin out."

"Don't think that much matters to him. From what I seen, he'd like to take the both of you right back home with him."

Alicia patted her mother on the shoulder and went into the house to put Jessica down for her nap. She laid the baby in her crib and kissed her gently on her soft cheek. She often wondered if she had done the right thing, taking her away from that strange man who had deserted her. But as the months flew by; Jessica had blossomed in the clear desert air and with all the love the Cunningham family gave this child, Alicia was sure she had made the right choice.

"Momma, momma," the sleepy baby mumbled, as she looked up at Alicia through droopy eyes.

"Yes darling, go to sleep now. Mommy's here."

One day, she would have to worry about a birth certificate, or some documentation to get her into school, but for now, knowing she was safe here at the ranch was enough.

*Part
Two*

Chapter Thirty-Eight

Clear Water Cove

"Mom, Justin asked me to marry him, again."
Jenny and Carolyn were sitting in front of the roaring fire Tom had laid in the massive stone fireplace. The living room was cozy and warm, but outside the cold rain beat hard fingers of wetness on the wide picture windows. The storm had come in the night before and it was whipping the water of the lake into foaming whitecaps.

"Well, darling, he has been very patient, you know. It's been five years since you two first met. I think it's about time you made up your mind. You couldn't find a more loving man, or one who can take such good care of you and Alexis. You know he adores that child."

"I know I haven't been fair to him, Mother. He's allowed Alexis and me to spend a few weeks at the ranch every summer and it's been wonderful, but I feel that if I leave here I'm giving up on finding Ava."

"Darling, you can't keep this up. You have to get on with your life, and Alexis's. You have to think of her, too."

Tears sprang to Jenny's eyes. "Do you think they are taking care of Ava or…" She couldn't continue. The horrible scenarios that had played out in her mind since the day Ava had gone missing still streamed through her subconscious.

Carolyn went over and sat on the couch beside Jenny. "It doesn't do any good to keep thinking like that. I prefer to think that whoever took her is taking good care of her, and she is doing fine. Nothing else is acceptable."

"She would be five years old, Mom. I have missed her first steps, her first word, and her first five birthdays. If I ever find her, those are things I will never get back. I've lost part of her life forever." She put her head down on her knees and sobbed. Would the pain ever go away? How was she going to make a life for herself and Alexis?

"Maybe, my darling girl, it's time to move past the tragedy and look to a wonderful and exciting future for you and the daughter you have."

The phone rang and Carolyn got up to answer it. She put her hand over the receiver and smiled at Jenny. "Speaking of the devil, it's Justin."

Jenny picked up the receiver, pausing a moment to compose herself before she answered. Her mother was right. She needed to move on. Justin was a wonderful man and she loved him.

When she finally said, "Hello", she knew the next time he asked her to marry him the answer would be yes.

Later that night, she lay awake in her bedroom going over the conversation she had with Justin. He wanted her to come out to the ranch for dinner on Saturday with

Alexis. She knew he would propose again. She hoped she was doing the right thing for both her and Alexis. As she stared out into the night, she thought she smelled a familiar perfume. She sat up in bed, her heart racing and looked toward the door leading to the hall. A shadowy figure moved just beyond her field of vision.

"Sirena, is that you? "

She jumped out of bed and stood there shivering, afraid, but excited. "Sirena, if you're here, please, tell me if I will ever see Ava again. Is she all right? Please, talk to me! I have done everything I know how to do to keep Evan from looking for your necklace. I had nothing to do with any of that. Please, if you know anything about Ava, tell me." Desperately she looked around for a glimpse of the ghost.

The faint sound of laughter came from the hallway and the smell of perfume faded. Jenny dashed to the window and looked out at the dark water of the lake. There was no moon. The night was black and overcast, but far out beyond the pilings a bright light glowed and then faded. Jenny knew that for whatever reason, Sirena had been here.

Chapter Thirty-Nine

Eagle's View Ranch

Justin awoke in high spirits. The morning sun flooded through the wall of glass that took up one entire side of his large bedroom. It was going to be a beautiful day. Today he was going to ask Jenny to marry him. This time he was sure she would say yes. He yawned and stretched, then leapt out of bed. Today was special. He had waited five years for Jenny. The time for waiting was over. He loved her and he loved her daughter. He knew it wouldn't be easy. Jenny would always carry the burden of losing a child, but they would have children of their own, and in time her pain would ease.

Glancing at the bedside clock, he saw it was almost eight. Jenny would be coming at ten. He had plenty of time, but he wanted everything to be perfect. After he showered and shaved, he put on a new pair of jeans and the deep blue shirt he knew Jenny liked. It complimented his blonde hair and blue eyes. Looking in the mirror, he grinned. "Not too ugly, if I do say so myself," he said out loud. They would have beautiful children. He wanted a lot of them. He would teach them to ride, sort cattle and run the ranch. He paused in thought. What if they were all girls? He frowned. He wouldn't go there. Not a chance. But even if that happened, he would teach the girls. His thoughts were interrupted by a knock on the door.

"Justin? Are you up?" his mother called.

"Yeah, Mom, I'll be out in a minute."

"What time are Jenny and Alexis coming? Do you want me to tell Maria to fix breakfast, or lunch?"

Justin opened the door and gave Laura a peck on the cheek. "Lunch would be perfect, Mom. They should be here around ten. I have a favor to ask."

Laura waited a question mark on her face.

"Would you watch Alexis for us for a couple of hours? I want to take Jenny for a little picnic. Maybe Maria could fix a lunch basket for us. I'm going to ask Jenny to marry me again today, Mom, and I want it to be special."

Laura's eyes filled with tears. "Darling, that's wonderful. It's taken such a long time. Your father and I have been hoping for you and Jenny to get married. We love Jenny and you know how much we adore little Alexis. She is such a beautiful and sweet child. Of course I will look after her. You take as long as you want. She's no trouble at all. I will have one of the ranch hands saddle Patches for her and she can ride around the corral. She loves the horses so much. That will keep her busy, and then we can make cookies. Don't worry about a thing. Go on your picnic and bring me back a new daughter-in-law." She hugged Justin tightly, and brushing the tears from her cheeks, she smiled. "You look very handsome. How could any girl resist?"

"I hope *one* can't. Keep your fingers crossed. I feel like it's my lucky day."

When Jenny's little red jeep pulled up in front of the imposing house, Justin was already out on the front steps waiting for her. He waved and ran down to open the door on the passenger's side. A small bundle of energy leapt into his arms, and he grabbed Alexis before she could tumble to the ground.

"Hey, be careful, bunny!" he laughed, giving the golden haired little girl a big hug. Then, as he was setting her down his heart caught in his throat. Jenny was standing in front of him smiling, her red gold hair catching the sunlight like a halo. She was wearing jeans and a yellow tee shirt with rhinestones across the front in a cross design. She literally sparkled.

"Well, don't just stand there. Give me a hug, too!" Jenny laughed.

Justin took her in his arms and kissed her soft, sweet mouth. He could feel her melt into him. "Humm, better stop before I ravish you right in front of your daughter – and probably my parents too, whom I am sure, are watching out of the window!"

Jenny giggled, but did not move from his arms. "They'll have to get used to me kissing you. It's not like we haven't been doing this for a long time!" She stroked his cheek and looked into his eyes. "I love you so much. Do you think they know that?"

Justin was at a loss for words. Jenny didn't often tell him she loved him, especially in the cold light of day. It had only been in the heat of passion that those words had been whispered. Now more than ever, he was sure she meant them. Grabbing her hand he motioned toward the house.

"Come on, Mom and Dad are waiting for us. I have a little surprise for you both."

"Really? In that case, let's hurry. I love surprises."

When the threesome entered the vast hallway, Justin grabbed Jenny's hand. "Come this way."

He led them down the long cool hall into the den, where Jordan and Laura were having a late morning cup of coffee. Both rose as they entered the room, and Alexis flew into Jordan's arms.

"Slow down there, little filly!" Jordan pretended to stagger backward, but a forty-pound little girl was no threat to his still muscular, six foot two inch frame. "Guess what? We get to entertain you all afternoon while your mommy and Justin go on a picnic!"

"You're going on a picnic? I want to go, too!" she pouted, stomping her feet. "That's not fair!"

"Honey, don't be rude. I'm sure Justin won't mind if you come." Jenny's face flushed with embarrassment. Alexis didn't usually make a scene.

"Actually, I had other plans for her, Jen. I think when Alexis finds out what Mom and Dad have in mind, she won't mind staying here." He pulled a strand of Alexis's red gold hair, so like her mother's, he thought. Alexis looked at Laura doubtfully.

"I had one of the ranch hands saddle up Patches for you, baby. We thought you would like to ride for awhile and then you and I could make chocolate chip cookies." Laura bent down and smiled. "Patches told me he has really missed you, and can't wait for you to get down to the barn."

"Well," Alexis said thoughtfully," If Patches needs

me; I guess I have to stay here. Can I give him a cookie, if we make some?"

"You bet you can, darling. Come along. We'll get started right now. By the time you have ridden and made cookies, your mommy will be back. We are going to have a lot more fun than going on a dumb old picnic."

Alexis grabbed Laura's hand and waved to her mother. "Okay, Auntie Laura, let's go. We shouldn't keep Patches waiting."

Laura winked at Jenny. "You two have fun; you deserve to have a little time alone. We'll see you for dinner."

Jenny breathed a sigh of relief. They were so good with Alexis. She couldn't have picked better grandparents. But, she told herself, she was getting a little ahead of herself. Maybe Justin wouldn't ask her to marry him today. Or, she smiled to herself, maybe he would!

Chapter Forty

Afternoon sun shone down on the couple as they lay side by side on the red and white stripped Indian blanket. Towering pine trees sheltered them from the brightest rays, but didn't keep the warmth from reaching their bare flesh.

Safe from prying eyes, they were relaxed and satiated. They had made love after a hasty attempt to eat had been foiled by their impatience. Sex had been wonderfully fulfilling for both of them since the first time they had slept together, and the years had only brought them closer.

Justin's hand lay gently on Jenny's exposed breast, his fingers idly stroking her. He could feel himself growing aroused, once again. This beautiful woman fed his desire like no one ever had before. Looking over, he saw her eyes were closed and a smile played around her lips.

"I know what you're up to, you lecherous man," she whispered.

"You do? Just what is that?" he whispered back,

drawing her closer as his hand moved down her soft belly.

"Whatever it is, don't stop." Her voice was low and husky. "This place is like an enchanted forest. Enchant me again!" Rolling over, she pressed her body against him and began kissing his ear, running her tongue inside.

"Hey, watch out! That tickles. You're asking for it, girl."

Pulling her over on top of him, he nuzzled her neck and pushed her legs apart, sliding into her gently. "Don't move. Let's just lay here like this for a while. You feel so good." He ran his finger over her lips, and raising his head kissed her roughly, his tongue probing her mouth. She returned his kiss and the heat rose in his belly. He lifted his head and looked into her half closed eyes. "I love you, Jenny."

"I love you too, Justin," she breathed.

He began moving slowly inside her. He felt her body respond, and her hips began to move in rhythm with his. He held his breath. He wanted to climax with her. Her breasts brushed his chest and he caught one in his mouth, gently sucking on it until he heard her moan and felt her orgasm begin. He tossed her over on her back and mounting her, held her hands over her head. Moving faster in rhythm with each other, they flew up over the cloudless sky and melted back down into the blissfulness that followed. Justin fell back and breathed into her neck, biting gently. "How can we still have this incredible sex after five years? Every time seems like the first."

"I know, sweetheart, I hope it's always like this for us. I wish this day could last forever." Jenny slid out from under him. "However, I need to breathe." Her laughing blue eyes looked into his, and he knew the time was right.

"Jenny, I want this to last forever too, my darling. I want you to marry me. Will you, Jen? Marry me?"

"Yes, of course I will. Who else could make me feel like the most desirable woman in this whole world, and love my daughter as much as he loves me? Besides, I need to be able to justify all this wild and wicked sex. You need to make me an honest woman."

Justin felt the world spin and caught her up in his arms once more. "You *are* the most desirable woman in my world, Jen. And I do love your daughter, but there will never be anyone in the world I love as much as I love you."

Chapter Forty-One

Justin and Jenny were married in a close family ceremony at Eagle's View Ranch. Justin's sister Julie, her husband, and their two children and Jenny's parents were also there to witness their happiness. Julie was Jenny's maid of honor and Evan, Justin's best man. The ranch hands had all turned out in their best Levis and starched shirts, their boots shining with new polish, wanting their boss to know how happy they were for him.

The ranch house had been turned into a flower garden with massive bouquets of yellow and white roses, lilies, and baby's' breath adorning every possible nook and cranny.

Alexis was the center of attention as she walked slowly down the hallway into the enormous living room in her pink taffeta dress, with a pink and white crown of tiny roses on her red curls, scattering rose petals as she went. Behind her came Jenny in a cloud of white lace and tulle, accompanied by her misty-eyed father. The minister stood in front of the fireplace. He looked out over the small group of guests that were seated in the comfortable living room chairs.

"Is there anyone here who objects to the joining of this man and woman?" he intoned solemnly, as he stared into the faces of the family. "If so let them speak now or forever hold their peace." After waiting a minute or two, he smiled. "Well, then, I now pronounce you husband and wife. You may kiss the bride, Justin."

Justin took Jenny in his arms and lifted her off her feet. He whispered in her ear. "Hey, Mrs. King, welcome to the family!"

Jenny felt tears sting her eyes. Their families were now tied together in this ancient ceremony of love and trust. The only one missing, thought Jenny, was Alexis. She should have been here. She was still part of their family, no matter where she was, or who she was with. A cloud passed over the sun and the room darkened for a brief moment. Jenny felt a chill. Was it an omen? No, she wouldn't let herself think like that, not on this, the happiest day of her life. She saw Justin looking at her and smiled, "Thank you, Mr. King. I am very happy to be here."

The couple turned and faced the room full of people who loved them so much. With all the good thoughts coming their way, how could anything spoil this day?

After the wedding, Evan drove back up the mountain to Clear Water Cove, his stomach churning. He didn't realize he would be so upset seeing Jenny get married. He had always looked at their relationship as a close friendship, and nothing more. Now, too late, he knew it had been something more. He had been too busy with his law practice and casual relationships to stop and analyze his feeling for her. He felt like an idiot. Why hadn't he made more of an effort to make her fall in love with him, instead of standing back, watching her being snatched up by Justin? Well, not exactly snatched up. It had been five years! He was just a slow mover, and because of that, he had lost someone who had always been very important to him. They had been close since childhood, now that would never be the same. He sighed. The newlyweds were on their way to their honeymoon in the Bahamas, and he was headed back to San Francisco and his law practice. He had to take his mind away from the images that persisted, images of Jenny and Justin making love. "It stinks!" he yelled out loud.

He had one more week of vacation at the cove. Maybe he would make one more attempt to dive for that damn necklace. It would take his mind off the honeymoon he didn't want to think about. Yes, that was a great idea. Tomorrow, he would get his diving gear together, get back out on his boat and look some more. It had been some time since he had made any further attempt to find the diamonds, mainly because Jenny had asked him not to. The ghost, she so believed in, hadn't made any further appearances as far as he knew, and it was probably all a bunch of hooey anyway. Now that she was married, Justin could take care of all her nightmares. He didn't feel obligated anymore. Yes, that would be the perfect distraction.

As the sleek Corvette gained speed, he straightened up in his seat and put a CD in the player. An old Blood, Sweat and Tears song blasted from the stereo. "Spinning wheel turning round." The wheel was turning, but maybe this time it would turn in his direction.

Chapter Forty-Two

Nassau, The Bahamas

Tonight was their last night on the island and Jenny had never felt happier or more fulfilled. They had gone scuba diving, snorkeled along the reefs and stuffed themselves full of great food, then danced the nights away. It was the honeymoon of Jenny's dreams. Lying in the luxurious king sized bed, she glanced over at Justin. He was sleeping soundly after another wonderful session of lovemaking. The moon was bright through the sliding glass doors and she could hear the gentle lapping of the ocean waves as they broke against the shoreline. Unable to sleep, she got up and tiptoed to the open door, and out onto the balcony. She stood looking out over the moonlit ocean. The tide was in and the water high up on the beach. Warm, tropical air brushed her hair from her face, and she breathed in deeply. It had been a fantastic two weeks, but she missed Alexis terribly and was anxious to get back home. She put her elbows on the railing and cradled her head in her hands. Suddenly the air smelled sweeter, and she straightened up. The smell was familiar. Her skin crawled. It couldn't be! Not this far from the cove! Not here! Not on her honeymoon! A light touch on her shoulder made her whirl around. There in the shadows by the door, stood the figure she was least prepared to see.

"What do you want?" Jenny whispered. Her voice quivering as she took in the all too familiar woman, in the century old dress.

"You must tell him to stop looking for my necklace. If you do not, you will never see your daughter again." The voice was faint, but it sent cold chills down her back.

"Which daughter do you mean? Ava? Alexis? Who? Tell me!"

The woman just smiled. "You will know if you are not successful in keeping my necklace safe." Then, just as quickly as she had appeared, the figure vanished. Jenny cried out and fell to her knees sobbing.

"Jenny, darling, what is it?" The sobs, coming from the balcony had awakened Justin, and he rushed to her side. Taking her in his arms, he held her tightly.

"It was her, Justin! It was Sirena! She was here. She warned me again about Evan and the diamond necklace. I don't know what to do? If he is trying to find it again, how can I stop him? She said if I don't, my daughter is in danger, but she didn't say which one! I am so scared."

"Come back to bed, darling. Tomorrow, we'll be home and you can see if Evan is still looking for that damn thing. Don't let it spoil our honeymoon."

"I know you probably don't believe me, but she was here. If she means Alexis, will I lose both my babies?"

Crying harder, tears pouring down her face, Jenny let

Justin lead her back inside. He sat her down on the bed and took her hand.

"I do believe you, Jen. You're my wife. I know what you saw was real, but how much she can affect us, is only how much you let her. We'll talk to Evan just as soon as we get home. If he is looking for the necklace, I will take care of it. Trust me. I won't let any harm come to Alexis."

As Justin held his new bride in his arms, he wondered if this ghost had any powers and if so, just how much of his promise he could keep.

Chapter Forty-Three

Eagle's View Ranch

Before the cab could come to a complete stop, Jenny had the door open and was flying up the long flight of stone steps to the King's front door. She had called the morning of Sirena's visit and Laura had told her Alexis was doing just fine and enjoying their company, but she had to make sure. Something, anything, could have happened during the time it took for them to travel back to the ranch.

Out of breath, she opened the door, not bothering to knock, and ran down the hall calling out for her daughter. Justin paid the cabby and ran into the house after her. Jordan almost ran into her as he rounded the corner of the circular hallway.

"Whoa! Jenny! You're home!" Then, seeing the terrified look on her face, he grabbed her by the shoulders. "What's the matter? Is everything all right? Where's Justin?" He dropped his hands and Jenny pulled away, heading for the kitchen to find Alexis. Jordan saw Justin coming down the hallway. "What's going on, Son?"

"Its okay, Dad. Jenny just had a nightmare about Alexis. She has been a nervous wreck ever since last night. As soon as she sees that Alexis is fine, she will be, too."

"I'm sorry to hear she's been worried. Your new little daughter has been having a great time. She's having a peanut butter and jelly sandwich with Laura in the kitchen. Come on, we'll go join them and you can tell us all about your trip." Patting Justin on the back, the two men headed for the kitchen.

Jenny was well ahead of them. She burst into the kitchen. Seeing Alexis sitting calmly at the table eating her PB&J, she collapsed on a chair beside her.

"Mommy, Mommy! You're home! I missed you sooo much!" Alexis climbed off her chair and fell into her mother's arms. Jenny kissed her cheeks and stroked her hair. "And I missed you too, darling. I am so glad to see you." Tears of relief pricked her eyes, and she brushed them aside quickly. "Thank you so much for taking care of her, Laura. I hope she was a good girl."

Laura looked at Jenny anxiously. Something was off. It wasn't like Jenny to be so emotional, but then she had been away for two weeks. "She was an angel. We had a wonderful time. Let me get everyone a snack. Jordan and I can't wait to hear all about the trip."

After recounting the honeymoon for Jordan and Laura, the newlyweds packed up Alexis's small suitcase and got ready for the drive back up to the cove.

"Thanks again, Laura. We'll see you soon." Jenny kissed her mother-in- law on the cheek and hugged Jordan, as the new grandparents stood at the door and waved goodbye.

"Hurry back." Laura called. "As soon as you have a

visit with your parents, we need you all back here. Jordan has a whole passel of jobs waiting for him. He's ready to hand the ranch back."

Jordan nodded solemnly. "Yep. This old cowboy is plumb worn out."

Both Justin and Jenny laughed. Jordan, the millionaire college graduate had definitely let the ranch take over his life.

Chapter Forty-Four

Clear Water Cove

On the drive up to the lake Alexis was full of questions. Her little mouth never stopped until they turned into the gates of Clear Water Cove. Jenny was glad for the distraction. The first thing she was going to do when they got to the house, was to see if Evan was home and make sure he was keeping his promise to her not to do any further exploring in the lake.

Over dinner, they recounted all the details of their trip one more time for Carolyn and Tom, then Jenny put Alexis to bed. She kissed the sleepy little girl and tiptoed out of her room, making sure she left the door slightly open, just in case. If there were even a tiny disturbance, she would hear it.

Her parents were sitting beside the wide, stone fireplace, talking and laughing quietly as Justin regaled them with even more stories from their trip.

"Come; sit down with us awhile, Jen. I know you're

tired, but indulge us for a few minutes longer." Her mother held out a hand to Jenny.

"In a minute, Mother, I want to call the Burney's and see if Evan is here this weekend. I have some things I need to discuss with him."

"Oh well, hurry up, honey. I haven't seen him, but that doesn't mean he's not up here." Carolyn looked over at Justin. "What could possibly be so important that she can't wait until tomorrow?"

Justin paused before he spoke. How much should he say about Jenny's obsession with this ghost, Sirena? She had told him her parents were the ones who were originally involved in trying to recover the necklace. She had also told him they, or at least Carolyn, had seen Sirena. He drummed his fingers on his lap.

"It's about Sirena, Carolyn." He saw her give Tom a startled look and then waited for him to continue.

"Jenny thinks Sirena was somehow responsible for Ava's kidnapping, how I have no idea. Now, she believes she is threatening to harm Alexis, if Jenny doesn't keep Evan away from his determination to find her necklace. She told me the ghost lady has visited her several times, and she is half scared to death. She believes if she doesn't stop Evan from trying to find the diamonds, Alexis is in danger."

"Oh dear!" Carolyn gasped. "My poor baby. Tom, can that ghost really do anything to Alexis? Could she have had something to do with Ava's kidnapping?"

Tom got up and put his arms around Carolyn. "No, no, and positively NO! If she is haunting Jenny, it's just a hollow threat. Ghosts can't harm anyone, if they even exist. All they can do is frighten us. I'll have a talk with Jen. She has to make this ghost see she is not afraid of her threats. Maybe that will end this. In the meantime, let her try to talk Evan out of his crazy quest. It's dangerous to say the least. If she can convince him to stop, then the ghost has done everyone a favor." He hugged his wife again and sat back down. "Let's wait and see how this plays out, if and when Jenny gets a chance to talk to Evan."

In the kitchen, Jenny was listening to the phone ring at Evan's house. It was a short walk to the big house that had been a gift to Evan from his parents. If he didn't answer, she would grab a coat and walk over. Just as she was about to hang up, she heard Evan's familiar deep voice come on the line.

"Evan? It's Jenny. I need to see you right away. Can I come over?"

"Not a good time, Jen. What are you doing here? I thought you were on your honeymoon with the rich cowboy." His words were slightly slurred, and Jenny could tell he had been drinking.

"We just got back this morning, but I really need to see you."

"Have to wait until tomorrow, baby. I have company tonight. Okay?"

Jenny's heart sank. She was hoping to get a promise from him tonight. The sooner she could make him listen to her, the safer she would feel for Alexis and Ava.

"I, I guess so. What time could you meet me?"

"Meet me at the club for lunch and bring your new hubby along. You can both make me jealous telling me how much fun the Bahamas were."

"See you tomorrow then. I'll be there at noon. Don't forget, please. It really is important."

"I won't forget, love. Now I have to get back to my, ah, friend. See you mañana."

"Bye, Evan." Jenny sighed and hung up the phone.

She wouldn't sleep very well tonight, but hopefully by tomorrow this would all be settled.

After spending a few more minutes with her parents, the newlyweds asked to finish their tale the following morning at breakfast and went to their bedroom. Snuggling close, Justin put his arms around Jenny. "I know you're too tired to make love darling, but don't worry, we have a lifetime ahead of us. Just relax and go to sleep. Tomorrow, you can deal with your ghost."

Jenny would have answered, but exhausted, she had already fallen into a deep sleep. Despite her best intentions, if Alexis cried out during the night, it would probably be Justin who heard her.

The golfers were occupying every seat in the clubhouse when Jenny arrived, but Evan was already seated at a table near the window. Seeing her come in, he waved and stood up. Jenny hurried over. He pulled a chair out and sat back down opposite her.

"You look beautiful as usual, my love," he said, admiring her closely fitting white slacks and pink flowered shirt, which revealed a modest view of her bosom. Her cheeks were flushed from the walk over to the club, making her skin glow, but despite that, her blue eyes looked anxious.

"Hi, Evan," she said, reaching over to take his hand. "I have to bring up an old subject that I know you would rather not talk about, but I have to. After I tell you about Sirena's last visit, you'll understand."

"Oh no, not that old girl again? What's she up to now?"

"Don't make fun of me, Evan. This is serious. I know she had something to do with Ava's disappearance. Now, she is threatening even more harm if you don't stop trying to find her diamond necklace. Please, Evan. Tell me you won't keep up this stupid and dangerous search!"

Evan looked into those amazing big blue eyes and his heart turned over. How had he let this beautiful woman get away? They had been friends since childhood, why hadn't they ever become lovers? It was too late now to be lovers, but not too late to remain friends. Even before today, he had decided to give up his childish dream of finding the piece of jewelry that had already taken his father's life. He was glad he hadn't told Jenny though, since he wouldn't be here with her now if he had. Maybe it was just lunch, but he would take advantage of every minute he could spend with her.

"So, what did the devil woman have to say this time?" He smiled into her eyes and held her hand tighter.

"If you let go of my hand, I'll tell you." Jenny glared at him. He was acting like this was a big joke, and it was making her angry.

"Sorry, Jenny, it's been a long time since I've seen you. I still care a lot about you."

Jenny's eyes softened. "Remember, I just got back from my honeymoon."

"Yeah, I'm well aware of that. So, let's get down to the bottom line. What did she threaten to do if I kept looking for her prized possession?"

"She warned me that more bad things would happen. I would simply die if anything happened to Alexis, so please promise me you will give this up."

"I already have, my dear. I promise you the necklace and its secrets will die with us." He picked up her left hand gently and touched the big diamond engagement ring, turning it around the glittering diamond wedding band.

"You did okay, Jenny. Are you happy?"

Jenny took a deep breath. "Thank you, Evan. You don't know how important this is to me, - and yes, I am very happy. Now, I'm also relieved beyond measure and I hope to never see that ghastly woman again. Maybe she will go away for good." Withdrawing her hand once more Jenny settled back, finally able to relax. Picking up a menu, she smiled, "I'm hungry, how about you?"

"After last night, I'm starving!" he grinned at her boyishly, and she blushed.

"I'm sorry if I interrupted anything, but I had to see you."

"Not a problem. Things went quite well after that. Thinking about you made it a lot better."

"You are so full of baloney, Evan, but I still love you and always will. We will always be best friends."

The waiter came to take their order, and during the rest of their lunch, Jenny told Evan all about her honeymoon trip.

Justin found Jenny on the couch that afternoon, playing Monopoly with Alexis. The sky had darkened and thunder rolled in the distance.

"How did your lunch go with Evan?" he asked lightly, trying not to show how jealous he had felt this afternoon, knowing Jenny was with her long time friend.

"I'm glad to say, it was successful," she beamed at him. "Evan promised me he would stop his *'research'*." She used the word research with a knowing glance at Alexis, who was studying the Monopoly board, pretending not to listen.

"Well, that's wonderful. So, does that mean we can go

back to Eagle's View? Mom and Dad are anxious to leave on their new adventure, but they can't until I'm back to look after the ranch. They have postponed it long enough for us" He looked out the window at the wind whipped waves that were growing in size and capping with white foam, signaling the approaching storm. "Looking at this weather it might make sense to stay here tonight, at least until this storm blows over."

Jenny stood up and put her arms around him. "I love you so much; you know that, don't you? I want to do what is best for both of us, but most of all I want to make you happy, as happy as you have made me. If going right back to the ranch will make you happy, we'll go tomorrow. I've done what I came here to do. I think I can go back now and sleep peacefully. At least as peacefully as you'll let me!" she kissed him playfully on his nose.

"Hey, you two, stop that! Mommy, get back here and finish our game. I'm winning!"

Jenny and Justin laughed at their precocious young daughter, and they settled down on the couch while Jenny let her daughter win the game.

Chapter Forty-Five

The next morning, Justin came into the kitchen, a big smile on his face. He leaned over the chair where Jenny was eating breakfast with Alexis. "Guess what, my darling?"

"Oh, I don't have to guess. From the sound of your voice, you can't wait to tell me," she teased and gave him a kiss.

"Hum, well you're right about that. Mom and Dad might buy the house next door! When they get back from Europe they want to look at it."

Jenny almost dropped the fork she had been eating with.

"You're kidding! How did they know it was for sale? We didn't even know that!"

"Sweetie, it's been months since we have been at the cove, the whole place could have gone up for sale and we wouldn't know about it."

Jenny laughed, "You're right about that."

Justin pulled out a chair and sat down, giving his daughter a kiss on the top of her blonde curls. "I think

Dad is ready to kick back and enjoy life. He has put his heart and soul into the ranch, but I think he may be ready to retire. And I can't think of a more beautiful spot than Lake Tahoe."

"They were lucky to find out about the house," Jenny said. "I don't remember a lakefront home coming up for sale, ever!"

"You can thank your mother. The Adams told her they were leaving for Seattle to live closer to their grandchildren and she got right on her cell phone to Dad and told him."

Jenny looked closely at her husband. "What do you think about taking on all the responsibility of Eagle's View?"

Justin pinched her cheek. "I'll love it. I won't have to ask Dad for permission to do anything I want to update the place, but he will be close enough for advice if I need it."

"Well, I hope you know what you are getting into. Without your dad around, the responsibility will be all yours."

Jenny got up and took her dishes to the sink, then glanced over her shoulder at Alexis. "What do you think, baby? Will you miss your Grammy and Grandpa?"

Alexis was thoughtful for a minute, then smiled. "Not if it means I will get to spend more time at the cove. And, Mommy, I will be able to see all my grammies and grandpas at the same time!"

"Smart girl," Jenny laughed, "I should have thought of that, myself."

Chapter Forty-Six

Eleven years later
Yerington, Nevada

From a distance, the big black and white gelding and his slender rider looked as if they were molded together as they raced across the desert and up the side of a hill, coming to a stop at the crest of a ridge. Closer observation would have revealed a stunningly beautiful girl, with flowing, black curls that hung to her waist and whipped around her face in the desert wind. Her long lashed, dark eyes surveyed the valley beyond. She rode the horse with only a rope halter and lead rope, wearing cutoff jeans and a short white tank top. Her long legs were bare, tanned to a deep brown from the sun. On her feet were light sandals. No saddle came between her and the sleek sides of her horse. As they rested on the top of the hill the gelding pawed the ground with his hooves, anxious to be off again.

"Hey, Comanche, calm down. We'll go in a minute." Jessica murmured, stroking the nervous horse.

Hopping down off his back, she led him to the edge of the ridge. She tossed her head back, breathing in the soft, sage scented spring air. It was too early for the summer heat to make a morning ride unbearable, but soon the temperatures would rise to 90 and above during the day, limiting her rides to early mornings and after sunset. Comanche lowered his head and began to graze on the short grass produced from winter snow and rain. Before long, it would dry up and be worthless, but for now the paint horse, and all the other desert inhabitants, would grow fat and sleek on its short life.

A movement in the distance caught Jess's attention. Comanche lifted his head. His ears pricked forward and he whinnied loudly.

"Forget it, bud. You're mine now. There's no going back to the herd." She spoke quietly and rubbed his shoulder as they watched a band of wild horses drifting across the valley floor, grazing as they went. A blood bay stallion trotted a short distance behind the band, snaking his head along the ground, driving them forward, guarding the small group of mares and long legged foals. She felt a lump in her throat. Summer would bring less and less food for them. The herds were in danger of starvation. There were too many horses for the available feed. It was a long-standing problem that no one seemed able to solve. The wild horse advocates wanted them left alone, but the ranchers and Bureau of Land Management, the BLM, wanted them thinned out any way they could. Helicopter roundups were harsh and frightening for the horses, causing many deaths among the older mustangs, pregnant mares and young foals. Even so, it was the easiest way to round up and pen the horses, so it was the method used by the government.

Jess sighed. She loved this land beyond reason. It was part of her soul, and had been her home for as long as she could remember. But things change, and one day the wild horses would no longer run free here or anywhere else. Comanche himself was a mustang that she had rescued from the BLM pens as a yearling. He had been wild as a cougar when she brought him home, but her gentle ways and long years of experience with the ranch horses, had won him over. No one else had ever ridden him, or ever would, if she had her way.

She stayed on the hilltop watching until the mustangs disappeared into the distance, covered up by a cloud of dust, then grabbing onto Comanche's long mane, she swung herself up onto his back. She tightened her legs around him, and he bolted forward down the hill toward home. As they ran across the desert, the smell of sage and the feel of the warm wind filled her heart with such happiness, she felt they could fly. Racing toward the ranch, she hoped this would be her home forever. She had lived here all sixteen years of her life and if it was up to her, she would never, ever leave.

As they neared the ranch house, she saw her mother and stepfather waving to her from the porch. When Jessica was six, Alicia had finally married Steve Foster. Alicia's mother and father had died five years before in a car accident so now Steve and Alicia ran the ranch. All in all, it had worked out well. Steve was a strong, ruggedly handsome man, and he adored Alicia. He wanted to formally adopt Jessica and never knew why Alicia denied him that. But Alicia didn't dare risk letting it be known that she didn't have a birth certificate to prove Jess was her daughter. Going to court to let a judge see the gap in her parental rights was not an option.

Jessica slid off the big gelding with ease and led him up to the front porch.

"Hey Mom, Steve, what's going on?"

Steve took the lead rope from her. "Get a shower and put some traveling clothes on. We're going on a short trip. I'm sure you'll want to come along." He smiled at the quizzical look on Jessie's face. "Don't worry, you'll love it. We're going to a ranch out of your dreams."

Jessie laughed. "Oh, right. I'm sure. Who would invite us to a big fancy ranch?" Her dark eyes sparkled with humor.

"Just wait," Steve said. "You won't want to miss this one."

"Okay, okay, if you say so. I'll be ready as soon as I put Comanche away and get showered and dressed."

Don't worry about your horse; I'll take him to the barn. You just get yourself all prettied up. Don't be long."

Steve smiled as he watched Jessie run into the house, excited now. *She didn't have to do much to get "prettied up",* he thought to himself. Jessica was a beautiful girl. Although she didn't act as if she knew how lovely she was, she would soon realize it when the local boys began to start nosing around. He grimaced; he wasn't looking forward to that. At sixteen, boys could only think of one thing, and he wasn't about to allow that to happen. He swung up onto the gelding and trotted off to the barn to put him away. As he slid off and put the tired horse into his cool, shaded stall, he realized too late, he had horse hair and sweat on his jeans. He would have to change again, but he would still be ready long before Jess.

Half an hour later as Steve and Alicia sat on the old porch swing waiting for their daughter to appear, the door burst open and Jessica came flying out. She had on a clean pair of jeans and a bright, red checked, Wrangler shirt. Her long, black hair was shinning, and curled charmingly around her tanned, oval face. She never wore makeup, but with her dark brown eyes, framed with thick, black lashes, and her full, naturally pink mouth, she didn't need any enhancement.

"Do I look alright?" she asked dutifully. "Think I'll be allowed on this big, fancy ranch?"

"Darling, you would look perfect in a rag, but fortunately, you haven't gone quite that far. Anyone would be privileged to have you as their guest."Alicia smiled as she looked at her adopted daughter, ruefully noting that she looked nothing like her. She was such a gift, one she hoped she would have forever. She and Steve had been unable to conceive a child of their own, which made Jessica that much more special. Thinking about how she had taken Jessie from the hotel so many years ago, always made her shiver with apprehension. In the back of her mind, hidden deep inside, was the constant fear that one day someone would come forward to claim her. A fear she refused to see the light of day, but it still remained. Every time someone was puzzled by the lack of family resemblance, and asked who Jessie took after, her stomach twisted as she tried to make up excuses.

Putting her worry aside, she grabbed Steve's hand and pulled him to his feet. "If we're going to get to that ranch by noon, we had better get going."

Together, the three piled into their old beat up Ford F250 pickup truck. With a wheeze and a groan, the truck started up and they took off for Eagle's View Ranch. A visit none of them would ever forget.

Chapter Forty Seven

Eagle's View Ranch

"Cut out those two over there, Roger!"

Seated on his big, black stallion, Justin's voice rang out, as the two cowboys helping him spun their horses around. Twirling their ropes over their heads, they raced after two young bull calves. Justin was going to try and sell them to a couple that was coming to Eagle's View today. They were looking for some new blood for their herd of crossbred cattle. His purebred Angus would be a great addition to their stock, but they were expensive cattle. He didn't know if the arriving rancher had the money to purchase the husky, young bulls. Even so, he had to get them down to the barn corrals where they could be properly looked over.

"Hey, Dad, do you need some help?"

Justin turned in his saddle and waved at the approaching rider. "Sure, honey, come on. We can use all the help we can get." He watched as Alexis tore after the other two riders, her horse cutting in and out of the herd of young, male Angus like a whirlwind. Her long, reddish blonde hair flying out behind her, she managed to co-ordinate so well with the cowboys that the two, rowdy young bulls were soon cut out of the bunch and were being driven up the canyon toward the barn. If it hadn't been for her long hair and obvious developing figure, she could have just been another wrangler.

He loped his horse slowly up the hill after them, enjoying the beauty of the early summer morning. The sun was barely above the horizon and the dew was still damp on the thick grass and pine branches. As he passed under the trees, small droplets fell on his cowboy hat and he could smell the pungent odor of the tall Ponderosa pines that lined the hillside. Blue lupine dotted the hillsides, and blankets of wildflowers decorated the valley. He breathed deeply, taking it all in. It was his favorite time of day and place to be. He was in no hurry to get back to the ranch house. Jenny was probably still asleep, he mused. After last night, she deserved to sleep in. He smiled to himself; their love life was still amazing.

His stomach grumbled, and he realized he was hungry. He urged the big stallion to a faster gait, and in minutes, he caught up with the other three riders and helped them move the young calves towards home.

Jenny yawned and stretched. Rolling over, she reached for Justin's familiar body. Not feeling him next to her, she realized he had probably gotten up early to round up the bulls for some prospective buyers. She glanced at the alarm clock. It was only six a.m. Dawn was just beginning to light the sky. The automatic window coverings were still closed. Justin must have left them closed, so she could sleep late. She could still smell the scent of their lovemaking from last night, and wiggled her toes with pleasure, remembering. How could she have been so lucky? She never stopped thinking about how she might have let him go, because of losing Ava. She had been in a dark, scary place, but he had reached down with determination and loving arms, pulling her back into a life more wonderful than she deserved.

She was about to throw back the covers, when a rustle in the corner of the room caught her attention. Fear gripped her as she became aware of the, all too familiar scent that immediately brought back the ghost of Sirena. Heart racing, she sat up, pulling the blanket around her to cover her nakedness. Peering into the darkness of the shuttered room, she saw the figure of the dance hall girl standing with one hand on her hip. Her dark hair almost covered her face, but Jenny could see her black eyes staring at her with amusement.

"Hello, Jenny. It's been awhile. Don't be alarmed. You have kept your part of our bargain. No one has gone looking for my necklace in years, and besides, I have moved it to a much safer place. I am tired of guarding such a precious object. I am ready to move on now." She drifted closer to the bed and Jenny could see the glowing light surrounding her.

"What do you want this time, Sirena? If you are going to do anything else to my family, tell me now." Jenny's voice trembled, and icy fingers of fear ran over her body.

"I had nothing to do with what happened to Ava. It was the evil of men, not ghosts that caused you to lose your baby. Actually, my dear, we are quite harmless. I was only trying to scare you into making that man, Evan, keep from falling into the death trap that took his father.

209

So much greed and trouble followed my lovely diamonds. Ah, well, it's over now. I won't trouble you any longer, but although physically we ghosts are harmless, we can see much more of the future from this side, things that are hidden from your eyes. I have become rather fond of you, Jenny, and I have something to tell you."

Jenny sat forward. Cold sweat beaded on her forehead. This wasn't happening, she must still be asleep. Once again, she pinched her thigh under the blanket, and gave a start. That hurt, she must be awake. Anxious to get rid of the apparition, she spoke to Sirena in a shaky voice.

"Tell me what you have to say then go away. I think it's time you went into the light. I can see it surrounding you. Give yourself some peace and give us some as well."

"Exactly what I intend to do, but first listen closely. There will be events happen today that you should watch closely. A stranger will look familiar to you. Do not be fooled by what is said. Lies will be told; all will not be what it seems. Follow your heart. If you pay close attention, your long search will be over. This is the last time I'll visit you. You won't be seeing me again. Goodbye, Jenny."

As she said the last line, Sirena's shadowy figure became fainter and the light became brighter. In less than five seconds the light faded and she was gone.

"Wait, wait! I don't understand! What are you saying? Please come back and explain!" Jenny jumped out of bed. Ignoring her nakedness, she ran to the corner where she had last seen the ghost, but it was too late. There was no sign of her.

"Oh please God, help me understand. I need to know if this is about Ava. Are the people coming to the ranch today somehow connected to my daughter, and if so, how?"

She pressed the button that drew back the wall to

ceiling window coverings, and bright morning light flooded the room. She blinked. She had to find Justin. Had to tell him about the strange message Sirena had given her. Without washing her face or combing her hair, she threw on some jeans and a wool shirt and headed for the barn. She hoped the men would be back with the young bulls by now.

As she flew down the long curving hall of the big house, she called out for Alexis, but got no answer. *That girl*! She thought as she ran, she must have gone with the men.

With her mass of curling, red blonde hair and black lashed, wide, blue eyes, Alexis was a stunning young woman. Her creamy complexion never seemed to suffer from her long hours in the sun. Her long legs and already developed curves turned the heads of every male in town. Despite all that, Jenny knew she would rather be out cutting cattle than sitting at a dressing table primping in front of a mirror, or calling up the young boys, who were always calling her.

"Guess I should count my blessings," Jenny muttered out loud. "All that will come soon enough." Gripping the heavy brass, door handle, she pulled the front door open and ran down the steps to the barn.

Just as she arrived at the barn, she heard a whistle, and looked out to see the crew bringing in the bulls. They herded them into a corral, and she saw Alexis drop from her horse to close the gate behind them.

"Good job!" Justin called to his daughter. He saw Jenny standing by the barn and kicked his horse forward.

"Thank goodness you're home," she said. "Come up to the house. I have to talk to you. You won't believe what just happened."

Justin looked at Jenny's pale face, even paler without

makeup. He noticed her disheveled hair and wild-eyed look.

"What happened? You look like you just saw a ghost." He smiled, "I'll be up as soon as I put Diablo away. Hope breakfast is ready, I'm starving."

"Please, hurry. It's really scaring me. You're exactly right. I *did* just see a ghost, and it won't take too much imagination to guess who."

Justin took off his hat and scratched his thick, blonde hair. "You mean you had another visit from our old friend, Sirena?"

"That's exactly what I mean, Justin. What she told me might be important. It might have something to do with Ava!"

Justin frowned, he wasn't sure he believed any of the ghost stuff, but he certainly believed Jenny had seen something. It had been a long time since he had seen her upset like this.

"I'll be up in a minute, sweetheart. Calm down, we'll figure it out."

Jenny breathed a sigh of relief. She knew she could count on Justin to make sense of Sirena's weird warning.

Chapter Forty-Eight

"So you think your ghost lady is telling you that the people coming to look at the bulls have something to do with Ava? Isn't that pretty far out, love?"

"I don't know. All I know is, she said that today there would be something I needed to pay close attention to, and that it would bring me closer to finding something I have been missing for a long time - or something like that. I was too scared to remember exactly what she said."

"Darling, I know you believe in this ghost, but how on earth could the visitors from a ranch outside of Yerington who run cattle for a living, have anything to do with Ava?"

"I told you, Justin! I don't know!" Jenny replied, annoyed that Justin still didn't believe in her sightings of Sirena. "If you can't take this seriously then I will have to try to figure it out for myself." She sat rigidly on the high backed, wooden chair in the bright kitchen, upset and confused.

"If it's any consolation, I'll check them out on the internet before they get here. That way, we'll see exactly who they are and what they've been doing all their lives." He patted her shoulder. "Now, will you just breathe normally? Let me worry about this."

Jenny gave him a slight smile and nodded. "I'm going to go take a shower and get dressed. I want to be on my toes when these people arrive in case there is anything I need to, as Sirena said, pay close attention to."

Jenny got up and put her arms around Justin, kissing him gently on his mouth. "I love you, you know. You have been the best, all through my awful ordeal of losing Ava. I could never have survived it without you. I keep hoping and praying somewhere, sometime, I will see her again. Maybe that's why Sirena's words are so important to me. If there is even a chance I will find something out about where she is, from anyone, I want to be aware of it. I have to keep hoping, it's the only way I can live with it."

"I know, honey, and if I hear or see anything that might give us a clue, I will be the first to tell you. Now, go get slicked up, you never know, this rancher guy might be a handsome, charming fellow!"

"Oh pooh, not a chance he could hold a candle to you." She eyed him up and down. "Nope, there's not a chance."

Then hugging his lean hard body once more, knowing how lucky she was, Jenny left him standing there amused and went to take a shower.

As she left the kitchen, the back door burst open and a mop of bright, red gold hair appeared. "Hey, Dad. When are our visitors arriving?" The youngsters are waiting in the corral. I tossed them some grass hay to keep them busy while they wait. Don't want them to get into any mischief. They are snorting and pawing. They aren't used to being penned up."

Justin smiled at his lovely young daughter. At sixteen,

she was the image of her mother. The same thick, curly, red-gold hair, long lashed blue eyes and long elegant legs. He wished he and Jenny had children, but so far that had not happened. Sometimes, he thought it might be because of her loss. Ava was never far from Jenny's mind. He had legally adopted Alexis shortly after he and Jenny were married and as soon as she was old enough to understand, they had told her about Ava's abduction, and a little about her real father. Justin knew that as far as Alexis was concerned, he was her father. She had never expressed any interest in finding the man who had deserted her mother before she was born.

"I was just about to get on the Internet and look up our visitors. Your mom wants to know a little more about them."

"Why?" Alexis asked, curious as to her mother's interest in people she didn't even know. They had many buyers come to the ranch to look at their horses and cattle. Her mother seldom got involved in the process.

"Oh, I don't know. Maybe their name sounded familiar to her, or something. Anyway, want to come with me?"\

"Sure, Dad, it might help us sell the bulls. Never hurts to know who you are dealing with."

Putting his arm around her slender shoulders, Justin walked her down the hall to his office.

Sliding behind the heavy mahogany desk, he sank into his leather chair and flipped open his laptop. Alexis plopped into a comfy, overstuffed sofa opposite him and munched on a cookie she had swiped from the kitchen, her cowboy boots dangled carefully off the cushions.

In minutes he found what he was looking for. He reached in the top drawer and took out a legal pad and pencil.

"Well, Alexis, here's the scoop. Their name, which by the way I already knew," he winked at her and she giggled, "is Foster. They run the C Bar II1 ranch in Yerington.

Wife's name is Alicia, and they have a daughter…" he paused struck by a sudden chill.

"What, Dad?" Alexis sat up. "What's wrong, you look shocked? What about the daughter?"

"Nothing, honey," Justin took a deep breath and continued. "They have a daughter named Jessica. She's your age, honey."

"Wow, neat. Maybe they'll bring her with them. I could show her Firefox and the new foals while you guys are bargaining over the bulls."

Justin had a strange feeling about the new information. He was thinking about what Jenny had told him. Could there be a connection to this girl? She would definitely get his close attention.

"Sounds like a great idea. Come on, let's go back to the kitchen and rustle up some breakfast. I only had a cinnamon roll and coffee, before we went out this morning, and I know you didn't eat anything."

"Sure, Dad, I'm not hungry, but I'll sit and watch you stuff you face. You never gain an ounce, whereas me, I have to watch every bite." She made a face as they exited the den.

Justin watched her from the back as they walked. Her tall slender body, and slightly curving hips showed no sign whatever of being overweight. He sighed; teenagers always thought they were too fat. He would have to talk to Jenny about it. He sure didn't want her getting too thin. Now that summer was here and school was out, she rode every day. Sometimes just for fun, but mostly helping the cowboys with fence mending and sorting cattle. She was as much help on the ranch as they were. One of these days, Alexis would stop being such a tomboy, and realize how beautiful and interesting she was to the opposite sex. Things would change, but he wasn't ready yet.

Chapter Forty-Nine

The old Ford truck came to a grinding halt outside the imposing gates of Eagle's View ranch. Jessica's eyes widened as she took in the tall stone pillars that flanked the entrance. A black post light sat atop each pillar and two black metal eagles graced the ornate iron gates with outspread wings.

"Wow!" she breathed. "These people must be really rich. Wonder what the rest of the place looks like?"

"As soon as I figure out how to open the gates, we'll find out." Steve said, as he got out of the truck to look for someway to enter. Spotting a small square box on a post by one of the pillars he walked over and looked at it, a puzzled look on his face.

"I think this is some kind of intercom," he called back to the two waiting in the truck, "but I don't know how to use it!"

"Let me see, Steve." Jessie flew out of the truck; impatient to find out what lay ahead. "Here, push this little button. Someone should hear you and let us in."

Sure enough, when Steve pushed the button a voice

came over the speaker asking them to identify themselves. As soon as whoever was on the other end heard his name, the big iron gates began to move slowly inward.

"Aren't you the smart little cookie?" Steve said hugging Jessie. They got back into the truck and Steve drove through the gate which closed behind them.

"Hope we don't have to leave in a hurry." Jessica said. "It's a little like being trapped in paradise."

Steve patted her on the knee. "Not quite like our ranch, but then again, I prefer the desert," he replied, as they drove down the mountain. The road was lined with tall Ponderosa pines and softly rustling Aspen trees. As they neared the bottom of the hill the trees thinned and ahead they could see a beautiful green valley where a herd of black cattle grazed peacefully. As the truck rounded the curve at the bottom of the hill, all three sucked in their breath simultaneously.

"Oh my gosh!" Alicia was the first to speak. "Look at that house! I've never seen anything like it. It looks like a giant glass bird's nest sitting on the top of the hill."

"Guess that's why they call it Eagle's View," Jessie giggled nervously.

As they got closer, a state of the art twelve-stall barn came into view.

"I'll take that!" Jessie said, still awed by the grandeur of the ranch. "I don't think I could live in such a huge house, but the barn...I'd live in that any day of the week."

The truck came to a halt in front of the barn where they were met by a smiling Justin and a curious Alexis.

"Good morning," Justin called, and walked over to the truck. He leaned into the open window and shook Steve's hand. "Glad you're here. The boys have the young bulls out by the side of the barn. Come and take a look."

As the three visitors got out of the truck, Alexis stared

at the dark haired young girl, whose long legs matched her own. Realizing she was staring, she came forward and smiled. "Hey, I'm Alexis, and you are?"

"I'm Jessica, nice to meet you." Jessie was also sizing up the cowgirl with the reddish blonde curls and the wide blue eyes, so different from her own dark brown ones.

The adults were moving towards the bullpen, Justin talking up his prize herd. Jessie started in their direction.

"Wait, if you aren't too interested in cattle, would you like to come to the barn with me and see my guys?" Alexis offered.

"Your *guys*?" Jessie frowned.

"That's what I call my horses, they're like my family. I have my own favorite. Do you ride?"

"You might say that," Jessie smiled, "Ever since I was old enough to sit on a horse."

"Me too!" Alexis laughed. "Come on. Since you know about horses, you'll appreciate mine."

Alexis took Jessie's hand and led her down to the wide-open barn doors. Strangely, as she gripped Jessica's soft hand it felt familiar, not like the hand of a stranger.

"My dad always says I would rather be in the barn than in the house," Alexis said, as they entered the airy open aisle, where interested sleek heads peered out at them from the twelve stalls.

"Your barn is amazing," Jessie said with a trace of envy in her voice. She walked over to one of the stalls and rubbed the nose of a big, black stallion. "He's a beauty. Do you ride him?"

"No, he's my dad's horse. My girl is over here."

Walking to a stall half way down the aisle, Alexis stopped and reached her hand in the open half of the

Dutch door. "Come here, Fancy, come meet my new friend."

A bright bay mare nickered softly at the familiar voice and trotted up to the door. Her large brown eyes fastened on Alexis and she nuzzled her hand.

"She's lovely. Is she an Arabian?" Jessie reached over to smooth the mare's thick, black mane that flowed almost to her shoulder.

"Yep, she's a straight Russian Arabian. I'm going to get an awesome foal from her one of these days, but in the meantime, she's my riding horse."

"Well, she's just beautiful. I have a black and white gelding that I raised from a baby. I got him from a wild horse gathering north of Elko. He's not elegant like your girl, but he's my best friend, and a great ride. He never tires and never needs shoes. Mustangs are tough as nails."

"That's what I hear. I haven't had much contact with them, but I'll bet they are great," Alexis replied.

The two girls stood there admiring the mare, not noticing that Jenny had come into the barn looking for them.

"Hey you two, would you like anything to eat or drink? The men will be tied up for awhile."

As both girls turned towards Jenny, she caught her breath. They looked so much alike! Even with the difference in coloring, they could have been sisters.

Jenny took a deep breath. Lots of teenage girls were tall and slender, some even as beautiful as these two. No coincidence there. But as she came closer, the resemblance became even stronger.

"Mom, this is Jessica. I was showing her Fancy. Like me, she's been riding since before she could walk. Wish we had more time, I'd take her for a ride around the ranch."

"Hello, Jessica." Jenny steeled herself. She couldn't help staring at the girl, seeing a face so familiar. Her heart pounded. Oh, God! It was like looking at a female version of Diego! The words of Sirena echoed in her mind. No. It wasn't possible. She was letting her imagination run away with her. This girl couldn't be her long lost daughter, could she? Trying hard to get a grip on herself, Jenny walked over to Fancy and stroked her soft nose. She thought quickly then taking a deep breath, she turned to Alexis.

"I don't see why Jessica couldn't stay for a day or two. You have so few friends that love horses the way you do. It would be fun. You could show Jessie the ranch on horseback. I'm sure we have something she would enjoy riding."

Alexis looked at Jessie. "What do you think? It would be fun. We have lots of room. We could drive you back home. I'd like to see your horse and where you ride."

"I don't know," Jessie said, a frown creasing her forehead. "Mom and Dad have never let me stay away from home overnight."

Alexis looked at her amazed. "Never? Wow, that's *so* like my parents, huh, Mom? Let's go ask them anyway. Maybe they will let you just this once."

Jenny followed the girls out of the barn and down to the corral where Justin, Steve and Alicia were watching the calves as they paced the perimeter of the pen. Somehow she had to convince Alicia to let Jessie stay. She needed to know more about her.

Chapter Fifty

"Hello!" Jenny called out to the group at the corral. She smiled brightly as she came up to the pretty dark haired woman standing with the two men. "You must be Alicia, so nice to meet you." Jenny searched the woman's face, trying to see a resemblance between her and Jessie. Despite the dark hair, the short, stocky woman's features and body were nothing like her daughter's. She turned to look at the husband, Steve. Again nothing matched. The blonde haired, blue-eyed man looked nothing like his daughter. Still, she reminded herself, those things happen.

"Nice to meet you, too, Mrs. King." Alicia said politely. "You have a beautiful place here. And your husband has bred some amazing cattle. Steve and I think we might buy both the young bull calves. We need some new blood in our herd, don't we, darling?"

The man smiled fondly at his wife. "You know, Mrs. King, she knows as much about the business as I do, but neither of us are as knowledgeable as our daughter." He put his arm around Jessie and hugged her. "She's been running our place since she was born."

"Oh? And when was that?" Jenny couldn't help the question. Alicia's answer surprised and shocked Jenny. Her breath stopped.

"Jessie's sixteen. Steve and I weren't married when I had her, but he thinks of her as his own."

Jenny let out her breath. That must explain it. She probably looks like her real father. Relief flooded her, then a sense of despair. She had thought for a minute…, but that was just wishful thinking. She still had to go through with the offer to let her stay, after all she had asked.

"Alexis is sixteen, too! The girls seem to get along so well. I was wondering if you would consider letting her stay over for a few days so they could ride around the ranch. Alexis doesn't have many friends that enjoy riding. It would be a real treat for her, and for us.

Alicia looked up at Steve, a worried frown on her face. "What do you think, honey. It would be her first time away from home, but it's so beautiful here, and the King's are such nice people."

"That's fine with me, sweetie. You're the one who never wants her to go anywhere. Then there's the problem of getting her home."

"Oh, that won't be a problem," Alexis piped up. "Dad and I can drive her back home."

"In that case, I don't see why not," Steve said. "It would be a chance for her to see how someone else runs a ranch. Probably pick up some good ideas."

Still Alicia hesitated. She looked at the two girls standing together, waiting for an answer and felt a sense of foreboding. But that was silly. They seemed so alike, they would get along fine. It was a great opportunity for Jessie to get to know people like the Kings.

Pushing aside her persistent feeling of unease, she forced a smile.

"I suppose if her first trip away from home is to stay in a place like Eagle's View, then it's a yes from me, too.

"Yeay!" Alexis shouted, giving the startled Jessie a hug. "Come on, Jess. Let's go find a horse for you!"

The girls ran back to the barn and the four adults turned their attention to the young bulls, and to the negotiations necessary to purchase the pair.

Chapter Fifty-One

That night they celebrated the sale of the two, very expensive young bulls at dinner. The new Mexican maid, Crescencia, had gone all out. After an appetizer of fully loaded nachos, they were served a huge prime rib roast from the King's herd of cattle, homemade albondigas soup, tortillas with refried beans, corn on the cob, a sweet potato casserole, and for dessert they dove into a sumptuous apple pie topped with vanilla ice cream.

Steve leaned back in his chair groaning; he couldn't eat one more bite. He put his arm around Alicia, who was seated next to him at the long cherry wood table. He was watching the two girls, who were laughing and talking animatedly across from him. They acted as if they had known each other all their lives. They even resembled each other, he thought. He felt a tug on his arm.

"Steve, we'd better get going. It's a long trip home," Alicia said quietly. She too, had been watching the girls and the same nervous feeling came creeping back. "Are you sure you are okay with Jess staying here for a few days?"

Alexis heard the conversation and piped up quickly.

"Oh, please! I really want her to stay. We'll take very good care of her and we'll bring her home as soon as she gets tired of us."

Alicia smiled faintly, "I suppose I'm being silly, it's just that it's her first time away and we'll miss her." She turned to Jessica. "What will you do for clothes? You didn't bring anything extra to wear?"

"Jessica and I are almost the same size," Alexis piped up again. "I have tons of jeans and shirts she can borrow. I even have an extra pair of boots if she needs them. What size do you wear, Jess?"

"I might borrow a shirt, but my jeans usually stand up to at least a couple days wear. As for the boots, I won't need any, but thanks anyway." She stuck out one foot from under the table, showing Alexis a well-worn and scratched, Justin boot. "These are my old faithful when I ride with a saddle. Usually though, I ride barefoot and bareback."

Seeing the look on Alicia's face, she laughed. "Oh, Mom, don't worry; I'll ride with a saddle. Look around! This place is amazing. I can't wait for Alexis to show me everything on the ranch. I'll be fine! It's only for a few days."

"Your mother and I have agreed you can stay," Steve said, squeezing Alicia's arm under the table. "We want to thank you for asking her, Jenny. I know she'll be in good hands." He pushed his chair back and stood up. "We really must get going. I wish I had a trailer to take the bulls, but I appreciate your offer to bring them with you when you bring Jessica home."

Justin got up from the table and shook Steve's hand. "My pleasure, I have a stock trailer that will do nicely. The ranch hands can help me load them. It will make it easier all around. Are you sure I can't talk you into coffee before you go?"

"Thanks, but no. You have been more than hospitable as it is. We didn't expect to be invited for dinner. Your cook did a great job. If I don't leave now, I'll fall asleep half way home!"

"Don't want that, my friend." Justin said.

Everyone left the dinner table, stopping by the kitchen to compliment Crescencia on her cooking skills. When they reached the front door Alicia stopped and took Jessica in her arms, hugging her tightly, then kissed her on both cheeks.

"I love you so much, never forget that, darling."

"I love you, too, Mom. Drive carefully, Dad. See you in a few days."

Justin opened the front door, and he and Jenny walked the couple to their truck. The two girls had already taken off for the guest rooms to see which one Jessica would like. Alexis was going to make sure it was the one closest to hers.

After more handshaking and hugs between Jenny and Alicia, the Foster's got into their truck and started up the long private road to the main highway.

Alicia turned her head to watch the King's return to their magnificent house. It all looked so perfect. Still, she had a premonition that she couldn't shake a feeling that leaving Jess was a bad idea.

She sighed, and moved closer to Steve. Jessie was as much her daughter as if she had given birth to her. No one must ever know the secret of how Jessica had come into her life. When they decided to make this trip she had not anticipated leaving Jessie behind with strangers she barely knew.

Little did she know the impact her decision would make on all their lives.

Chapter Fifty-Two

"When's your birthday, Jess?" Alexis asked, as the two girls sat on Alexis' bed. Although Jessica had settled on the room next to Alexis', they had ended up spending the evening in Alexis' large room, where the décor was most definitely horse oriented. Pictures of various ranch-bred horses hung on the walls, and a silver embellished western show saddle sat on a stand in one corner. The gold and tan bed cover was printed with various breeds of horses. It was a far cry from the usual girly room one might expect from such a lovely and feminine young lady.

"March fourteenth. When's yours?" Jessica asked.

"Wow, that's amazing! Mine's March eighth!" We're almost the same age! Were you born in Nevada?" Alexis asked, unaware that Jessica's birth date was one Alicia had guessed at.

"Mom says I was born at Lake Tahoe. That was before she married Steve. He's my stepfather, but he's the only father I've ever known, so it's like he's my real dad."

"Oh, gosh. Do you ever see your real dad?" Alexis' eyes widened.

"No, he left when I was just a baby, so my mother brought me back home to the ranch. I have no idea where he is, and you know what?" she looked up defiantly, her brown eyes fixed on Alexis. "I don't care. He obviously didn't want me. I don't ever want to hear from him, ever!"

Alexis' face reddened. "I'm so sorry, Jess. I didn't mean to get personal. It just seems like you and I have so much in common, you know, the horses, being raised on a ranch, and if you can believe it, just like you, Justin isn't my real dad! He and my mom were married when I was a little girl. I don't remember my real dad, either. That is so weird. Maybe that's why I feel like you and I are so alike. Well, I don't care who your real dad is, or mine either, the only thing I want to know is…" she leapt up off the bed and danced over to the long closet, "What do you want to wear tomorrow when we explore the ranch?"

Jessica relaxed and slid off the bed. "Let me see." She sucked in her breath as Alexis flung back the sliding door, revealing dozens of Wrangler, Cruel Girl and Dusty Rose shirts. "Wow! I've never seen so many beautiful shirts." She began to pick through them, settling on a blue and white striped, long sleeved Wrangler shirt that had blue pearl snaps. "Could I borrow this one?"

"Absolutely, anyone you want." Alexis was happy to see Jess had forgotten the obviously painful conversation. "Try it on. If you want, pick out a pair of jeans, too," she said, as she slid open still another part of the closet, revealing a rack of carefully stacked Levis.

"I can wear mine another day, but thanks, it looks like you have enough here for years!"

Alexis smiled. "Yeah, my mom and dad sort of spoil me. I'm the only kid here, so they get carried away."

Jessica took her shirt off and tried on the crisp blue and white Wrangler.

"Now that's what I call a perfect fit. Looks great with your dark hair," Alexis commented.

Jessica looked in the mirror that hung above the triple dresser and examined her reflection. "It's the nicest shirt I've ever worn," she said quietly.

"Tell you what, Jess. You keep it. I have so many I'll never miss it,"

"Oh, no, I couldn't. It's too nice. It would just get ruined on our place." She took it back off and folded it gently; laying it on a brown velvet chair.

"Whatever," Alexis said, disappointedly. "But, you will wear it tomorrow, won't you?"

"Of course, thanks." Jessica sat back down on the bed. "So, Alexis, how come your mom and dad never had any more kids?"

Alexis sat down beside her, and her shoulders sagged. "I did have a sister once, but she was kidnapped when we were babies. We never found her. I think it's been too hard for Mom, thinking about losing Ava. That was her name."

"How awful! I'm so sorry. My mom can't have anymore kids, so I guess we were meant to be spoiled brats!" She patted Alexis' knee and grinned. "It's really not so bad, is it?"

Alexis ducked her head and smiled shyly. "No, I suppose not, but it would have been fun to have someone to talk to, like I can talk to you."

"Yeah, I know what you mean. Do you think your mom would let you come and stay at our place for awhile? It's only fair, you know." She hugged the fair-haired girl, so opposite in coloring from herself, yet so strangely familiar.

Alexis smiled a true smile this time, "That sounds great. We'd better turn in, or we'll sleep too late tomorrow. I like to ride out early with the ranch hands. I hope that's okay with you. It's fun to follow them around for a while, and then we can take off on our own. That way, you can see how we do things here."

"Sounds like a plan to me," Jessica said. She got up and walked to the door. As she reached for the doorknob, she turned back to Alexis. "My room is amazing. Can't believe I have my own bathroom and everything. Thanks so much, Alexis."

"Whoops, forgot your shirt." Alexis ran to the chair and grabbed the shirt from where Jessica had laid it. "Don't forget to set your alarm. Six o'clock sharp. Breakfast will be waiting for us."

Jessica took the shirt, and not knowing what else to say she waved goodnight and walked out of the room. She walked down the hallway a few yards and entered a bedroom like those she had only seen in magazines. She twirled around and jumped on the big four-poster bed. "Wow, unbelievable!" she chirped. She tossed her long hair back and fell onto the thick, blue comforter. She glanced out of the floor to ceiling windows that were a feature of every room in the house. The valley below was lit by a full moon, revealing the grassy pastures and surrounding, pine-covered hills. She gave a sigh of pure pleasure. She couldn't wait to explore this paradise tomorrow. She loved her desert, but her new friend, and this new and exciting place were going to be very interesting.

Chapter Fifty-Three

At exactly six o'clock the next morning, the two girls appeared in the big warm kitchen, where Crescencia was frying bacon and stirring up a big batch of sour dough pancakes.

Dressed in Levis and long sleeved shirts, the girls could have passed for sisters, Crescencia noted. Except for the difference in coloring, their features and body shapes were amazingly similar.

"Come, sit and eat," she beaconed to them. "The men have already been and gone, but you have plenty of time before they ride out. They are loading bulls." She laughed. She loved having the new young lady here. She knew how lonely it was for Alexis.

Although she never admitted it to anyone, Crescencia could tell Alexis needed someone her age, not just the ranch hands and her parents. On rare occasions she brought a friend to stay overnight, but Crescencia had never seen her bond so well with a friend before, or so quickly. She filled their plates with stacks of thin sourdough pancakes and slices of crisp bacon, beaming as she watched them wolf down their breakfast. Both girls had hearty appetites. That was good, she thought. It meant they were healthy, and she didn't have to worry about anyone falling off their horse, faint from hunger. Her job was to feed this family, and although she was new here, she intended to do just that, as well as she knew how.

Watching the girls eating and talking so animatedly, Crescencia puzzled over the resemblance. Somehow, these two must be related. But that couldn't be. Mr. King had a twin sister, but she and her children lived in San Francisco. This girl and her family came from a ranch in Nevada!

Oh well, she thought, none of her business. Maybe Mr. King had fooled around as a young man? Her face flushed. What a terrible thought! *Muy Malo*! She scolded herself. Some people just look alike. She heard tell everyone had a double somewhere in the world. Maybe this was Alexis' look alike. She jumped, as she heard her name called.

"Hey, Crescencia, how about more pancakes. These are delicious."

Both girls were holding up their empty plates. With no more time for puzzling over her new guest, she grabbed the bowl with the pancake batter and began pouring more sourdough on the griddle.

When they had finished with their breakfast, the girls thanked Cresencia and left for the barn.

Jenny stood at the tall bedroom windows that overlooked the entire valley, including the barns and paddocks, where the mares and foals played in the bright morning sun. She watched the two girls run down the steps that led to the barn, and her breath caught in her throat. The shape of their bodies, the slender shoulders, long legs and narrow waists were so alike. She remembered Sirena's words. She was undoubtedly being foolish, but she had an urgent need to know more about this girl.

Justin was in the den going over paperwork from the sale of his bulls when Jenny entered the room. He looked up and smiled.

"That went well, don't you think? We got twenty thousand for our two young fellows and a friend for Alexis, at least for a couple of days."

Jenny sat down by the desk. "I know you'll think I'm going crazy, but I have to find out more about Jessica."

The troubled look on her face made Justin put aside his paperwork.

"What do you mean, sweetie? What is there to find out?"

"I want to see her birth certificate."

Justin looked confused. "Her what? That's crazy, baby! We have no right to do anything like that - even if we could."

"Just humor me, Justin. There must be a way to get a copy of it to find out who her real father is. I can't ask Alicia. Please, don't you know someone at the court house that would do you a favor?"

Seeing how upset Jenny was, Justin sighed and shook his head. "I can try but I don't know... Judge Hargrove owes me a favor or two; maybe he could get a clerk at the records department to research it for me. If it's that important to you, I'll try."

Seeing the relief flood Jenny's face, Justin stood up and come over to her. He put his arms around her and held her tightly.

"I know how hard it's been all these years, darling. Every time you see a girl Ava's age with dark hair and dark eyes, I see how you react, but you can't keep doing this. One day you might have to realize it's quite possible we may never find out what happened to her. Maybe that's for the best."

"NO, I'll never stop trying to find her! Never! Unless someone shows me proof that she's dead!"

Giving a strangled cry, Jenny pulled away from Justin and started out of the room. Justin ran after her and grabbed her arm, turning her to face him.

"Listen. I told you I'll try to find out everything I can about this girl, but just because your ghost lady has put ideas in your head, there's no reason to think she is anything other than Steve and Alicia's daughter."

"I just have this feeling. I can't shake it, Justin." Jenny shrugged off his arm and raised her chin defiantly. "I have to see that birth certificate. Please, do it as soon as you can, before she goes home."

After Jenny left the den, Justin stood quietly for a minute thinking about the possibilities. What if this girl was Ava? What then? Were they going to open a can of worms they would all regret? He shrugged, he had promised Jenny he would try, and so he would. Going back to his desk, he picked up the phone and dialed Ben Hargrove.

Chapter Fifty-Four

Two hours later, Justin received a call back from the county clerk. The news was not good. There was no birth certificate on record for Jessica. There was a marriage license on file for Alicia and Steve Foster, but researching her maiden name had not brought up any record of a baby born to Alicia Cunningham sixteen years ago, either in Douglas County, which was the Lake Tahoe region, or Lyon County which included Yerington. The clerk had even tried Washoe County, which was the Reno area. Justin thanked the clerk for the information and hung up the phone. It was possible she had been born elsewhere. He didn't want to tell Jenny the news. It would only exacerbate the problem.

He was mulling over his options, when a thought struck him. What about a DNA test? That would prove positively whether or not Jessica was Jenny's daughter, wouldn't it? Should be fairly easy with her here at the ranch. He rubbed his chin. He wasn't sure how legal it was without parental consent, but he was willing to do whatever it took to put Jenny's mind at rest,. He would wait for the results to tell her. It would probably take longer than the Fosters were willing to have Jessica stay, but still, in the end they would know for sure. In the meantime he would tell Jenny he was still working on it.

Comfortable with his decision, Justin sat back down at his desk and continued to review his profitable sale.

Unable to sit still, Jenny walked down to the barn to wait for the girls to return from their ride. She got a bucket of horse treats and went down the breezeway, pausing at each occupied stall to give out a handful to each horse, patting their soft noses and whispering in their listening ears.

It was comforting being in the big warm barn, with the smell of clean shavings and horses. She decided to take her favorite mare out of her stall and groom her while she waited. It relaxed her.

Just as she reached for the halter and lead rope, a clattering of hooves made her wheel around. Two puffing horses, their riders shrieking with laughter, flew into the barn and skidded to a stop a few yards from her.

"Mom, Jessica is such a good rider! She beat me home! We raced clear from the meadow. Course, since she was my guest, I kind of let her." Alexis winked at Jenny and jumped off her sweating horse.

Jessica sat on her horse, trying to quiet it from their run. "Doesn't matter who won," she giggled, "we had so much fun!" She patted her horse's neck, and then slid down off his back. "I'd call it pretty even. Alexis is as good a rider as any I've been around, and that's saying a lot!" The girls hugged, and then led their horses off to the wash rack to unsaddle them and rinse off their damp backs.

Jenny watched them go. She fought off the urge to take Jessica in her arms and hug her tightly. The bond she felt kept growing. Whatever these feelings were, something strange was going on. She remembered how close the twins were when they were babies. She remembered how Alexis had cried for days when Ava was taken. She was so lonely without her sister. It had taken months for her to return to the happy little person she had always been. As she watched the two girls laughing and working closely with the horses, she felt certain there was a connection, and was almost certain she knew what is was.

Dinner that night was a festive affair. The girls were in high spirits. They were already making plans for the next day's ride to explore the hillsides surrounding the ranch. Jenny's blue eyes followed Jessica's every move, trying to see in this young girl a resemblance to her or Diego. The more she watched, the more she was sure there was one. Was it her imagination, or were those Diego's same long lashed, dark eyes? Weren't the two girl's smiles just alike and the short, perfect noses exactly the same?

Alexis had noticed the way Jenny was watching them, and was getting irritated. "Mom, what is it? You keep staring at us like you've never seen me before? Are you okay?"

Jenny felt her face redden. "I'm sorry, darling, I'm just happy to see you two getting along so well and having so much fun. It's been a long time since you had a friend over. Sorry, I didn't mean to be rude."

"Well, don't' look too closely, you'll probably see what a pair of goofs we are." Jessica laughed. "Alexis, your mom is the best. Don't give her a bad time."

Jenny made a face at Alexis, "I love you too, Jess."

As she uttered those words, her heart skipped a beat. Alexis looked at her with a curious glance. Realizing she might be giving away her feelings, she put her napkin down on her plate and pushed back from the table. "It's time to watch the news. Don't know why that is such a tradition with your father and me. There doesn't ever seem to be anything good happening in our world, but you two stay and talk all you like. Don't feel rushed. If you need anything else, just call Cresencia." And with that, she hurried off to the living room and the nightly news.

As Crescencia began clearing the table, Justin followed her into the kitchen. While she piled the dirty dishes on the sink, he took a napkin and picked up a fork. He had kept his eyes on it as it made its way from Jessica's plate to the sink. He put it into a plastic bag. Slipping the bag into his pocket, he joined Jenny in the living room. He smiled at her. He loved her so much. He hoped he was doing the right thing. Tomorrow, he would take the fork into town, along with some hair from Jenny's hairbrush. He was fortunate to know a lot of people in law enforcement. He would get the test done, no matter what the cost. If the DNA matched, it would change all their lives.

Chapter Fifty-Five

J enny stood on the wide redwood deck that encircled the entire house like arms that embraced the glass-fronted structure, protecting it from the elements. Resting her elbows on the railing, she looked out over the pastures, enjoying watching the mares and foals as they played in the afternoon sunshine.

The girls had been gone for over two hours on another ride. She wondered if they had any idea how connected they were? As she watched for the two riders to return, she saw a familiar candy apple red Corvette roar up the driveway and come to a halt at the front steps. The door swung open and Evan got out. As he glanced up at the house, she waved.

"Hey stranger, what are you doing way out here? Come in, the door's open."

Happy to see her old friend, Jenny ran back into the house and around the curving hall to the front door. Evan was already in the entryway waiting for her.

"I never get over being impressed with this beautiful

house, Jenny. Are you and Justin going to live here when Jordan and Laura get back from Europe?"

"We'll see. It gets difficult sometimes, living with your in-laws, but they are such wonderful people, it has mostly been fun. They mentioned buying a home at the lake and letting Justin run the ranch, but I'm not sure Jordan can give it up that easily."

"Where are Justin and that gorgeous daughter of yours?"

"Justin had to go into town, and Alexis is out riding with a friend. Come in the living room and sit down, Evan. I have something I want to talk to you about."

"You look serious. Has something happened?"

"I'm not sure. Wait until I tell you about your friend Sirena's latest visit and our new house guest." She hugged Evan, and then, taking his hand, led him into the living room where they settled on the soft leather couch.

"A couple came to buy some of our young bull calves the other day and they brought their daughter with them. Evan, I think she might be Ava!" A sob escaped from her lips and she wrung her hands.

"What! Jenny, are you serious? What would make you think this girl is Ava?" Seeing how agitated she was, he took her hands and rubbed them gently,

"Oh, Evan, wait until you see her! She looks so much like a teenage Ava. She and Alexis resemble each other so much, and they are exactly the same age. Then there was the visit I had recently from Sirena."

"Sirena, again! Isn't she ever going to leave you alone? Hasn't she done enough?" Now Evan was getting upset.

"This wasn't another warning, Evan. She told me I should be looking for something that would lead me to Ava. Then here comes this family, with a daughter that looks just like her."

Evan looked sternly into Jenny's eyes, lowering his ridiculously long lashes, which could still make her heart skip a beat. "Jen, I know how much you would like to think you've found your daughter, but be realistic, what are the chances she would just walk into your life? What proof do you have, other than she looks like Alexis? Do you know how many young girls look alike at this age?"

"You don't understand, Evan." She turned away. "Wait, you'll see. Have dinner with us and meet her. You can judge for yourself."

"What? You mean she's still here?" He looked at her amazed. "How did you manage that?"

"Alexis never has girls her age around. This was a perfect opportunity to get to know, "Jessica", as they call her."

"Oh for God's sake, Jen, I can't believe you would hijack their daughter just because you think she might be Ava." Evan got up and started pacing around the room. "As an attorney, I have to tell you, this isn't going to go well when they find out what you're up to."

"If she's not Ava, then nothing will be said, Evan, nothing. I feel this connection with her. It's a mother's sixth sense. I have to know."

"Okay, I'll stay for dinner and meet her, but then what? If by some remote chance she is Ava, how are you going to prove it? And then what are you going to do? Have you really thought this through? The girl is sixteen, Jenny. She has lived with this family since she was an infant. Exactly what will you tell her? Then there's the parents, are they the ones who kidnapped her? Will they face charges? How will that affect the girl?" He shook his head and stopped pacing. "You'd better think about this very hard. I don't believe for a minute you are right, but if you are, there are a lot of questions you need to answer before you confront anyone."

Jenny got up and leaned into Evan's arms. He pulled her close.

"I know, Jen. It's been hard for you, but I don't want you to do anything foolish." Seeing the tears running down her face, he kissed her cheek. "Go blow your nose. When the girls get back from their ride, I'll try to evaluate everything you've told me. During dinner we can throw some question at Jessica that might give us a few more clues."

"Thank you, Evan. Still my friend?" she sniffled.

"Always," he replied, and after she blew her nose, they both walked out to the balcony to see if they could spot the two girls.

Chapter Fifty-Six

South Shore, Lake Tahoe

Justin walked into the Douglas County Sheriff's office with the package tucked inside his briefcase. He had contributed a lot of money to Sheriff Frank Brewster's reelection campaign, hoping to have an immediate response if anyone caused trouble at the ranch, and also as compensation for the long hours his men had spent on their search for Ava.

After he and his sister, Julie, had been kidnapped from the ranch years ago, Justin was aware that there were people who might want to harm his family. He and the entire Sheriff's department had been wonderfully co-operative when Ava had been kidnapped. The case was still in their open files, and he had been assured they would keep looking as long as it took. It had been a long time. Justin felt sure she was either dead, or gone somewhere they would never find her. But he had to make sure Jenny was wrong about this young lady who did look so much like Alexis, and, he realized with surprise, like Jenny too! He shook his head. It just couldn't be. It was impossible that she would just walk into their lives after all this time.

He stopped at the front desk where a petite, dark haired girl was sitting at a computer.

"Is Sheriff Brewster in?" he asked.

"Yes. May I ask your name?" She smiled as she took in the tall, handsome cowboy in the Stetson hat. *Now, there's a catch*, she thought to herself.

"Justin King. It's personal. Please let him know I need to see him. It's important."

"Of course, sir, please have a seat. I'll be right back."

The girl recognized the name immediately. Most of the town knew about Eagle's View Ranch. It was famous for its well-bred horses and cattle. She hurried from behind her desk and disappeared down a long, white tiled hallway.

In a few minutes the girl returned, followed by a tall, lanky, stern looking man with a hawk nose, thinning black hair and receding hairline. When he saw Justin, his face broke into a wide smile that softened his harsh features.

"Hey, Justin, what's up? No trouble at the ranch, I hope?" He shook hands with Justin. "Come on back into my office. Whatever it is, I'm at your service, you know that."

"Thanks, Frank. There may be trouble, but not the kind you could imagine in your wildest dreams."

Frank patted Justin on the back. "Well, whatever it is, we'll try to fix it. Penny, get us some coffee, would you, please."

The dark haired girl batted her eyes at Justin and

pushed back her long hair. "Be there with it in five, Sheriff," she said as she hurried away.

Frank Brewster smiled, shaking his head, "Still turning the girl's heads, Justin. But I don't think you would trade that beautiful red headed wife of your for anyone."

Justin walked into the sheriff's austere office. "You got that right, Jenny could never be replaced. Actually she's the reasons I'm here. I think she is about to make a big mistake."

After Justin explained why he had come, Frank Brewster leaned back in his chair and gazed out the window. He thought about the impossible case scenario Justin had laid out for him. The implications were troublesome. All the questions Evan had asked Jenny were also going through his head. He swiveled his chair around, looking down at the plastic bag containing the dinner fork and some hair collected from Jenny's hairbrush.

"Of course, we'll get this tested as soon as possible. It might take a week or so, that's if I can expedite it. We probably have a year's worth of DNA evidence that has yet to be processed. I know how important this is to Jenny and you, but if this girl is Ava, you will have some serious issues to face."

"I know, but if there is even a tiny chance that she is, we have to know, Frank. What will happen from then on, well, we'll just have to take it a step at a time."

Justin rose to leave. "Tell Miriam and the kids hello for me."

Sheriff Brewster got up and shook Justin's hand again. "I'll do that. We'll have to come out and visit one of these days - soon."

"Great. We'll find a couple of gentle old horses for the kids to ride. They will enjoy that, I think." Justin smiled at his old friend. He knew he would be as good as his word and they would have their answer soon.

"Sounds like a great idea. You take care, Justin, and give that lovely wife a hug for me. She has been through more than I can imagine. All these years of not knowing…," his voice trailed off. "Sometimes I feel like it's my fault we didn't find Ava."

"Don't ever think that, Frank. You and your department did everything you could. We couldn't have asked for more dedication than your crew gave us."

Justin walked with the Sheriff to the front desk. Shaking hands again, he winked at the receptionist. "Thanks for the coffee, Penny."

Penny blushed and lowered her eyes. Why were all the best guys married?

"I'll talk to you shortly, Justin," the sheriff said. "In the meantime relax. I'm sure this is just Jenny's wishful thinking."

"You're probably right. Talk to you later, Frank." And with that, Justin left the office and got back into his truck for the long drive home, leaving behind him evidence that would change their lives forever.

Chapter Fifty-Seven

Eagle's View Ranch

The truck rolled up to the wrought iron gates, but Justin hesitated before pushing the gate control. Was he really prepared to face the consequences of this investigation? Would dinner tonight reveal anything that could help them? He sighed; sitting here in the truck wasn't going to solve anything. He pushed the gate opener and sped down the road toward his house where the mysterious girl in question was staying.

As he approached the front of the house, he saw Evan's Corvette parked along the drive. Wondering what he was doing here, Justin hurried into the house. He knew Jenny was over her crush on Evan, but still, he wasn't entirely trusting of Evan's intentions. No reason to leave him alone with her any longer than necessary.

The two old friends were seated at the long oak bar having a glass of wine when Justin entered the den. Evan stood up and embraced him with a bear hug.

"Justin, it's been too long. You two should come up to the cove once in awhile. After all, Jenny's parents do still live there," he said jokingly. "I manage to sneak away from the office a lot lately, but the firm seems to think I am doing a pretty good job, so they look the other way."

"You're right. We should. Trouble is, this ranch needs a lot of looking after, and with Mom and Dad in Europe, I really can't leave. So, what are you doing out our way?"

"I had a little time on my hands and wanted to come and visit my old friends. However it seems like I came at a troubling time."

Jenny swiveled around on her bar stool, taking a sip of her merlot. "You're always welcome, Evan. I think you came at the perfect time. I want you to meet this girl. See if you can pick up on the same vibes I have. The family resemblance is stunning. I mean it, Evan. Even though you never met Diego, I have to say she looks a lot like him, and she has a lot of the same features Alexis does. Also, they are getting along as if they have known each other forever. And then there's the message from our "friend" Sirena." She patted the bar stool beside her. "Come and sit, Justin. Have a glass of wine with us. I have Crescencia started on dinner. As soon as the girls get back Evan will have a chance to see for himself what I'm talking about."

Justin gestured to a bar stool. "You sit. Evan. I'll tend bar. I want to hear all about your newest case. Being a defense attorney must be interesting as hell, I couldn't do it unless I was one hundred percent sure the person I was defending was innocent."

Evan settled down beside Jenny. "Sometimes it's hard, but damn, Justin, someone has to do it. Believe me; I get well paid for compromising my moral integrity." He smiled and picked up his drink glass. "Here's to justice and our great legal system." He took a deep swallow and turned to face Jenny. "I'll make you a promise Jen. If we ever find out who took Ava, I'll switch from defensive to prosecutor in a heartbeat. The perp will never know what hit him."

Jenny forced a smile. "Thanks, Evan. I know you would help any way you could, but even if Jessica is Ava, then what? There are so many questions. How did she get to where she is now? Did that couple steal her? That's hard to believe, but if they did, then what? Do we ruin her life by telling her? If, in fact she is Ava, she has been with this couple for fifteen years. As far as she is concerned, they are her parents. She loves them!" She shook her head and took another drink of her wine. "As much as I want to know if she is my daughter, I'm afraid, really afraid, of what will happen if we find out she is."

A knock on the open den door made the three turn in unison. Alexis was standing there, windblown and glowing from her horseback ride, unaware of the conversation.

"Can I come in? Or is this a private party?" She laughed and ran to give Evan a hug. She stood back and looked at the familiar, tall, dark, good-looking man, whose sweeping eyelashes still amazed her. "You get more handsome every day, Uncle Evan." He was her favorite, non-family member and she referred to him affectionately as Uncle. "What are you doing here? It's a long way from San Francisco! But, I'm so glad to see you!" She gave him another hug. "Are you staying for dinner? Please! You can meet my new friend, Jessica. She's in her room right now taking a shower, which by the way, I probably should do, too."

Evan took in the slender, golden haired beauty, her blue eyes sparkling with fun. "Yeah, you are a little smelly. Kind of like sweaty horses, but I love you anyway." He patted her cheek. "I'm just kidding! You are beautiful as always- even if you are smelly."

"You're a brat!" Alexis grinned back at him and punched him on the arm. "You're right though, I probably do smell like horses," she winked at him, "It's one of my favorite smells!" she teased. "Believe it or not, Jessica and I both rode bareback. She's as good a rider as I am, and I'm not saying that to be conceited, it's true. Kind of amazing to find someone who likes all the same things I do. We are so much alike it's weird. Oh, well, I better get cleaned up. I saw Crescencia on the way in and she said to tell you dinner is in a half an hour." Going over to Justin and Jenny, she gave them both a hug and ran back out to take her shower.

"That's a stunning young lady, Jen. Better keep her under lock and key."

"Thanks, but life will happen eventually, whether we like it or not. Just hope her upbringing will help her make the right choices."

"I'm sure it will. Now, let me tell you about my latest case."

Justin and Jenny settled in to listen to one of Evan's tales, which were generally embellished, but very entertaining. Jenny found it hard to concentrate on the story. She was uneasy, and anxious for the dinner hour to arrive when she would have someone else to assess their visitor.

Chapter Fifty-Eight

The dinner conversation centered on the two girls and their day long horseback ride. Justin sat at the head of the table with Jenny at the foot. The girls were side by side across from a bemused Evan. Alexis sparkled with excitement as she told how much fun the two had riding through the hills, and how she had shown Jessica the secret places only she knew.

Jessica was more reserved, still overwhelmed by her surroundings. The elegantly paneled dining room contained a long dark mahogany table set with fine china and silver. It's heavily carved legs rested on a thick oriental carpet of deep blue wool. Overhead a sparkling crystal chandelier gave a warm glow to the diners. She was almost afraid to touch anything. It was a long way from the rough pine table in her kitchen at home where they ate all their meals. Her dark eyes were shining with pleasure, but she was hesitant to take the lead in the conversation.

"Tell them about your horse, Jess." Without waiting for her to answer, Alexis continued. "Mom, Dad, she raised her horse, Comanche, a wild mustang, from a baby and broke it to ride herself! Can you believe it! No one else has ever ridden him! I would love to do that!"

Jessica blushed and bent her head modestly, her long dark hair swinging over her cheeks. "It's not a big deal. Lots of people on the ranch take mustangs from the wild herds and train them. They make the best horses." Then realizing the Kings raised some very expensive horses themselves, she stuttered. "Oh, well, I mean, not to say your horses aren't wonderful. It's just that mustangs have to survive on their own without people to trim their feet, protect them from coyotes, keep them well fed and warm in shelters. They have to be tough. It makes them brave and easy keepers." She bit her lip. She hadn't meant to go on so, but she felt obligated to defend her cold-blooded, much loved gelding.

Jenny smiled gently at the girl, who obviously was not used to being around strangers, or in a formal dinner situation. She could tell Jessica was unsure of her table manners and still having a difficult time feeling at ease. "I think it's wonderful that you could do all that on your own. It must make Comanche a very special horse."

Jessica raised her eyes and looked at Jenny gratefully. "Yes he is, very special. I love him a lot. The ranch and my horse are my life. I don't think I would ever want to live anywhere else."

Jenny felt her throat tighten. Jessica's eyes shouted Diego and her fine nose and full sweet mouth matched Alexis's. If this was Ava, what were they going to do? She needed to talk to Justin after dinner. She would ask him again to try to settle this. The more she was around Jessica, the stronger the connection felt. Tomorrow Justin was planning on loading up the two young bulls and taking them to the C Bar III Ranch. Jessica would go back home. How could she let her go before she knew the truth? Yes, she must certainly talk to Justin tonight.

After dinner they all adjourned to the living room. Conversation turned to the ranch and the senior Kings' trip to Europe. Seeing the girls were getting bored, Jenny suggested they go do whatever they wanted; knowing the grownup conversation was boring them. Gratefully the two girls left for Alexis's room to listen to the latest MTV program on the 52-inch plasma TV.

As soon as she was sure they were out of earshot, Jenny interrupted the men's conversation. "Well, Evan, what do you think? Does she or doesn't she look like she could be Alexis' sister?"

"Sweetie, I don't know. Sure they could be sisters, but to me all teenage girls of the same build and similar looks could be Alexis' sisters. I never saw her father, Diego, so I can't see what you think looks so much like him. The problem to me as a lawyer is, if this girl is Ava, you will be stirring up a huge storm when you confront her parents. Are you ready for that?" Evan looked at his long time friend and his heart went out to her. Her blue eyes filled with tears. He knew how much she had suffered since the day Ava disappeared.

"I have already missed fifteen years of my daughter's life, Evan. If there is any chance this is Ava, I don't want to lose another minute. I know it will be a mess, probably a legal battle, but then, how can it be if she's my daughter? After all, she was kidnapped! Whether these people took her, or how she came to live with them, doesn't change that."

Justin had been listening to the discussion and knew it was time to tell Jenny about the test he had requested. He didn't want to give her false hope, but he wanted her to know he was on track to find out the truth. Letting her go on with not knowing would soon end.

"Jen, I wasn't going to tell you this because I didn't want to get your hopes up, but I took a fork Jessica used at dinner into Brewster's office along with a sample of your hair. He's going to test the DNA. We'll find out if Jessica's matches yours. The results won't be back before I take Jessica back home, but a few more days won't make that much difference. If this turns out to be a match, she should be with her parents when we tell her."

Jenny took a shaky breath. Although she had to know the truth, she wasn't sure she was ready for it. She put her arms around Justin and kissed him.

"Thank you, darling. You have been through so much for me. You adopted Alexis, and I know you would have adopted Ava. Maybe because of this you will have another daughter, and I will have my daughter back again."

The years of wondering what had happened to Ava, and the thousands of sleepless nights spent imagining nightmarish scenarios had left Jenny desperate for a solution, desperate for an end to the hurt and torment. Unable to help herself, she dissolved into tears.

Evan patted her shoulder. "Think I'll be going, guys. You know I'm here for you. If there is anything I can do to help, just let me know."

Jenny got control of herself and wiped her eyes. She gave him a kiss on his cheek. "Thank you, Evan. You're a good friend. I wish your visit could have been more fun. Next time you come we'll plan something you'll enjoy."

"I think it's your turn to come up to Clear Water Cove and visit. I know Tom and Carolyn miss you and their granddaughter. It's been awhile."

Justin and Jenny walked him out to his red convertible, and with their arms around each other they watched as it roared up the driveway and out of sight, then they went back into the house. Jenny was determined to spend the last bit of time with Jessica before she had to let her go. Although she was leaving tomorrow, she felt sure she would see her again soon.

Chapter Fifty-Nine

After Jessica's departure the days drug on slowly for Jenny. Waiting for the DNA testing to be completed was hard. Justin had taken Alexis with him to bring Jessica and the young bulls home to the C Bar III Ranch. They had not stayed long, but Justin had promised the Fosters he would bring Alexis back for a longer visit when he had more time. He was stalling. He wanted to have an excuse to come back no matter what the results of the DNA test were. Alexis had enjoyed Jessica's company so much; he wanted to make sure the two girls remained friends. On the same hand, if the test proved positive, he wanted to keep the relationship with the Fosters at arm's length. If this was Ava, the truth would be brutal for them.

Ten days after Justin left the package with the sheriff. Jenny was in the kitchen having a late morning cup of coffee when the phone rang. Crescencia answered then passed the phone to Jenny.

"It's for you, Mrs. King."

"Who is it, Crescencia?" Jenny asked. She felt lazy this morning and not in the mood for a useless chat.

"He did not say, misses. Do you want me to ask him?" The maid paused with the phone at arm's length.

"No, that's okay. Hand it over. I'll take it." Jenny reached for the suspended telephone. "Hello?" she said, hoping maybe it was her mom.

"Good morning, Mrs. King. This is Frank Brewster. I tried to reach Justin on his cell phone, but he must be out of range."

Jenny's heart skipped a beat and she stood up quickly. "Yes, he's out with the ranch hands this morning. They are doctoring cuts and bruises on the north pasture. There's only spotty cell phone service out there. What have you found out on the DNA test, Frank?" As she heard him clear his throat she rushed ahead. "It's okay, you can tell me. Justin told me he asked you to run the sample. I know all about it. Please, I have been counting the hours."

"Well, alright, Jenny. The test came back yesterday. I was waiting to tell Justin first, but if you already know about it I guess I can tell you. Jessica's DNA matches yours." Jenny sucked in her breath and waited for him to continue. "The chances of her being your long lost daughter are about one hundred percent positive. I think your instincts were correct. I believe Jessica is Ava."

Jenny's hand began to shake and she put both hands on the receiver. "Oh, Frank. What do I do now?" Trembling, she sat down in a chair.

"I need to talk to those people, Jenny. We have to find out how she came to live with them. They could be arrested and taken into custody for kidnapping."

"No, No. I can't let you do that. These are good people, Frank. There has to be a good explanation. Oh, God, I can't think straight. Don't do anything yet. Let me talk to Justin first. I don't want Ava, can I really call her that again, hurt anymore than she is going to be. Justin will be home by dinnertime. I'll have him call you as soon as we know the best way to handle this. And, Frank, thank you. Thank you."

Jenny hung up the phone and sat stunned, unable to move.

Crescencia ran to her side, pressing her hand on Jenny's shoulder.

"What is it, Mrs. King? Please, Dios Mio! Let me help you," she said, as her employer put her arms around the housekeeper and began to weep.

By the time Justin rode in from the north pasture, Jenny had calmed down, excitement taking the place of her tears. When she heard the front door open, she ran down the hall and threw her arms around him.

"Whoa, there, little filly!" he teased, dropping his voice to try to sound like John Wayne. "What's this all about?"

"Frank called. The DNA test came back. Justin, darling! Frank has found our Ava!" As the words spilled out of her mouth she began to cry again, this time they were tears of pure, unadulterated happiness.

Justin took her in his arms and held her tightly. "That's wonderful, darling. I don't know what to say." Pushing her away at arms length, he looked into her flooded blue eyes. "So, now that we know the truth, what are we going to do about it? Come into the den with me. We'll have a cocktail and talk about it. You look like you could use a drink right now."

The two settled down with their drinks in front of the fireplace that the maid had lit earlier. The warmth of the crackling fire and the alcohol began to relax Jenny, and she knew she was ready to make some plans.

"Frank wants to go out and talk to the Fosters, maybe arrest them for kidnapping."

"What! I hope you told him that wasn't what we want?"

"Of course I did. I think you and I should go out and talk to them first. Find out exactly how they came to have Ava. Oh God, how I love saying her name again. We have to figure out the right way to break the news to them that she belongs to us. Then we have to decide how to tell Ava."

Justin reached for her hand and held it tightly. "This isn't going to be easy for any of us, you know."

Jenny sighed. "I know, but we'll do the best we can. We have to start somewhere."

"Tomorrow I'll go to town and get the results from Frank. They will want proof of what we're telling them, even though they *must* know she isn't legally theirs. They have to know that one day someone would find out."

Jenny shivered. "We may be destroying three lives, Justin, but now that I've found Ava, I have to know the truth about what happened. I have to have my daughter back!"

Justin wrapped her fire-warmed body in his arms and smoothed her red gold curls with his hand. "That's exactly what we are going to do, my darling, and the sooner, the better."

Chapter Sixty

Yerington, Nevada

Alicia was carefully stacking the breakfast dishes in the cupboard when the front door flew open and Jessica ran in.

"Hi, Mom, where's Dad? I think Francis is about to pop out that baby."

Francis was the wild burro Alicia had rescued from the auction yard in Fallon six months previously. Although Jessica didn't know the burro was in foal when she bought her, it wasn't much of a surprise. Like the wild mares on the range, most of the female burros were bred as soon as they were able to conceive.

Alicia laughed at her disheveled daughter. "Slow down! Don't you ever walk?" She pushed Jenny's tangled curls away from her face. "That's good news. The poor little thing has been practically dragging her belly on the ground for weeks now. Your dad is up in his office. Do

261

you want me to come and take a look? It won't be the first foal I've delivered."

"Yes! Let me get Dad. We'll all go. Francis won't mind. She's in too much pain to care if we sit with her."

They had no need to worry. By the time the three got to the straw-filled stall, a shaggy wet foal was struggling to its feet, being licked dry and nuzzled by an exhausted Francis.

Alicia yelped quietly, not wanting to upset the new mom. "Oh, Mom isn't it cute! I have never seen a newborn burro. It's so tiny! I wish Alexis were here to see this. She would love it."

Alicia's stomach twisted. Ever since Jessica had been back from Eagle's View Ranch, she had done nothing but talk about Alexis. It made her very uneasy. There was something about Alexis that bothered her. The two girls were so much alike. Whenever Alicia saw a teenage girl that looked close to Jessica's age and had similar features, she got nervous. Somewhere, she knew there was a mother who had lost a child. Could it be possible that Jess had a sister? She had wanted her so badly she had never tried to find out about her mother. Some day that might come back to cause trouble. She had to get a birth certificate that looked legal. There had to be a website where she could get that done. She needed to get on it. Jessica was the only child she would ever have. She couldn't let anything, or anyone, take her away.

"Mom! Helllooo! Look! How cute is she?" Jessica had the new baby in her arms and was cradling her to help her stand. "It's a girl!"

Alicia turned her attention to the new foal. She could think about the birth certificate later when she had more time.

Chapter Sixty-One

Eagle's View Ranch

Bright morning sun flooded the deck and a warm pine scented breeze blew in through the open windows of the bedroom. Jenny yawned and stretched. She reached for Justin, but the bed was empty. He must have gone out with the ranch hands early this morning. As she threw back the covers to face the day, there was a gentle knock on the bedroom door.

"Mom, are you awake?" Alexis' sweet, high voice called from the hallway.

"If I was asleep, could I answer you?" Jenny jokingly answered. "Come in, sweetie, I'm getting up."

The door opened and Alexis peeked in. "Guess who just called? Jessica! They have a new baby burro! She invited me out for the weekend to come see it and go for a trail ride. I would love to go. Can I Mom?"

Jenny looked at her beautiful, young daughter. Seeing the peaches and cream completion, red gold curls and her own big, blue eyes, her heart filled with love. How lucky she was to have her. A sudden sense of sadness overcame her. She couldn't help but think about all the years she had missed while her other daughter had grown up in someone else's home, the years she would never recover. She smiled at Alexis, shaking away the sad thoughts.

"Maybe. Let me talk to your dad. Justin and I were thinking about going to the Foster's to see how the bulls are doing, and since I know how much you two girls enjoy each other's company, you should come with us."

"But, Mom, I want to stay a few days. Can't I?"

"Depends, baby, let me talk to Justin. Tell her you will let her know tonight."

"Well, okay, but try to talk Dad into it. By the way, did you know Jessica is home schooled? That must be interesting. Wonder why?" Alexis came over to Jenny and gave her a hug. "I'm going for a ride. It's such a beautiful morning. I'll be back in a couple of hours. Love you!"

Jenny watched her daughter race out of the room, the energy of youth so apparent. She sighed. She had a feeling she knew exactly why they home schooled Jessica. Public schools would ask for documents the Fosters couldn't produce. How was this going to go down? The invitation seemed like the perfect opportunity to confront the Fosters and find the truth, but was she, or any of them, ready for the truth?

"Dad, did Mother tell you Jessica invited me out to her place for the weekend?"

The three were sitting at the dinner table finishing up their dessert. Justin and Jenny had already discussed the invitation and decided it was probably the best opportunity they were going to have to face the Fosters. Where it would go from there was still unknown. Evan had offered to go along as their lawyer, but Justin didn't want this to be confrontational. Too many years had past. Their main priority was keeping Ava from being too hurt in this process.

"Yes, sweetie, we talked about it. I think it's a good idea. You can call her back and let her know we are all coming for a visit. I don't know how long you can stay though, that's a wait and see situation."

"What do you mean, Dad? Why couldn't I stay?" Alexis was puzzled by her father's reply. Something was going on here. They had been acting strangely ever since they had met Jessica and her parents. She really liked Jessica. Whatever their problem was, she didn't want it to stop her from being her friend.

"Sweetie, I know Jessica has invited you, but we haven't talked to her parents. I'm not saying you can't stay, all I am saying is, let's play it by ear."

"Huh. That's the best I get?" Alexis was a bit irritated at her father's indecision. Either she could stay, or she couldn't. What was the big deal?

"That's the best we can do for now. You're my daughter. I don't want to put you in a situation that might be uncomfortable." Justin knew he was hedging, but he didn't want to commit to something he couldn't make good. He had never reneged on a promise, and he wasn't about to now. The chance of the Fosters wanting Alexis to stay after they talked was remote.

Chapter Sixty-Two

South Shore- Lake Tahoe

As Alexis was making plans to visit her new friend, Diego Rivera was also making plans. He had arrived at Harrah's, the hotel at the south shore of Lake Tahoe where almost sixteen years ago he had left his baby daughter. This time Diego was determined to find his child and take her back to Spain with him. Although his mother and father had little money, his grandmother had been very wealthy. She had passed away a few months ago, leaving his father and mother an inheritance they were not likely to share with their wayward son. However, knowing Diego's character, his grandmother had left part of her enormous estate to her great grandchildren. Since Diego was her only surviving grandchild, this meant a considerable amount of money would go to his two daughters.

He was, as usual, broke. Since Ava was still a minor he

would petition the court to be in charge of all her money. His only problem now was finding her.

Before he left for the U.S. he had looked up the King family's web site. It was a well-formatted site, spelling out the history and background of the ranch, profiling all the prize cattle and horses they had for sale. As he paged through the site, he realized the daughter they called Alexis, was not the child he had taken from the house in Clear Water Cove. Who was the beautiful teenager in the picture? Could Jenny have had twins? The girl in the picture looked to be very close to Jessica's age, but was as blonde and blue-eyed as her mother. So, what had happened to Jessica? He was here at Lake Tahoe to find out.

He hadn't left any information with the young maid at the hotel, into whose care he had left the baby, but surely she must have turned her over to the authorities? Or had she? If she had called child protective services, Jessica would be back with the Kings. That meant only one thing. She had taken her, but where?

He pulled the rented Jeep Cherokee into valet parking at the hotel's front entrance. The young valet parker opened the door for him. He handed him the keys and headed inside.

The summer tourist season was in full swing and he had to wait ten minutes to get through the line at the front desk.

"I need to speak to someone who might be able to give me information on a former employee," he asked the tall, well dressed blonde lady, who was already pushing a pen towards him along with a room reservation card, while still talking on her headset.

Startled, she looked up. "One moment please," she

said, and put her caller on hold. "I'm sorry, but we can't give out any information on our employees."

"I need to find out what happened to a young girl who worked in your housekeeping department about sixteen years ago. Someone must remember her.

"I'm sorry, sir," the reservation clerk said briskly. "That's not possible. I'm not sure we even have records that go that far back. Now, if you don't need a room, please step back so I can help the next person in line." Giving him a dismissive look, she waved the next patron forward.

Diego turned away. There had to be someone here who remembered the girl, Alicia. He certainly did. A man doesn't forget the young virgins. She was a pretty one. He felt heat flare in his stomach as he thought about that day in the hotel room where he had violated her so cruelly. She had asked for it, he thought to himself. He had simply helped her out. He smiled at the memory. If she had Jessica and he could find her, maybe he could satisfy his pent up urges. It had been months since he had been with a woman. His supply of older rich widows had dwindled. His reputation as a user had traveled exponentially in the past few years and his once muscular fit body and handsome appearance that had so charmed the ladies, had turned to a flabby shell of what used to be. His face and body now showed the ravages of drugs and alcohol, and his thick black hair was turning grey, receding at his temples at a rapid pace.

As he lingered in the hotel lobby, he spied a maid standing at the end of a hallway that branched off from the main lobby. She was entering a service elevator that led to the upper floors. Walking quickly toward the elevator, he caught the doors just as they were closing and managed to squeeze through.

"You aren't allowed in here, mister," the middle aged maid said sharply. She was overweight and florid-faced with thinning hair that showed signs of once being dark brown. It looked as if she had worked hard all her life. Her hands were red and wrinkled. Probably from years of scrubbing toilets and dirty bathtubs, he thought with distaste.

"I'm sorry. I need to ask you a question. Have you worked here very long?"

"None of your business, mister, now get out of this elevator before I call security."

Diego reached into his pocket and pulled out a hundred dollar bill. "Maybe this will help you answer a few questions," he looked deeply into her eyes, giving her his winning smile that used to turn the ladies into giggling idiots.

The maid was unfazed. "Huh, depends on what you want to know. Maybe a hundred is enough, maybe not." She didn't reach for the money, but eyed him suspiciously.

"I'll tell you what, if you can give me some information about a former maid who worked here about sixteen years ago, I'll double the offer."

The elevator had reached the maid's floor and the doors slid open. The maid got out. As he expected, she didn't take off down the hall, but stood waiting for him. He followed her out into the hallway.

"That's a long time ago, mister. What was her name?"

"Her name was Alicia. She was a pretty dark-haired girl; young, maybe twenty-one or so. She did some babysitting for the hotel guests."

The maid looked away and then turned back. "I remember a girl by that name. She lived in a small farm town in Nevada. Let's see, I think she was from a ranch near Yerington. I'm from Carson City myself, so we talked a bit. Then one day she just disappeared, didn't give notice or anything. She just left. I remember her because it doubled my shift for that night, her being gone without notice and all."

Diego signed audibly. "That's not enough information for a hundred bucks. You don't remember her last name, or the name of her ranch?" He was still holding the one hundred dollar bill in his hand where she could see it.

"Nope, we don't get real personal with each other here. Mostly just work talk." Then, quick as a flash, she grabbed the bill from his hand, tucked it into her ample bosom and walked quickly away. As she hurried off, she turned back to him. "Don't think about called security. I'll tell them you tried to pay for my services."

Diego had to laugh. She didn't have to worry about him calling security; he certainly didn't want anyone to think he was desperate enough to proposition that old hag, however the information she gave him might be enough.

He took the elevator back down to the hotel lobby and walked out the front door. He signaled to the valet parker. He handed him his parking ticket and waited for his ride. The GPS in the rental car would take him to this town called, Yerington. The maid had described it as a small farming town. Someone would probably know a woman by the name of Alicia, who had a daughter named, Jessica. There couldn't be too many women in a small town that fit that description. Besides, he could still describe her down to her bare skin.

In Diego's alcohol damaged brain, he didn't take into consideration the possibility that if he was caught, he and Alicia could both go to prison for a very long time for the kidnapping of the King's baby girl.

Chapter Sixty-Three

Yerington, NV

Diego cruised slowly into the town of Yerington looking for a likely place to get some information. His eyes fell on a shabby diner that looked as if it was a local hangout. He slowed down and turned into the nearly deserted parking lot. It was almost noon, but evidently the lunch crowd hadn't shown up yet.

The waitress looked up as the well dressed stranger walked through the door. Diego gave her a warm smile and sat down on one of the faded red counter stools. The thin young waitress looked tired and worn out, her brown hair was pulled back in a bun and her stained apron hung loosely on her narrow shoulders. Her pale complexion and sad eyes spoke of a hard lived existence. Her lapel pin read, "Mary".

"Hello, Mary," Diego said softly. "Could I get a cup of coffee?"

Mary shrugged. "Sure, mister, can I get you anything

else?" His dark eyes gave her an appraising look that made her swallow hard. She hadn't seen such a well turned out man in this place, ever! Mostly, her customers were farmers or ranchers in boots and jeans, tired and sweaty from a hard days work. This man was not from around here that was for sure.

"Yes, actually there is, Mary," he leaned his elbows on the cracked counter; his eyes boring into her questioning, grey ones. "I am looking for a family who runs a ranch near here. The mother's name is Alicia. She has a daughter by the name of Jessica. Any chance you might know them? I have some good news for them," he lied smoothly.

Mary set a cup of steaming coffee in from of him, along with a small pitcher of cream and a container of sugar. She was wary of this stranger with his noticeable foreign accent, city clothes and Italian shoes. At least she thought they were Italian. She had never seen Italian shoes, but his looked expensive. She wasn't sure she should tell him anything about Alicia Foster. She had gone to high school with Alicia and knew exactly where to find her, but there was something off about this guy. On the other hand, he said it was good news. Heaven knew they could always use that. He was smiling encouragingly at her.

"You're sure it's good news you're bringing, and not just some sales pitch? She's a friend of mine. I wouldn't like to have any trouble turn up on her doorstep."

Diego laughed a deep, hearty laugh. "Trouble? That's the last thing I would bring her," he lied. "She's an old friend who's been left a fortune. I think she'll be very glad to see me." His hand tightened around the coffee cup. He was about to find out where his daughter was! What luck! This little floozy actually knows her! His story wasn't totally false; there was a fortune to be had, just not for Alicia.

"Well, in that case, I guess I can tell you where to find her. She and her husband and daughter, live on the C Bar III Ranch. It's about five miles out of town. I'll draw you a map." She pulled a chewed up pencil stub from behind her ear and grabbed a napkin. With a few stokes of her pencil, Diego had what he wanted, clear directions to Alicia and Jessica.

Diego drove slowly down the narrow two lane blacktop highway, looking for the sign that told him he had found the, C Bar III Ranch. The rolling countryside was sparsely populated, and barb wire fencing lined the roadsides. A few scattered head of cattle were grazing on the dry grass. As he turned a corner, he slammed on his brakes. A worm of excitement wove its way around his stomach. There on a rusted, sagging gate was a metal sign with, "C Bar III Ranch", in faded black letters. The gate was closed, but the chain that hung loosely around the wooden fence post was unlocked.

He got out of the car and walked over to the gate. Pulling the chain from the railings, he swung the gate open and returned to the car. Moments later he was driving down a gravel road that meandered across a shallow creek and down into a valley. He could see a little farmhouse with a large barn in the back. Stopping the car, he watched the house for signs of life.

As he sat watching, a movement from the barn caught his eye. He straightened up and leaned forward. His heart began to race. There, right in front of him, was the dark haired young woman he had deserted so many years before. There was no doubt it was Jessica. Her lithe young

273

body moved with the grace of a teenager, and her hair was the same color of his own. It had to be her.

He eased the car forward and pulled into the cleared area behind the barn. This was going to be easier than he thought. Alicia would have to let him take his daughter home to Spain. If she didn't, he would let Jenny know where she was, and they would turn Alicia over to the authorities for kidnapping. He knew that as long as the kidnapped child was recovered under the age of eighteen, there was no statute of limitations on prosecution of the perpetrator. He grinned as he exited the car and walked around the barn to the front of the small frame house Jessica had entered. The front door was open. Only a screen door was left between Diego and the interior of the house. He could hear sounds of someone rattling dishes in the kitchen. The smell of brewing coffee wafted out the door. He knocked gently. When no one came, he knocked harder.

"Just a moment," came a sweet, high-pitched voice. "I'm coming."

Jessica put away the dishtowel she had been using to finish up the lunch dishes and went to the door. When she saw the unfamiliar dark haired man standing in the doorway, she hesitated, not many strangers came around the ranch. Alicia and Steve were down at the barn doing chores, which left her alone and vulnerable.

Reluctantly, she approached the door. "Can I help you, sir?" she asked politely.

Diego's breath caught in his throat. His daughter was a beauty. Her wide, long lashed dark eyes and silky black hair were his, but the shape of her face, her nose and slender figure, were all Jenny's. She was tanned and glowing from the desert sun. Unexpectedly, he felt sadness and a sense of loss.

"Hello, Jessica. Is your mother home?"

Jessica's heart began to race. How did this stranger know her name? Who was he? For some reason he looked familiar, but why? She had never seen him before in her life.

"She's down at the barn. I'll go get her."

"I'll walk down with you." Diego smiled his most charming smile. He didn't want to panic her this early in the game. He stood aside as Jessica opened the screen door. Looking curiously at him, she led the way to the barn.

"Dad, There's someone here to see you," Jessica peered around the barn, and saw her mother and father hanging over the stall where the new burro baby and her mother were resting. Alicia and Steve both stepped back and turned to see who the visitor was. As Diego and Jessica walked closer, Alicia caught her breath. The color drained from her face. The man standing before her was the same man who had so cruelly raped her and then deserted his innocent baby for her to take care of. What was he doing here?

"Diego!" she barely whispered the words. "Why are you here? What do you want?" Trembling with fear, Alicia grabbed a startled Jessica and pulled her close.

Seeing that his wife was terrified of the stranger, Steve put a protective arm around her and glared at Diego.

"Who are you?" he demanded.

Diego grinned, "Why don't you ask your wife? Don't tell me she never told you who your little girl's father is, or how she came to live with you?"

Steve's face turned red. "What the hell are you talking about? Explain what you just said or I'll kick your ass out of here."

"Oh, I don't think you'll do that, mister. You see, I've

come to take my daughter back home to Spain with me. Considering the circumstances, I don't think you will want to stop me."

Jessica looked at her parents, her face frozen with fear.

"Mom, Dad! What's he saying? What does he mean?"

"Listen, mister, if you don't explain yourself in the next minute, I'm calling the sheriff," Steve threatened.

"Steve! No!" Alicia cried her face pale. She looked at him pleadingly. "Please, let's go up to the house. We have to talk!"

Angry and puzzled, Steve took Jessica by the hand. With his other arm still around his wife, he nodded. "Okay, I don't know what's going on here, but I aim to find out." Glaring at Diego he began walking toward the house with Diego trailing happily behind. Steve growled to Alicia. "I hope you have an explanation for why this guy is here."

Alicia nodded numbly. How had Diego found them? What was she going to tell Steve - let alone Jessica?"

The four entered the modest living room and Steve motioned for Diego to take a seat on a well-worn, leather chair across from the couch.

"Okay, buddy. Start talking."

"Wait, Steve! Jessica, please go to your room. This is between the three of us. It doesn't concern you. You don't need to hear all this man's nonsense."

"But, Mom," Jess protested.

"You heard your mother, Jess. Now go to your room!"

Steve's stomach was in knots, he had a really bad feeling about what was coming.

Reluctantly, Jessica left the room. As she exited the doorway she looked back over her shoulder at the strange man who looked troublingly familiar.

Diego leaned back in his chair while Steve and Jessica sat down on the couch across from him.

"I see your wife hasn't told you anything, has she? Not even the fact that Jessica isn't her daughter?"

Steve started to get up, but Alicia pushed him back down. This was her worst nightmare coming true. She had prayed this day would never come. Now here it was, and she was faced with the terrible fact that she had to tell Steve, and probably Jessica, the truth.

"Don't say another word you bastard," Alicia whispered to Diego. "Just shut up. If Steve is going to hear this, it's going to be from me."

"Fine, great, start talking, my dear. But don't take too long. I haven't got that much time. Jessica needs to start packing. I have plane reservations for us this evening. We'll be flying out of Reno."

"You'll take her over my dead body!" Steve slammed his fist on the arm of the couch and flew to his feet. "Get the hell out of my house!"

"Oh, I don't think so." Diego's eyes narrowed. "Let your wife continue. I think you will find it highly entertaining."

Hands tightly clasped in her lap, lips trembling, Alicia began to relate the details of Jessica's arrival in her life. When she got to the part of the rape, she just stared at Diego and let it go. Steve didn't need to hear about that.

When she was finished, Steve sat stunned. "I can't believe you have kept this from me all these years, Alicia. How did you think you would get away with it? Did you ever try to contact Jessica's mother, or anyone in law enforcement, or child protective services? My God, Alicia, you could be put in jail for life for kidnapping!"

Diego stood up and walked over to Alicia, putting a hand on her shaking shoulders. "No need for that drastic measure. I'm her father, and I intend to take her home. I'll not be pressing any charges. You've done well raising her." He tried to look repentant. "I should never have left her like that. It was a big mistake, but now I am here to rectify my bad judgment. Just let her go with me and your wife will not be blamed for anything."

Steve jerked Diego's hand from Alicia's shoulder. "You think you can just walk in her and take our daughter after you deserted her and never looked back all these years? You must be crazy. Sure, Alicia should have turned her over to the authorities, but that doesn't make her a kidnapper. What it does do is make you guilty of child abuse and neglect."

As the three glared at each other, a shadow at the door caught Diego's eye. "Well, Jessica, I guess you heard the real story, so what do you think?"

"Mom, is it true? Is he my real father? If he is, where is my real mother?" Jessica's face was gray. She had her arms wrapped around her chest to keep from shaking. Alicia just nodded; she didn't know what to say. With a wrenching cry, Jessica fled from the room.

"Better go round her up," Diego said. "If she's not back and ready to leave with me in thirty minutes, I'll call the sheriff." He pulled a cell phone from his pocket and brandished it in front of them.

Chapter Sixty-Four

Eagle's View

"Hurry up, Alexis. It's already nine o'clock. If we are going to get to Jessica's before noon we have to get going." Jenny called over her shoulder as she walked out the front door to where Justin was waiting in the Escalade.

"I'm coming, Mom. I just have to find my leather jacket. Have you seen it?"

"No, but you have more than one coat. Just take another one." Jenny shook her head. She knew it had to be the right one, or they would be waiting forever. She opened the front door of the car and poked her head inside. "Hold on for just one minute, Justin. Alexis is completing her wardrobe."

Justin shook his head. "I should have had another waffle. The girl is never ready when we are."

However, much to his surprise, as he was settling in

for a long wait, the front door flew open and Alexis ran down the steps, her gold curls streaming behind her.

"Found it! Let's go. I can't wait to see that baby burro and Jessica."

The drive out to the C Bar III ranch was uneventful. But, when they drove up the gravel road, they saw a new jeep parked behind the barn.

"They must have company," Justin remarked. "Hope they remembered we are coming. On the other hand, they won't be happy about if for long."

"What do you mean, Dad? Why not? They invited us?"

"We should have told her a long time ago, Justin. This is a mistake. We can't go in there with Alexis not knowing."

"Not knowing what! Mom, Dad! What's going on?"

"Pull over behind that jeep, Justin. We have to explain what this is all about before we go in that house and hit these people with the truth."

"You're right. Guess we got so caught up in what we were going to do about Jessica, I mean Ava, we didn't think very clearly about how it would be for Alexis to hear it. That was stupid."

"Jessica! Ava! What are you talking about, Dad? Ava was kidnapped years ago when she was a baby." Then realization dawned on Alexis and she gasped. "Dad, you mean Jessica is Ava?"

"We are sure of it, darling," Jenny sighed. "It's going to be complicated. These aren't bad people, and we don't think they were responsible for taking her, but we really don't know. We thought that we should bring you here to face the truth along with Ava. You two are already such good friends; we thought you could help each other accept the truth. We should have prepared you."

Alexis grabbed the door handle and flew out of the car. She raced toward the house and the sister she had never known.

"Go after her, Justin. We have to make sure this is done right. We can't have her barging in like this."

Justin nodded. He jumped out of the car and ran to catch up with Alexis.

The sound of crunching gravel signaled the arrival of a car outside by the barn. Distracted, the three people looked out the living room window to see if they could tell who it was.

Recognizing the gleaming Escalade, Alicia froze. What now? What was she going to say to the Kings?

'Expecting someone?" Diego asked. "Better get rid of them fast. I don't need anyone interfering. I was hoping I wouldn't have to resort to this, but just in case you try anything..." he put his hand inside his pants pocket and withdrew a wicked looked Glock handgun. Alicia gasped.

"There's no need for that," Steve said nervously. "I'll get rid of them. Put that gun away."

"Fine," Diego smiled. "But just in case, I'll step out of here while you tell them some story. Remember, I have this gun aimed at your back and I'm not afraid to use it if I have to."

Chapter Sixty-Five

As Alexis flew towards the house, she saw Jessica run out of the back door. Changing course, Alexis ran after her with Justin close behind.

Because Jessica was crying and stumbling as she ran, it was easy for Alexis to catch up with her.

"Stop, Stop! Please, Jess. I have to talk to you."

Jessica turned towards Alexis and stopped, tears obliterating her vision.

"I already know! Just leave me alone! That man made my mother tell us everything!"

"But, Jess! That means we're sisters! Doesn't that matter to you?" Alexis stopped, out of breath. "Please, we have to talk!"

"There's nothing to talk about. I have a family. I have a mother and father. I don't care what that man says!"

Justin caught up with the girls and heard the last few desperate words.

"What man, Ava? I mean Jessica. Who made your mother tell you about us?"

"He says his name is Diego. He's threatening to take

me back to Spain with him, or he says he will put my mother in jail for kidnapping. He says he's my father!" She fell to her knees and Alexis knelt down beside her. She put her arms around the terrified girl, hugging her.

"Diego is our father, Jess. I have never met him, either. He deserted our mother before we were born and Justin adopted me. But we have the same mother! She's been looking for you for years. She never gave up on finding you. Please come back to the house. We'll work something out."

Justin grabbed the girls. "Come with me. Hurry!" he said. Herding them in front of him, he ran back to the car. He had to let Jenny know Diego was inside. It was going to be a shock. He sensed danger. This could change everything.

Jenny watched as Justin ran to the car with the girls trailing behind him. She could see how upset Jessica, her Ava, was. "What's wrong, Justin? Has something happened?" She got out of the car, anxiously waiting for an explanation.

"I'm afraid so. We have a change of plans. Girls, get in the car. Lock the doors and call 911. Tell the sheriff we need him as fast as he can get here."

Still crying, but mindful of the authority in Justin's voice, Jessica followed Alexis into the Escalade. Alexis pulled the door shut and hit the automatic door lock, safely locking them both inside.

"Jenny, Diego's inside. He told Steve about Jessica. Evidently Jessica heard him so now she knows, too. He's demanding that she return with him to Spain. He thinks he can just walk in here and take her. I'm beginning to think it wouldn't be the first time he's taken her, either. I don't know how he found Steve and Alicia; all I know is he's here. We have to talk to him."

"Are you telling me that Diego, the twin's father, is inside this house, right now?"

"I'm afraid so, baby. Come on. The girls are calling the sheriff. We'll have backup if we need it. This guy sounds like he's lost his mind,"

"So, Steve knows how Alicia came to have Jessica?" Jenny was wide-eyed. How was this possible, she thought? After all these years he just shows up and wants her? She shook her head, this wasn't happening. The last person on earth she wanted to see was Diego Rivera.

Grabbing her arm, Justin walked swiftly towards the house. The sooner they got this settled, the better. In a way he was relieved. At least he didn't have to be the one to break it to the Fosters. Then he quickly realized that although Diego had told them he was Jessica's father, he probably hadn't told them Jenny was her mother and the woman whose kidnapped child Alicia had been raising as her own. What a can of worms. He shook his head. This wasn't going to be easy.

Unaware of the gun Diego was holding on the Fosters, Justin and Jenny approached the house and knocked on the frame of the screen door.

Steve appeared at the door but didn't open it to welcome them inside.

"Hi Steve," Justin said. "I understand we have a problem. Your daughter says there's a guy named Diego here. Can we talk to him?"

"How do you know this guy?" Steve said with surprise.

"It's a long story, Steve. We need to talk. Please, can we come in?"

Reluctant to disobey Diego's order to get rid of the newcomers, Steve shook his head. "Not a good idea right now, Justin. I'm sorry, but I think you should come back later."

"We really have to talk to you, Steve," Jenny begged.

From the hallway where he had been hiding, Diego heard Jenny's pleading voice and his stomach rolled. What the hell was *she* doing here? How did she know the Fosters? He stepped around the corner, not able to resist his curiosity. Standing in the doorway was the mother of his two girls, right here at this house! Maybe he should find out why. Stepping out into the living room, Diego could see Jenny's worried face pressing against the screen door.

"Well, well, if it isn't my long lost love. Come on in and join the party, Jenny. I am about to be reunited with our daughter."

Once more, Alicia gasped with shock. "What do you mean, Diego? What does Mrs. King have to do with Jessica?"

"Oh, well, I forgot to tell you that part of the story, didn't I? See, Jenny and I used to be a couple, years ago. When she found out we were going to have a baby, she took off and I never saw my children again."

Jenny jerked open the door, but stopped short when she saw the gun in Diego's hand.

"That's a lie, you bastard. You ran away when you found out I was pregnant, and I never heard from you again."

"Put that gun down, Diego," Justin warned.

"Or you'll do what?" Diego said with a nasty smile on his face. "If you think you are going to test my sincerity about taking my daughter back to her rightful family, forget it. I think the ball is in my park." He waved the gun at Justin and Jenny. "Now that you're in, come, sit down. We're just waiting for Alicia to get my daughter ready to travel, aren't we Alicia? Go do it now!" The smile disappeared from his face as he pointed the gun at Alicia. "I have no more time to waste. I took her once, I'll do it again."

Jenny looked at Justin with a growing realization, and then turned to Diego.

"You! You're the one who stole my baby from me! How could you! And now you want her back? Are you crazy? Don't you know you're going to jail for kidnapping?"

"I don't know about your laws here in America, but in Spain the father has a right to his child." He tapped his foot impatiently. "Hurry it up, Alicia," he called down the hall.

"You could have seen the girls anytime you wanted." Jenny said accusingly, "You had no right to take Ava and then just abandon her! How did Alicia come to have her in the first place?"

"It's a long story. You would find it boring. The fact is, I found her again and I'm taking her back home with me. By the way, where is my other daughter? The one you still have, what did the news article say her name was? Alexis? Nice name. Where is she? I'd like to meet her."

"Not a chance in hell," Justin growled. "You'll be lucky if you leave this place with anyone but the sheriff."

Alicia sat on the edge of Jessica's bed in her room. Where had she gone? What was she going to do now? Would Diego kill them if he couldn't have Jess? She buried her head in her hands. She looked up as Diego entered the room with the Kings and Steve in front of him. His gun was trained on all three.

"Where is she?" he thundered. "If you have hidden her somewhere you don't value your husband's life, or that of her *real* mother's." He kicked aside the window coverings angrily.

"I don't know where she went," Alicia sobbed. "She was so upset after she heard what you told us, she ran. Maybe she's out in the barn. I don't know. Please, don't hurt anyone. Let me try to find her."

"We're all going back into the living room, now! I'll secure the Kings and Steve, then you and I will go find her." He licked his lips. "I haven't forgotten what a delicious little virgin piece of ass you were. Guess that's one reason I left the baby with you. You were so anxious to jump into my bed; I thought you might want a baby. I just made your wish come true faster."

Steve started towards him, but Diego shoved the gun viciously into his ribs. "Stand back or I'll kill you. It really doesn't matter to me. The only one I care about taking out of here alive is Jessica. The part where you all stay alive is up to you, and depends on how cooperative you are. And, Steve, old buddy, if it makes you feel any better, she was a rather reluctant virgin." He reached over and stroked Alicia's breast with his free hand and smiled over at the helpless, livid Steve.

Justin thought about the girls in the car. If they left the house, Diego would find them quickly. Hopefully, they had convinced the sheriff they needed him right away. It was their only chance to save lives and keep Jessica from being taken from her family again. What would happen when this was all over was still a huge question. One he didn't want to think about right now.

Diego pushed Steve into a straight backed, wooden chair in the kitchen. Then grabbing some rope he saw laying on a shelf, he told Justin to tie his hands and feet to the table leg, forcing him into an uncomfortable, bent over position, while he held the gun on the others.

In the distance Jenny heard the wail of a siren. "The sheriff, Justin!" she cried, unable to hold back her relief.

Diego's eyes blazed. "Who called the cops? Which one of you?" he waved the gun wildly, looking around for a quick exit.

Seeing his chance, Justin made a swing at Diego's gun hand, and the weapon flew through the air. Both men hit the ground, grabbing for the gun as it skittered across the worn linoleum floor.

As the two men struggled, Jenny kicked the gun far enough away where she could safely reach it. She picked it up and leveled it at Diego's head.

"Get up you S.O.B. Don't try anything. It would give me great pleasure to blow your head off. You deprived me of all the years I could have had watching my daughter grow up. You also deprived me of the love I wanted to give her, and time I will *never* get back." She was shaking, but the gun was tight in her hands.

Justin released Diego from the chokehold he had him in and they both stood up.

"It's okay now, baby. Give me the gun," Justin said gently. "It's over. The sheriff is almost here. Diego is not going anywhere with anyone. The only place he's going is prison - for a very long time."

Jenny let Justin take the gun from her hand and she fell into a chair, her eyes still glued on the man who had stolen Ava.

Chapter Sixty-Six

While Justin held the gun on Diego, Jenny untied Steve. Just as they finished, the front door burst open and two-uniformed sheriff's deputies came into the house, guns drawn. One was tall and muscular with dark hair. The second man was shorter with sandy brown hair and intense blue eyes. Both looked like they could handle anything that came their way.

"In here, guys," Justin called not taking his eyes off Diego's panicked face.

The deputies entered the kitchen, but stopped short at the sight of Justin's gun pointing at a very frightened man.

"Put the gun down, mister," the sandy haired deputy said firmly, his gun trained on Justin. "We've got it under control now."

"Gladly, here, take it. It belongs to this fellow here. He's trying to kidnap this couple's daughter, who he claims is his." Justin handed the gun to the deputy and nodded in Alicia's direction.

"One of the young girls in the car?"

"Yes. They are both Jenny's daughters." Justin said, pointing to Jenny. "This man kidnapped one of them when she was a baby. These folks here," he nodded at Steve and Alicia, who were now huddled together, not knowing where this was taking them, "have raised her as their own. She just found out that she doesn't belong to them. If you don't mind, could you take this fellow out of here? We need a little time alone with the girls. This has been a quite a shock to them."

The sandy haired deputy spoke to his companion. "Troy, go to the car and get the girls. Bring them in. I don't know what's happening here." As the tall officer left to get the girls, the deputy looked at the nervous group and shook his head. "I'm taking all of you down to the sheriff's office. We'll take statements from everyone."

Justin put a hand up. "Fine, but let us have a minute or two with our daughters. Just take this guy out of here and secure him in your patrol car. Given what he's facing, there is no doubt in my mind he'll try to take off."

The deputy looked doubtful, but the only odd man out in the situation was Diego. The other four looked like they were telling the truth. As soon as Troy came back with the girls, he would find out more. Then maybe he would let these two couples have a few minutes to talk to them.

"Mom, Dad! Are you alright?" Alexis flew into the kitchen and into Justin's arms. \

"We're fine, honey. The deputies are going to take Mr. Rivera outside while all of us have a quiet little talk."

"Dad is that man, Diego, really my father?" she gave a little shudder and turned to Jenny. "Mom, is this really my sister, Ava?"

The two deputies looked at each other and nodded.

"We'll give you all a little time to figure this out.

Sounds like a mess to me," Troy said. "We'll get Mr. Rivera into the car, but don't be long."

Taking Diego by the arm, the two marched him out of the house.

"It's all my fault." Jenny looked at the group, her eyes filling with tears. If I hadn't had anything to do with that man, none of this would ever have happened."

Justin put his arms around her and pulled her close. "Don't say that, Jen. If you had never known Diego, we would never have had these two beautiful children," he looked at Jessica and Alexis, "who are now the center of a big decision."

Jessica had not spoken a word since she came into the house with the deputies. She looked pale and shocked, still unable to process what was taking place.

"Let's all sit down." Justin said, "I know this is a shock to the girls, and believe me, it's a shock to their mothers. I say mothers, because I know Alicia is as much a mother to our Ava, as is Jenny. I don't know why she was hidden out here for so long, but I will wait for Alicia to tell me before we point any fingers. Needless to say, Diego appears to be the culprit in the initial kidnapping of Ava, but why on earth didn't anyone try to find out who her real mother was? Do you have any idea what you have put our family though all these years?" Despite his efforts to remain calm, Justin couldn't help raising his voice.

Alicia was trembling. Jessica went to her and put her arms around her mother. "I made a terrible mistake, Mr. King" Alicia said tearfully. "I wish I had tried to find her real mother, but I was so afraid for her. Diego deserted her in a hotel room, for God's sake! He left her there with no contact address, telephone number, or last name. I was terrified the authorities would put that beautiful baby in foster care, or keep her as a ward of the state. I know

now it was wrong, but with a father like that; I couldn't imagine what her mother was like to let him take her away with him. I am so, so sorry. I know I can never make up for all the heartbreak I have caused you, Jenny, but I want you to know that Jess has been the joy of our lives. We have loved her so much. I think she's had a good life and has been happy living here on our ranch."

"Oh, Mom, what have you done?" Jessica stood up. "I find out I have a sister and a mother I have never known! "I love you and Dad, but what have you done! " Jessica stumbled back away from Alicia, a stricken look on her face. Then with a cry, she flew out of the room sobbing.

"I have to go after her!" Alicia said.

"No," Steve said sternly, catching her by the arm, "Leave her be. She has to have some time to think. She'll come around."

They stood there uncertainly, not sure what to do, when the front door opened again. They all turned at the same time, hoping to see Jessica, but it was Troy, the tall deputy.

"Sorry folks, times up. We need to talk to everyone down at the station. I suggest you call your attorney as soon as we get there, if you have one. Until we are sure what Mr. Rivera's role is in this, we might have to arrest the man who was threatening him with a loaded weapon." The deputy's eyes rested on Justin.

Justin took a deep breath. "We'll see about that. We have waited almost sixteen years to find our daughter. We have the man who stole her under arrest in your car. If I had to take a gun away from him to keep him from stealing her again, then you can arrest me, too."

The deputy held up his hands. "Not saying I'm going to arrest anyone. I'm just suggesting you get legal counsel to help straighten this out. Now, if you don't mind, follow me to the car. Kevin will take Mr. Rivera in the patrol car. The rest of you folks can ride back with me in your car."

As they left the house the deputy stopped and looked around. "Hey, where is the other girl?"

"She's probably taken off on her horse to try to make some sense out of what she has learned in the last hour or so," Steve said. "She'll be back. She has nowhere else to go. Don't worry about her. She knows this ranch like the back of her hand. The only place she ever goes when she's upset is the desert. If you really need her, we'll bring her in to you later."

"Guess I don't have any choice, do I? Come on, let's get going. The sooner we straighten this mess out, the better."

"I agree," Justin said. Taking Jenny's hand firmly in his, he led her to the Escalade, followed by Alicia, Steve, Alexis and the deputy.

As they all climbed into the car, Jenny looked out the window and caught sight of a horse with his rider bent low over his withers, her long black hair whipping out behind her, racing across the desert as fast as Comanche's strong legs could take them.

Chapter Sixty-Seven

On the way into the Yerington Sheriff's Office, Justin pulled out his cell phone and called Sheriff Brewster at Tahoe. After he got him on the line, he told him what had happened and asked if he could call the station to explain the situation to the deputies.

Brewster was shocked to hear the news they had been waiting so long to hear. He assured Justin he would take care of it and make sure they would be free to leave. Then Justin called Evan at his office in San Francisco. He didn't think he, or Jenny would need a lawyer, but he knew for certain that Alicia Foster, and maybe even her husband, Steve, would. Evan was in court, but his secretary promised to have him call the minute he was able to get to a phone.

When the group arrived at the station the deputies took everyone inside. The sheriff had already received the call from Brewster. He handcuffed Diego and told him he was under arrest for the kidnapping of Ava. Then he told Alicia he was holding her for accessory to the crime. Since there was no proof that Steve had any hand in the kidnapping, he and Justin were free to go. Alicia was crying as they led her away to a jail cell. Steve ran to her, but the deputy with the sandy hair held him back.

"Sorry man, we have to do this. Mr. King says he is getting your wife an attorney. As soon as he arrives we can question her. Maybe the judge will set bail. Until then, you will be better off at home with your daughter."

Angrily, Steve brushed away the deputy's hand. "If anyone so much as lays a finger on her…, "his voice trailed away. He clenched his jaw. What had just happened here? Why hadn't Alicia told him the truth about Jessica a long time ago? God! Kidnapping! What had she gotten them into? He turned and walked quickly past Jenny and Justin, then realized he didn't have a ride back to the ranch. With his eyes brimming with tears, he asked quietly, "Mr. King. I have to ask you a favor. Would you mind giving me a ride back home? Jess might be back by now and if she is, she'll need me."

Jenny put a hand on his shoulder. "Of course we will, Steve. Remember, she's our daughter. We need to talk to her, too."

"Yeah, I guess you do. But, just so you know. She may be your daughter by birth, but she has been our daughter for almost sixteen years. I don't know how she's going to accept the fact that she was born to some other woman."

Tears filled Jenny's eyes. "What do you mean by, "Some other woman"? I'm her mother!" Her voice shook with anger. "She has a twin sister. I have been searching for my baby for fifteen years! I know this is a shock to you, mister, but certainly not to your wife! However right she thought she was in keeping Ava, she was wrong, so very wrong! Now we are all going to pay the consequences. *Me*, for all the years I have been deprived of my daughter. *Ava*, for all the years she didn't know her sister and mother, and you, Steve, for you may lose her." She hugged herself tightly. Filled with anger and sorrow, she could only stare at the man who Ava thought of as her father.

"This isn't helping anything." Justin said. "Let's get in the car and drive Steve back to the ranch. This is difficult for all of us. I think the best thing to do is talk to Jessica and let her make up her own mind about what she wants to do. The last thing Jenny and I want, is to tear her away from a life she knows and evidently loves. As much as we want our daughter back with us, this is not going to be an easy transition."

Jenny walked stiffly to the car, emotion roiling through her. She couldn't think straight. It was possible her own daughter might not want to live with her! After all this time, after all the sadness and loss, she still might not get her back.

Jenny rounded up Alexis, who had been waiting patiently outside the office, and Steve and Justin followed her out to the Escalade. They drove silently back to the C Bar III, all four lost in their own thoughts.

Chapter Sixty-Eight

Jessica sat on Comanche's warm back. Her long legs stuck to his damp, heaving sides. They had run for a long time. Realizing she had to let her horse take a breather, she pulled him to a stop on top of a ridge. From her vantage point, she could see clear across the valley. Her home for the past fifteen years was barely visible in the distance. She patted his sweaty neck.

"What am I going to do, Comanche? I don't even know these people. *My mother*! My mother is Alicia. My father is Steve, not that awful man, Diego, who came to the house." She put her head down on his neck and began to cry. "What if they make me leave here? I can't go!" She straightened up. "I won't go! If they try to make me I'll run away. They think they had a hard time finding me before, ha, they'll never find me next time. You and I will go somewhere."

Then realizing how ridiculous her reasoning was, she sat there looking off into the distance. She watched as the breeze blew fluffy white clouds across the robin's egg, blue sky, casting shadows that fled across the desert floor.

She threw back her head and looked up at the sky, letting the wind blow her hair away from her face. Breathing in the sage scented air, she made a decision. This was her land, her ranch. Somehow, she would find a way to stay here. Pulling Comanche's head around toward the ranch house, Jess dug her heels into his side and instantly they were off again, this time racing back home. She had to talk to Steve; she had to convince him not to let those people take her away from here. She was going to make sure they knew her name was Jessica. It would never be anything else!

As she neared the ranch, she saw the gleaming Escalade parked in the gravel drive in front of the house. The Kings were still here! Hadn't the Sheriff taken them all away? What were they doing back here? She trotted around to the barn and slid down off Comanche's back. Easing the bridle off over his ears, she turned him out into the corral, and watched as he pawed the ground, then lay down with a grunt and rolled over in the dirt. She couldn't help smiling. He was wet with sweat, and dirt stuck to his smooth coat. He looked like a big mud pie. That was okay; she would rinse him off, brush his mane and tail and put him up later. She had ridden him pretty hard; he needed to scratch his itching back.

The house was quiet as she opened the front door and walked inside. From the living room she could see into the kitchen where the three adults were sitting around the scarred and worn kitchen table. When Steve heard her come in he jumped up and ran to her, wrapping her in a bear hug. He stroked her windblown hair and whispered in her ear. "It's going to be okay, sweetie. They just want to talk to you. Come on. Chin up. We're going to give this our best shot."

He pulled away and looked down into her troubled

dark eyes, so unlike his own green ones, but so like those of the man who had just been arrested by the Sheriff. His stomach turned over. Lord, help us get through this, he prayed silently, then taking her by the hand, he led her into the kitchen where Justin and Jenny were waiting to talk to a daughter they hadn't seen in fifteen years. A daughter who was no longer the baby they remembered, but a young woman with a mind of her own.

Emotions poured through Jenny as she watched Steve lead Jessica into the kitchen. All she wanted to do was jump up and throw her arms around her daughter and hug her until her arms got tired. Although she hadn't seen her since she was a baby this was still her child, one she was determined to know again, hopefully take back to Eagle's View where they could become a family. She clasped her hands tightly under the table to keep them from trembling, but there was nothing she could do to stop the sick feeling in her stomach as Jessica seated herself at the far end of the table, her eyes dark and angry. Before Jenny could think of what to say, Jessica spoke directly to her and Justin.

"I really don't know who I am anymore. I don't know who you are either, Mrs. King. You may be my birth mother, but this is my home and this is my father. They had better not arrest my mother! I thought a lot about everything while I was out riding Comanche. I want to get to know my sister," she looked over at Alexis and gave her a tiny smile, "and I feel obligated to get to know my real mother, but I am not going away from here. This is my home. You can decide if you would like to have me visit you, or come here and spend some time with us. If you press charges against my mother, I will make sure you never see me again. The only person responsible for all this mess is that man, Diego. You can do whatever you feel you have to, to punish him, just leave my mother out of it." Jessica finished talking and sat straight and defiant in her chair, daring anyone to argue with her.

Jenny sighed deeply. "My darling," she began, tears choking her words, "if you only knew how much we love you, and how difficult it has been to live without you for fifteen years, you wouldn't be so hard on me. I realize you have never known any parents, other than Steve and Alicia, but please, give us a chance to have you back in our lives." She gulped, this was tearing her apart. "You're my baby, the baby I lost so long ago." Her eyes pleaded with the angry girl.

Jessica's face softened a bit, but then she stood up, ignoring Jenny. "I'm going down to the barn. Want to come, Alexis? You haven't seen the baby burro yet." Then she turned back to Jenny. "If my mother isn't back home by tonight, you can forget about coming back here, ever. I don't care who you are, you have no right to come here and tear our lives apart." She turned to leave, motioning for Alexis to follow her.

Alexis looked at her mother, who nodded. "Go ahead, honey. Go with your sister while we try to straighten this out and get her mother back home."

After the girls left for the barn, Jenny spoke to Steve, "I don't want my daughter to hate us. I also tend to believe Alicia was only doing what she thought was best for our baby. It was wrong, but not in her eyes. If we are ever going to have a relationship with, "Jessica," she swallowed as she said Ava's new name, "we can't let Alicia go to jail, but I am determined to see that Diego goes to prison for all the harm he has done."

Justin hugged her, "When Alexis and Jessica come

back we'll go to the Sheriff's office and see what can be done to get her out of there tonight. I'll see if I can get hold of Evan and let him know what's going on. I'm sure we can do something."

"Thank you both," Steve said. "I wouldn't have wished this on you for the world. I had no idea."

"We know that, Steve," Justin said, "We'll all work together to right what has been a terrible wrong for Jessica, Alexis, for you and Alicia, but mostly for Jenny."

Chapter Sixty-Nine

"Are you sure you don't want to pursue charges against this woman who has kept your daughter illegally for fifteen years?" Evan said disbelief in his voice.

Justin flipped his cell phone to his other ear and looked over at Jenny. "That's correct, Evan. Jenny and I had a long talk, and we decided to drop all charges against Alicia Foster. If we have any hope of reestablishing a relationship with our daughter, we simply cannot put her mother in jail." He pulled the car over to the side of the highway to continue the conversation safely out of traffic. "We're on our way back to the ranch. I'll call you back when we get home."

"Okay, but I hope you know what you're doing. She had to know the baby had a mother somewhere!" Evan sounded angry. He had, after all, been at Clear Water Cove when Ava was taken and had been part of the search party that had spent weeks looking for her. He also knew how much Jenny had suffered since the event.

"I'll tell you one thing, Evan, that young girl loves her

family. They have raised her just like we would have. She is a remarkable young woman."

"Alright then, I'll handle it. Call me as soon as you get home. We need to talk about Diego. You both have to be prepared to testify against him. Don't know how Jenny is going to handle that one. At one time, I'm sure she thought she was in love with him, and he *is* the twin's father."

"Maybe legally he is, but that's as far as it goes, Evan. Believe me Jenny has no sympathy for the guy. I don't think there will be any problem with her testifying against him. He stole a part of her life she will never get back."

Justin clicked off the call and turned the big car back onto the highway.

"Dad?" Alexis put her hand on his shoulder.

"Yes sweetheart?"

"When can we ask Jessica to visit us?"

"I don't know, sweetie. We have to see how things smooth out. I don't imagine she'll want to leave her home until everything settles down."

"Oh." Alexis frowned and slumped back into the seat, disappointed. "I have so much lost time to make up. I just found out a sister I thought I would never see again, is living just a few hours away! I want to be with her, to talk to her, to see how her life has been and let her know about mine."

"I know, Alexis, and we are going to make sure that happens. You just have to be patient. When she's ready to come, she'll let us know."

The three drove the rest of the way back to the ranch deep in their own thoughts about the child and the sister, who had come back into their lives so unexpectedly.

Chapter Seventy

Eagle's View Ranch

The sun shone brightly, but dark clouds skimmed across the sky, blown in from the West by a freshening wind. The tall pine trees that fronted the house creaked and swayed, scattering needles down on the meadow. It felt like a storm was coming in, Jenny mused, but the storm that had been swirling around her for so long had thankfully blown away. Her girls were together again, and if she was lucky, Jessica just might come to love her. Not pressing to have her returned had been a difficult decision for Jenny, but after seeing how much Jessica loved her family and her way of life, she knew letting her stay with Alicia and Steve had been the right decision. Because of her heart breaking decision, Jessica had agreed to come often and get to know her mother and twin sister. It was all working out.

Jenny was standing on the deck in front of the house, her curly red hair forming a sunny halo around her face.

She put her hands on the railing and leaned over, calling to the riders on the two eager prancing horses below her.

"Be careful, girls. Be back before dark. It looks like a storm is brewing." She smiled and waved. The two waved back and cantered off down the road toward the hills. Jenny hugged herself tightly. It was hard to believe it was only a month after Diego's arrest and Jessica was here at Eagle's View. She had promised to stay a week.

Diego's trial was still months away, but he was in jail and safely out of their lives for now. Evan had made sure Alicia was cleared of any blame in the kidnapping and she was safely home. The judge had not been kind in his court room comments to her but without Jenny pressing charges; he had to let her go. The inheritance Jessica was going to get from Diego's grandmother's would help the Fosters with their ranch, and if she decided to go to college, it would more than pay for any school she chose to go to. With the fortune Jordan would leave to Justin and Julie, Justin's twin sister, all the children would be well taken care of They did not need the Rivera's money.

Jenny's parents, Carolyn and Tom, had asked if the twins could spend some time with them at Clear Water Cove and Jenny had told them she would try to see if this was possible. Jessica should get to know her grandparents. But, there was still time for that. Jenny didn't want to share any of the little time she had been able to spend with her daughter. Maybe Thanksgiving they could all go up to the cove, she would ask the Fosters to come, too.

The door to the deck slid open, and Justin walked over to where she was standing, still looking after the disappearing riders.

"Wonderful, isn't it darling?" he said. "It's as if they have never been apart. They act like they have known each other forever. I am so grateful to the Fosters for raising Jess just like we would have."

"Letting her stay with them was the hardest thing I have ever done, Justin, but you're right, it has been wonderful."

Justin bent and kissed her wind-pinked cheek. He loved this woman more than life itself, and to see her finally be so happy and free from the ghosts of the past was a blessing.

"It was the perfect decision, my love, it was a decision only you could make."

Jenny looked up at her husband, "Remember when Sirena told me I was going to have a daughter, and a son?"

"Yes, well, she was wrong. I'm very happy with what we have." Justin said with conviction.

"Oh, Then I guess I shouldn't tell you that she might have been right!" And Jenny gave him a big grin.

Epilogue

Clear Water Cove

Carolyn woke with a start. The bedroom was filled with shimmering light. Pulling her robe from the chair beside the bed, she cautiously got to her feet, shrugging into her robe as she stood up. This time the light seemed to be coming from the windows that looked out over the cove. She tiptoed across the room, trying not to wake Tom. However, he was sound asleep and snoring loudly.

She went to the window and looked out at the lake. The full moon threw a runner of bright silver across the water that stretched to the foot of the mountains on the far shoreline. She gasped, there closer to shore was a pale figure that appeared to be suspended above the moon's shimmering path and she could make out the shape of a woman with long, dark hair. The woman's arm was raised, as if in a gesture of farewell.

Carolyn sucked in her breath. It had to be Sirena.

What could she possibly want now? They had found Ava, and she was becoming reacquainted with her mother, and thank God, her Grandmother and Grandfather. It was such a blessing. Please don't let anything else happen now, she prayed silently. As she watched fascinated, the figure seemed to rise farther up from the surface of the lake. Suddenly a strong blaze of light beamed from the sky and with a flash, the apparition vanished up the path of light into the heavens.

"Tom, Tom, wake up." Carolyn's pulse was racing.

"What!" Tom leapt from the bed, startled and alarmed at the sound of Carolyn's frightened voice.

Carolyn ran over and pulled him to the window, but it was too late. Except for the path of moonlight on the water, the lake lay calm and dark once again. The light had vanished and with it, the figure of the woman Carolyn was sure had to be Sirena.

"Tom, I know you're going to think I'm seeing things again, but I swear I saw Sirena's ghost rise from the lake and follow a path of light up into the sky!"

Tom hugged her tightly. "Well, my dear. I certainly hope you're right. It's about time your ghost from the past left us for good." He nudged her ear with his nose and whispered. "Now can we go back to bed?"

"You never will believe she had anything to do with what happened here at the cove will you, Tom? But I know what others and I have seen. Hopefully, she has decided to leave this earth and is finally at peace. Perhaps she has figured out that you can't take it with you. After all the trouble her earthly treasure has caused, I think she has finally decided to leave it behind. Hopefully she will find bigger rewards where she's going."

"Yep, I believe that, anyway. Now come on, my darling. Tomorrow the girls are coming to visit. You'll need all the rest you can get to keep up with your two grandchildren." Tom kissed her cheek and steered her back to bed, where she curled up beside him.

She was very excited to see Ava. She would have to get used to calling her Jessica. The vision of Sirena's departure had somehow comforted her. Without that supernatural presence their lives were going to be far calmer. Even so, the experience had frightened her, and it was a long time before she drifted off to sleep, holding close the knowledge that she would see her Ava again soon.

Eagle's View Ranch

In her newly constructed art studio, Jenny stood before an easel, brush in hand, her painter's smock streaked with all the colors of the rainbow. With a final stroke of the brush, she finished the painting. Her heart filled with an overflowing feeling of love as she looked at the work with approval.

The two children in the painting sat with their arms around each other in a field of golden poppies. Lake Tahoe lay blue and serene in the background, guarded by the snowcapped Sierra Nevada Mountains. The two babies were not more than ten months old. One fair and blue eyed – the other dark with brown eyes. It was the portrait Jenny had started before Ava was taken. She had put her talent on hold for sixteen years, haunted by her loss, but now she was once again ready to paint. She smiled at the two beautiful children and they smiled back at her from the canvas.

A touch on her shoulder made her smile. "Justin," she whispered, "Aren't they lovely?"

Justin put his arms around her, gently touching her swollen stomach, feeling the life growing inside her. "Yes, my darling girl. Now our son can be your next project!"

They stood hand in hand in front of the portrait, filled with happiness at the prospect of a new life that would forge an even tighter bond between their families.

About the Author

This is my fifth novel.
I still live and work with my Arabian horses and three
little Shih Tzu dogs in Reno, Nevada.